# The Heirs

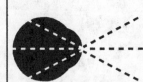

This Large Print Book carries the
Seal of Approval of N.A.V.H.

# THE HEIRS

## SUSAN RIEGER

**THORNDIKE PRESS**
A part of Gale, a Cengage Company

**GALE**
A Cengage Company

Farmington Hills, Mich • San Francisco • New York • Waterville, Maine
Meriden, Conn • Mason, Ohio • Chicago

**LIBRARY OF CONGRESS CATALOGING-IN-PUBLICATION DATA**

Names: Rieger, Susan, 1946– author.
Title: The heirs / by Susan Rieger.
Description: Large print edition. | Waterville, Maine : Thorndike Press, a part of Gale, a Cengage Company, 2017. | Series: Thorndike Press Large Print Basic.
Identifiers: LCCN 2017028779| ISBN 9781432844011 (hardback) | ISBN 1432844016 (hardcover)
Subjects: LCSH: Large type books. | BISAC: FICTION / Contemporary Women.
Classification: LCC PS3618.I39235 H45 2017 | DDC 813/.6—dc23
LC record available at https://lccn.loc.gov/2017028779

Published in 2017 by arrangement with Crown, an imprint of Crown Publishing Group, a division of Penguin Random House LLC

Printed in Mexico
1 2 3 4 5 6 7 21 20 19 18 17

*To Lydia P. S. Katzenbach*

# CONTENTS

# CONTENTS

The real represents to my perception the things we cannot possibly not know, sooner or later, in one way or another.

HENRY JAMES, PREFACE, *THE AMERICAN*

# CHAPTER 1
## ELEANOR

He that dies pays all debts.

WILLIAM SHAKESPEARE, *THE TEMPEST*

When he was dying, Rupert Falkes had the best care money could buy. His wife, Eleanor, saw to that. After the last round of chemo failed, she installed him in New York–Presbyterian in a large, comfortable, private room with a window facing the Hudson. She could have put him in hospice but she knew that in his rare moments of lucidity, he'd want to be in a hospital. He'd fought the prostate cancer tooth and nail, and even when it took over his bones, inflicting almost unbearable pain, he fought on. He wasn't ready to go. He was only sixty-five. "Why can't you stop them," he had said to the oncologist when the third off-label drug didn't shrink the tumors. He fiddled with his wedding ring, worrying it like a loose tooth. The doctor gave a small guilty shrug. He was out of drugs and words. "How much time do I have?" Rupert said. "Will I see in the millennium?" It was a week to Thanksgiving. The doctor nodded cautiously. "If things progress as I expect, you should make it, with a bit to spare." Rupert rubbed the top of his head, shiny and bald from the chemo. "I remember when Nixon declared war on cancer. It must have been thirty years ago." He shook his head. "I voted for the bugger."

Eleanor's sons — she had five — knew her as playful, even mischievous, but in the presence of others, even close friends, she rarely revealed that part of her, except in her sly, darting wit. The qualities that drew people to her were her democratic manners, her openhandedness, and her attention to the comfort of others. Often, these qualities passed mistakenly for charm, but charm is natural, innate, a gift. Eleanor was like a ballet dancer; what she did was hard work, born of arduous training, made to look as effortless as breathing.

As she had always reliably primed the social pump, so she made Rupert's last months easier for everyone. She bought Starbucks cards, spa gift certificates, pizza, and wine for all the aides, porters, and nurses on the floor. Rupert had always been fastidious — understandably, Eleanor thought, but overly — and though he slept most of the time, she rallied the staff to spare him the indignities of his body's failing systems. The aides kept him spotlessly clean, changing his diapers and sheets when they needed changing, and turning him over gently to prevent bedsores. The porters took care as they mopped and scoured not to bump his bed. The nurses were attentive, never stinting on the morphine. Unless he was so medicated that he barely breathed, Rupert couldn't bear touch. Most days, Eleanor was unable to tell if Rupert sensed anything other than pain. Still, three times a week, she brought in fresh flowers, unseasonal and riotous, to put at his bedside; and she kept a radio humming by his ear, tuned to WQXR. Every afternoon she looked in to see him and read him short stories, Updike, Cheever, Munro. His doctors made it a point to drop by when she was there. Afterward, she often went to the movies.

Eleanor belonged to that class of New Yorker whose bloodlines were traced in the manner of racehorses: she was Phipps (sire) out of Deering (dam), by Livingston (sire's dam) and Porter (dam's dam). Born in

1938, during the Depression, to parents who had held on to their money, she was never allowed to buy anything showy or fashionable. It had to be good and it might be costly, but not obviously so to someone outside the walls of New York's Four Hundred families. She went to Brearley because the women in her father's family had gone there and because Brearley girls wore shapeless, navy, hand-me-down, Catholic-school uniforms and brown oxfords.

Eleanor's upbringing had been conducted by a martinet mother and a succession of brisk English nannies who drilled her daily on grammar, hygiene, deportment, and dress. In truth, she wasn't so much raised up as subjugated, yoked to a set of rules and rituals that rivaled Leviticus for their specificity, rigor, piety, and triviality. On the subject of manners, Mrs. Phipps swore by Emily Post's diktat that the Chief Virtue of Children was Obedience.

No young human being, any more than a young dog, has the least claim to attractiveness unless it is trained to manners and obedience. The child that whines, interrupts, fusses, fidgets, and does nothing that it is told to do, has not the least power of attraction for any one. . . .

When possible, a child should be taken away the instant it becomes disobedient. It soon learns that it cannot "stay with mother" unless it is well-behaved. This means that it learns self-control in babyhood.

When, years later, at Vassar, Eleanor read Mrs. Post's 1922 monumental *Etiquette* in a sociology class, she saw the "it" as the key to her upbringing. She wrote her term paper on obedience, "Portrait of the Debutante as a Young Dog." Her professor gave her an A. His only comment was: "So, Miss Phipps, what do you think it would have been for you, as one raised under authoritarian principles, in WWII? Hitler Youth? White Rose? Kinder, Küche, Kirche?" Eleanor showed her roommate. "The creep is flirting and insulting me at the same time," she said.

Mrs. Phipps, had she known, would have bridled at the "authoritarian" epithet the professor had so slickly applied to Eleanor's upbringing. She was no narrow dogmatist, doing unto Eleanor as had been done unto her. She never struck Eleanor or locked her in a closet or made her stand in the corner. Her childrearing regimen was up-to-the-minute and scientific, based on the sound-

15

est principles of "child development." An early and avid subscriber to *Parenting* magazine, she was a votary of the psychologist J. B. Watson and kept his book *Psychological Care of Infant and Child* by her bedside. She took to heart his nostrums against hugging and kissing and often quoted to Eleanor his most famous axiom: "Mother love is a dangerous instrument that can wreck a child's chance for future happiness." Everything she did was for Eleanor's own good.

Deference to males, no matter their age, was an article of faith in the Phipps household, and by the time she was twelve, Eleanor, with no show of temper, would lose regularly at tennis to boys who weren't nearly as good as she was. With similar equanimity, she would never argue with a boy or, worse, correct him, no matter how thick he was. At most she'd allow herself a "Do you think so?" then clear her throat. Mrs. Phipps took the hard line against female intelligence, thinking it suspect in a woman, unpardonable in a girl. Vulgarity was the besetting sin, the mark of the ill-bred, covering a range of behaviors extending well beyond conspicuous consumption to reading French novels, confusing a fish fork with a dessert fork, nodding off at the opera, using "lay" instead of "lie," and wearing white shoes after Labor Day.

Adolescence offered no escape for Eleanor from the maternal dragnet except in furtive play. Pre-Kinsey, she didn't have a name for it; she only knew she wasn't to do it. "No decent person does it," Mrs. Phipps told her. "Only perverts." Eleanor's response, by now second nature, was to slip into silence, which passed for submission, and take long baths.

Her mother always blamed Vassar for Eleanor's marriage to Rupert, and certainly it contributed to her general "Bolshiness," as her mother called it. In truth, the path was laid down when she was sixteen in a setting Mrs. Phipps would have thought, if not entirely wholesome, then safe enough.

Eleanor was spending the night at the home of a Brearley classmate, Clarissa Van Vliet. Clarissa's parents, despite impeccable antecedents, were by Mrs. Phipps's lights "Bohemian." They lived on the Upper West Side, not the Upper East. Their living room bookshelves held books and not antique Chinese export pottery. Their three children, ages eleven to sixteen, regularly ate dinner with their parents. They socialized with Jews and homosexuals.

That evening at dinner, Mrs. Van Vliet

directed her conversation toward Clarissa and her guest, telling them about "a terrific book" she was rereading, D. H. Lawrence's *Women in Love*. "It's as good as I remember — I first read it when I was at Vassar, English 225, I think," she said. "The professor was advanced." Her husband looked up from his plate, amused. "Very advanced, even for Vassar. Isn't it what we called in my day a 'dirty' book?" he asked. "Well, of course it is," Mrs. Van Vliet said. "How are young women supposed to learn anything?" As she said this, she knocked her water glass to the floor, where it shattered into scores of tiny, spiky shards. "Oh, shit," Mrs. Van Vliet said. The hair on the back of Eleanor's neck stood up. She'd found the whole conversation exhilarating, but this last outburst was thrilling. She'd never heard anyone's mother use a swearword, and she had believed that if one ever slipped out, a thing almost unimaginable, the woman would be filled with chagrin, falling over herself to apologize. Not this mother. Mrs. Van Vliet laughed and called to the maid to sweep it up. The next day, Eleanor went to Scribner's and bought *Women in Love*. She stayed up all night reading it. When she'd finished, she told her mother she was going to go to Vassar. Years later, Eleanor would think of that dinner at the Van Vliets' as her Emma-Bovary-on-the-road-to-Damascus moment.

Eleanor's first act of open rebellion was to vote for John F. Kennedy in 1960. No one in the family, not since McKinley, had voted for a Democrat. Her second was to marry Rupert Falkes, a penniless Englishman.

Rupert Falkes had only one social rule, which he observed punctiliously: a gentleman is never unintentionally rude. He was equal parts charm and rudeness, and in his prime, he was rude at some point or other to almost every person he knew, and many he didn't. Occasionally, he larded his insults with obscenities. The exceptions were Eleanor, the boys, and her father. He knew that Eleanor wouldn't tolerate rudeness to herself or the boys. She had made it clear early in their marriage when he criticized their firstborn's table manners. "He's not fit to eat at table," he said to Eleanor. The child, Harry, was sixteen months at the time. He had scant control of the spoon, but insisted on using it, carrying his porridge to his nose as often as to his mouth. When Eleanor tried to help, he pushed her hand away and shook his head. "Self," he said.

19

"Right," Eleanor said. "Off to boarding school with him then." Rupert took the warning. "I'm not used to eating with babies," he said. His explanation passed for an apology.

Eleanor never minded his rudeness to others, shrugging it off. "It's like Tourette's or hiccups with him," she would say if a friend mentioned it. "Raise it with him, if you like. He might respond well."

Rupert had had the good fortune he'd always say of being an orphan. A foundling, he'd been left in the English winter of 1934, when he was no more than a month old, on the steps of St. Pancras in Chichester. He was fair and rosy, healthy, and nicely swaddled, and the priest who'd found him, the Rev. Henry Falkes, was sure his mother would have a change of heart and come fetch him. She didn't. Rupert grew up in St. Pancras's Home for Orphaned Boys, a childhood no more brutal than one offered in the Depression years at a Church of England prep school. Whatever the weather, the boys wore shorts. Whatever the games and season, they bathed once a week in communal tubs. Until he came to America, he didn't know that chilblains were frostbite.

Rupert had a lovely boy's soprano voice that made him stand out from the unruly, runny-nosed, scabrous little boys he lived with. It would prove not only the saving of him but the making of him. When he was seven, Reverend Falkes made an application for him to the Prebendal School and he was accepted as a chorister. From there, he went to public school at Longleat on a scholarship, and then to Cambridge, as a scholar. Holidays, he spent with Reverend Falkes, who was proud of Rupert and always kind to him but unaffectionate in that wooden way of Englishmen sent off to boarding school before they cut their second teeth.

Rupert emigrated to America in the summer of 1955, when he was twenty-one. Reverend Falkes had died without warning on Boxing Day the year before and there was nothing to keep him in England. Twice abandoned and orphaned, he had no home, no one looking out for him, no useful connections. Despite his first-class education, his prospects, if he stayed, would be limited. And he was made for America. Americans loved his accent and his Cambridge pedigree and regarded his orphaned status almost as an asset, the stamp of authenticity of the self-made man. The first time Eleanor saw him weep was when he read *The Great Gatsby.* "We don't read this in England," he said. "Witless arrogance."

Rupert never talked about his first year in America, and Eleanor was never sure how he'd got on. The story he would tell was that he met the dean of Yale Law School, Eugene Debs Rostow, on a train that first year, and talked his way into a scholarship there. Rostow would not regret the decision. Rupert made the *Law Journal,* clerked for Judge Friendly on the Second Circuit, and then went to work for Maynard, Tandy & Jordan, where he practiced antitrust law in the golden age of antitrust. He made a lot of money, and when he retired at sixty-five, he endowed three chairs at Yale, one in honor of Dean Rostow.

Eleanor was attentive to Rupert's needs, pushing aside all feelings of loss until they could not be ignored. She would miss him, she knew, but she could not wish him longer life. She wondered what the boys were feeling. They were now men, the oldest thirty-seven, the youngest almost thirty, and they no longer confided in her. Sam, the middle son, would take it hardest, but she didn't believe Rupert's death would be wrenching for the others, except perhaps in the feeling of what-might-have-been-and-now-never-will. But that is loss too, she thought.

Harry and Sam, the two boys living in

New York, visited him at the hospital at least three times a week, usually before or after work, and Sam often stayed through dinner and read to his father, picking up where Eleanor had left off. Will, Jack, and Tom came from Los Angeles, Austin, and Chicago every few weeks. Although Eleanor had been, they would tease, an overly fond mother, she had not rejected all the lessons of her childhood, but had instilled in the boys a sense of responsibility to family and community. "We do what decency requires," she regularly said to them. "Never less." The boys loved Rupert — he was, after all, their father and he had always looked out for them — but he had been, for so much of their early lives, so little there, they had few childhood memories of him. They remembered their mother and grandfather. Eleanor had taught them to ride their bikes and serve a tennis ball. She had held them when they were sad and kissed their scrapes. Poppa took them to baseball games and museums. He'd let them sit on his lap at dinner. A natural Watsonian, Rupert never hugged or kissed his sons. When they were two, he patted them on the head; when they were seven, he met them with a handshake. He couldn't help it, much as he cared for them in his buttoned-up English way. Elea-

23

nor told them not to take it personally and, except for Tom, the youngest, they didn't.

"Did you ever change a diaper?" Sam asked his father, one evening at a family holiday dinner, everyone there, wives and partners, not long before Rupert fell ill. The question held no rancor, no accusation. Sam was curious.

Rupert turned to Eleanor. "Did I?" he asked.

"No," Eleanor said.

"I didn't think so," he said. Everyone laughed.

Harry once said to his mother that he never remembered, as a young child, going anyplace with his father by himself but he did remember, as he got older: their arguments about politics, serious but never querulous; Rupert's interest in whatever Harry was doing, even debate; and Rupert's encouragement to take risks in life. Eleanor thought the others would say the same. Rupert believed in his sons, and his belief in them was the greatest thing he gave them. He simply couldn't show them affection. It seemed inevitable to Eleanor that Rupert had managed in his final illness to make physical touch impossible, as if he'd been traveling toward that point his whole life. His last coherent words to her, a week before he died, were lawyers' words: "Settle my just debts."

Eleanor had not been in love with Rupert when she married him, but she was twenty-two, and there was no one else she liked better or liked being with more. She had confidence in him — in his appreciation of her and in his ability to get on — and he made her feel safe.

They met at her cousin's wedding; he was a law school classmate of the groom. Still blond at twenty-six, he was good-looking without being too handsome. He had high cheekbones and Arctic eyes, giving him the glint of a wolf. All the girls and women at the wedding noticed him as he moved about the room with the easy gait of an athlete. Though he insisted, laughingly, that he had bought his dinner jacket secondhand from Moss Bros., he wore it with the elegant carelessness of a young Olivier. He spotted Eleanor early in the evening, the loveliest girl in the room, and, without waiting for an introduction, approached her. "Hello, you," he said. He was a wonderful dancer, which left her breathless, and he talked easily and wittily. He seemed older than the groom and the other young men and had read everything. "He comes from nowhere," the bride whispered in Eleanor's ear, "but if he offered to run off with me, I'd go. Right now. He's a man, not a boy."

Eleanor's expectations of marriage were by then hardheaded: So long as it is less awful than my parents', she thought. She wanted contentedness not ardor. She had had ardor and it had set her back on her heels. The summer before her junior year, she'd fallen in love with a Jew, a Russian major at Yale, beautiful, brilliant James Cardozo. Both families were dead set against the match, his even more than hers, and the young couple couldn't see making their way in the world on their own. Jim was planning on going to medical school; like all the young women she knew, she had no plans, other than marriage. The breakup was a watershed for Eleanor. She would marry the next man who asked her, as long as he could kiss and hold down a job.

Carlo Benedetti could do both. Three months after she broke with Jim, they started dating. He was in his last year at Columbia Law. They had known each other from childhood; his father did business with her father. Her mother pulled the plug the first time Eleanor brought him home. "Stop it now. He's not one of us," she said. "What do you mean," Eleanor said. "He's descended from Popes. He goes everywhere." Mrs. Phipps held up her hand. "Not St. James's," she said. Rupert was a godsend, an Episcopalian her mother disliked more than the Catholic, as much as the Jew.

The Falkeses' marriage looked like many marriages of their generation and class. Eleanor loved being pregnant and loved her babies; Rupert worked hard, leaving at seven, coming home at eight. By their third anniversary, they had achieved, without words, an easy, unguarded relationship, animated by a deep sexual connection. Their friends might have said they loved each other, but brought up without family warmth or affection, neither had the vocabulary of ordinary, everyday happiness. They were very good at sex, it turned out, but no good, with each other, at casual touching. It suited them both.

Their division of labor was conventional; Eleanor didn't read *The Feminine Mystique* until after the last baby. Rupert was the breadwinner; she raised the boys and ran the household, as she had been raised, with help from nannies, maids, cooks, and drivers. They were kind, supportive, and respectful to each other, publicly and privately. Handsome, clever, and rich, they were popular with friends and colleagues. Eleanor's lineage allayed any questions about Rupert's idiopathic origins. Over time Rupert's friends diagnosed his rudeness as "an English thing," like eating Marmite, and paid it little mind. At the law firm, the associates kept lists of his taunts and insults, comparing them almost as badges of honor. They pined for his praise.

Eleanor and Rupert had a floor-through apartment in the Hotel des Artistes, the old studio building on West Sixty-Seventh. In pursuit of Van Vlietism, Eleanor had wanted to live on the Upper West Side. Her father approved and bought the apartment, originally two apartments, as a wedding present. He put it in her name. The boys never knew another home. Their attachment to it was primal. After Rupert's death, they all worried that Eleanor might sell it. "Who will buy it if she does?" Harry asked his brothers. They all offered although they knew it was unhinged sentimentality.

"Do we keep it as a shrine to our childhood, never changing anything?" Will asked.

"It must cost a fortune to run and maintain," Sam said.

"I love it," Tom said, "but I couldn't live in it. I'd feel like an imposter."

"Who'd get to sleep in their bed?" Jack asked.

Eleanor's old boyfriend, Jim Cardozo, didn't marry until 1975, when he was thirty-six and had finished his residency in cardiology. His wife, Anne Lewisohn Lehman, was also a Vassar graduate, six years behind Eleanor, a biology major. She was short, blond, sturdy, and kind. They were married at Temple Emanu-El, the Reform German Jewish synagogue that looked like a bank on the outside. Reading the wedding invitation, unexpected and unwelcome, Eleanor felt a twinge of irritation, realizing, after fourteen years of marriage to Rupert, she hadn't thought about Jim in years. Her heart had broken and then it mended, good as new. I was twenty, she thought. I didn't know there was sex without love. Jim had loved her, she knew, more than she had loved him, but she couldn't believe he harbored at this remove anything more than passing wistfulness for their ardent youthful selves. Perhaps he wanted her to know he had landed on his feet.

The Cardozo reception was at the Harmonie Club. There were six hundred guests, including Eleanor and Rupert. Their gift, from the registry, was a sterling fish server, in the same pattern as her parents'. Jim and Anne spent all their holidays with her family, an uncomplicated bunch who loved tennis, sailing, practical jokes, and charades. Anne loathed Jim's parents. Meeting the young Cardozos for the first time at their wedding, Rupert pronounced Anne a "good sort." He never said what he thought of Jim, except to say "damp handshake."

Eleanor thought of her marriage as a stroke of luck, sweeter for being unexpected. In her romance with Jim, she had seen herself as the victim of selfish and uncaring parents, more interested in their comfort than in her happiness. As she grew older, she acknowledged her conventionality and her cowardliness — and Jim's too. She had been bred for marriage; even her high-powered Vassar education had only served to make her more marriageable to the right sort of man, and she hadn't known what else to do with herself. She hoped she might come to love Rupert, and by the end, her attachment to him passed for love. To her delight, he had turned out to be sexually gifted. Who taught him? she wondered.

Rupert married Eleanor because she was the girl of the year in 1960, because all the other men he knew wanted her, because she knew the difference between sarcasm and irony, because she was a knockout, because she'd read George Orwell, because she was sexually electrifying, because he could talk to her. She was like an Arabian racehorse, angular and lean, almost as tall as he, with dark hair and eyes. Reverend Falkes had been dark, probably Welsh. Seeing the photo of him that Rupert carried in his wallet, Eleanor thought, dark and tall like me. Makes sense. Rupert's blondness was one of his minor selling points, the un-Jim.

Rupert understood from the start theirs was a marriage not of convenience exactly, more of mutual benefit, and all in all, he thought they'd both held to the bargain and made it work. Once, years into the marriage, he asked her whether she was fond of him. She was quick to answer. "Of course I'm fond of you," she said, "and I admire you." He nodded and smiled at her, then took her hand in his. Later, she marveled at the oddness of this exchange, after so many years together. The meagerness of his expectations — or sadder, his desires — was painful to her, as was this unexpected, transient willingness to expose himself. He didn't risk asking whether I might love him, or could love him, or did love him, or ever loved him. Her thoughts took a sharp turn. Of course, I've never asked him if he loved me. Did I mean to marry a man who didn't love me? She wondered sometimes whether he'd ever been unfaithful. She had never required fidelity, only discretion. Their sexual bond was the glue of the marriage, but almost a thing apart from their emotional connection and requirements. In their couplings they were like world-class athletes. They didn't think about what they did. Eleanor thought downhill skiing came closest to sex with Rupert.

Rupert and Eleanor disagreed now and again — politically, Eleanor was more liberal — but never acrimoniously. There wasn't enough heat to raise the temperature of an argument and there was so much money smoothing the way. The boys were a source of pride. "Not a duffer among them," Rupert would say, "even if they're all Democrats." Henry (Harry) came first, in 1962, eleven months after they were married; the rest followed in two-year intervals: William (Will), Samuel (Sam), John (Jack), and Thomas (Tom). When Tom was a year, Eleanor had her tubes tied. "I take it there will be no Guy," Rupert said. "Five in ten years is an excellent sufficiency," she said. They were good-looking boys — tall, dark, and lean, like their mother, athletic and brainy. People used to say they had Eleanor's looks and Rupert's brains. My brains too, Eleanor thought, but she let it pass.

Rupert took mild exception. "Where are the rosy-cheeked towheads?" he would ask now and then.

As expected, Eleanor's mother disapproved of Rupert and the match, but her father, who had been a phantom presence in her childhood, gave his blessing, firmly quashing any maternal interference. He insisted on having a big wedding and then offered to support the young couple for the first five years while Rupert was getting his footing. Eleanor wondered if he was making amends for closing ranks with her mother against Jim; she drew closer to her father. Rupert never forgot this kindness, and his regard for his father-in-law, as with Reverend Falkes, approached love. They lunched together at least three times a month and Rupert went to Mr. Phipps for advice on investments. Mr. Phipps had spent his career, more than forty years, at the family bank, Phipps & Co. He had studied chemistry in college, thinking he would be a doctor or scientist, but his father and grandfather pressed him to join the bank and his early marriage forced his hand. His wife would be expensive. He had a genius for identifying coming companies and industries, which his father and grandfather recognized, and by the time he was thirty, he was director of new investments. This position, with its spending clout, kept him from growing restless or careless. At fifty, he was chairman of the bank. He made himself and many others very rich. In 1966, Mr. Phipps recommended that Rupert invest eighty thousand dollars in McDonald's, and offered to loan him the money interest-free if he didn't have it. Rupert took the loan and bought the stock. By 1973, it was worth five and a half million dollars. Rupert insisted on paying back Mr. Phipps; he gave him five hundred and fifty thousand dollars. Mr. Phipps gave the money to Eleanor. "A sunny-day fund," he said. Both men loved to sail and would often spend their Sundays together on the Sound, off Kings Point, where the Phippses had a house and Mr. Phipps kept a sloop. The second and last time Eleanor knew her husband to weep was at her father's funeral.

Mrs. Phipps grew wary of Rupert, who played with her as a cat with a mole. If she was in a hectoring mood, criticizing one of the boys or, more likely, Eleanor, he would deliver a "Granny slap-down," as the boys called it, asking her repeatedly to repeat herself — "I'm sorry, I didn't hear you" — until she sounded stupid even to herself. At those times, Eleanor felt something approaching real love for him. Only once did Rupert lose his temper with his mother-in-law. It shut her down in his presence. She never again said anything to him other than "How are you?"

In marrying Rupert, Eleanor had accepted his limitations. He was capable of expressing gratitude, appreciation, generosity, even affection, but not stronger emotions, even if he felt them. He had decided, at twenty-one, he would be a successful man in ways New York society respected, and this he had achieved. He did what he could with what he had.

Their last conversation before the morphine shut him down was fittingly valedictory. Afterward, Eleanor wondered if he had planned it, holding out as long as he could. She was sitting by his bed in the hospital. Schubert's *Trout* was playing on the radio.

"I wasn't always a good man," Rupert said. "I wanted to be but couldn't do it."

"Good enough," Eleanor said.

"My life turned out to be much better than I had any right to expect," he said.

"Mine too," she said.

"Thank you," he said.

Eleanor leaned over and kissed him. He reached up and touched her cheek.

"I wish I could stay," he said.

"I do too," she said.

Eleanor's boys not only looked like her, they looked like one another. Acquaintances seeing the older or younger brothers together often took them for twins, even triplets. Ancient cousins frequently got their names wrong. Eleanor found this annoying but she came to see that on the surface, by their looks and close age, they invited confusion in the inobservant. Her mother was always mixing them up, whether out of weakmindedness or spite Eleanor couldn't tell. Her father, embracing grandfatherhood, kept them straight, buying each of them every year the perfect birthday gift. For Sam's ninth, Mr. Phipps bought him a real stethoscope, sending Sam into paroxysms of joy.

To Eleanor, the boys were nothing alike, each vividly himself. Harry taught law at Columbia, specializing in constitutional law and conflicts of law, "Torts for Pedants," he called it. He was smart, canny, competitive, confident, at ease everywhere, a quick study, and a natural leader. Job offers came his way often; he was good at lunch. His law school colleagues saw him as a future law school dean or circuit court judge. He married Jewish. "We were sent to Trinity to meet

Jews, right?" he said to his parents one night at dinner, graduation looming. He had invited Jane Levi to the senior prom. He thought he was his mother's favorite, the fulfillment of the famous Freudian dictum: "A man who has been the indisputable favorite of his mother keeps for life the feeling of a conqueror." He felt a conqueror. *Post hoc, ergo propter hoc.*

Will was literary, witty, astute, and stealthily ambitious. At eleven, he announced at dinner: "I'm a Marxist." The table fell quiet; everyone looked at him. He grinned. "A Groucho Marxist." Will had been an editor in New York at Random House, but then went off to L.A. to be a talent agent. He loved making deals; he felt most alive in the middle of a deal. Every year on the anniversary of the day he sold his first book to the movies for a million dollars, he and his wife, Francie, went to dinner at the Polo Lounge. He'd gone there to celebrate with his boss after that first big sale. The place never changed; it was Hollywood, unapologetic and unadulterated, with its dry martinis, aged steaks, plush banquettes, and lavish flowers. "I read Dickens and Eliot in college so I could sell Thane and Gordon," he told Eleanor. "Plot," he said. " 'A gun in the first act.' " In 1999, he had three best-selling authors with seven-figure movie options. Eleanor thought he was the smartest. He was the most intellectual, Thane and Gordon notwithstanding.

Sam was a scientist, an MD/PhD researcher in infectious diseases. Eleanor thought of him with remorse, as the outlier, neglected in the tumult of three boys under five; but hers was a minority view. Rupert, in his stiff way, and her father, in his, had worked to fill the void she had left, and in their coalition, they had, remarkably, succeeded. Sam was insightful and observant, his senses alive to those around him, with a barbed sense of humor and a stubbornness that often passed for principled objection. He was slow to anger but, once aroused, slow to forgive. Like his brothers, he loved his mother, almost without criticism. He saw himself less as the odd one out than as the gravitational center of the five brothers. "I am the keystone," he told his mother when he was ten. Of the five, he was closest to his father and, Eleanor thought, his father's favorite. He was, if not his brothers' favorite, then the one they found least irritating.

Jack, the only artist, was the most talented, the most driven. A jazz trumpeter, he was interested in little besides music. People, hearing he was from a large family, pegged him as the youngest; he had the sweetness and self-centeredness of the baby, indulged by older brothers as well as parents. "I love the trumpet more than I love food," he told his mother. "It's the brassiest of all instruments. It struts." My id, Eleanor thought.

Tom, who was the baby, missed having someone below him to push around and often felt the weight of the older four as oppressive. He would refer to himself as the runt of the litter, though he was the tallest and the best athlete. There was never any unalloyed good news, no winning without losing for Tom. He was the only one of the five who'd been in therapy. Among his grievances, he resented that he was born in the '70s, not the '60s like the others, a different generation. He was a federal prosecutor, working in the white-collar crime unit in the Chicago US Attorney's Office, "having a not-too-bad time of it" going after insider traders. Eleanor wondered if his decision to be a prosecutor was his way of arming himself against his big brothers. He too married Jewish, a niece of Jim Cardozo's wife, Anne.

All five had gone to Princeton — Harry, Will, and Tom as tennis players. Eleanor had wanted them to go to Yale, their grandfather's old school, while Rupert, along with Trinity, their high school, had pushed Harvard. Harry, being Harry, beat his way to Princeton and brought the rest along. Growing up in New York City, they liked the country all right while they were there, but after graduation, they gravitated to cities. Tom insisted he'd never have gotten into Princeton if he wasn't a legacy, seeming to forget he had been a highly ranked tennis recruit with 1400 boards; in fact, it was Jack, with a patchy academic record, who presented a challenge to the admissions office. Still, Princeton took him. They didn't want to risk losing Tom, who'd be applying in two years, or alienating the older brothers; and the head of Trinity's music department told admissions that Jack was the most talented music student he'd ever taught. "Reject him and regret it," he wrote.

For thirteen years, from 1980 through 1992, there was at least one Falkes on campus; for nine of those years, there were two. Harry blazed the trail, writing his way into a junior history seminar in the fall of his freshman year and making the varsity tennis team in the spring. The younger ones walked onto campus already celebrities; everyone seemed to know who they were. Harry joined Quadrangle — he didn't want to join an eating club that didn't have women members, and he didn't like bicker. His brothers followed but even Quadrangle was too elitist for Tom, who dropped out. Harry liked Princeton best, then Will, then Sam, then Jack, then Tom. After Rupert's death, Harry endowed a scholarship at Princeton in his father's name. The others thought he was gunning for a seat on the board of trustees.

"Why did we all follow Harry to Princeton?" Tom asked Sam when his fifth reunion was coming up. He wasn't planning on going.

"Habit," Sam said. "We always did what Harry did back then. Also laziness."

Will graduated summa and won a Marshall, spending three years at Cambridge, which pleased Rupert no end. Harry and Sam graduated magna and went on to Yale, Harry for law, Sam for medicine. That too pleased Rupert, who joined the Corporation after Sam was admitted. Tom graduated cum and was awarded the Scholar-Athlete Award at graduation. "Rafa Kohn, the soccer player, should have got it; he's brilliant. I just wallop the ball," he told his parents. He went to Berkeley for law school; "I want sunshine and fresh air," he said. Jack graduated "with great relief," but clinched his place in the Princeton pantheon by being invited onstage to play with Wynton Marsalis at a jazz concert his junior year. Marsalis told the crowd he'd heard there was a "white trumpet prodigy at Princeton."

The family money was part of the constellation — the boys all had Phipps as one of their middle names, a kind of calling card of its own — and Rupert and Eleanor gave generously. But there was more to them than the obvious markers; a dashing, romantic aura hovered about the five Falkeses, the kind usually ascribed to quivers of remarkable or highly marriageable sisters, like the Mitfords or the Cushings; other boys and men were always having crushes on them.

They'd all married or partnered in their twenties or early thirties, and there was the whiff of Eleanor or Rupert in all their choices. Except for Sam's boyfriend Andrew, they were all fond of their in-laws, who went the second, third, and fourth mile to welcome them to the family. Andrew felt toward Eleanor and Rupert the antagonism of the provincial boy. "Who still uses fish forks?" he asked Sam the first time he had dinner at West Sixty-Seventh Street. "And is there always a maid serving dinner and a cook cooking it?" Sam regarded both questions as rhetorical bloodletting and didn't answer them directly. "My father was an orphan, left on the church steps," he said. Andrew snorted. "He's a hero, then, completely self-made. I know where I came from, and so do they: the other side of the tracks." When Eleanor and Rupert gave Andrew an elegant Omega gold watch for his thirty-fifth birthday, an expensive gift but not embarrassingly expensive, Andrew decided the acuity of the choice was an insult. "It's too thoughtful," he said to Sam. "I'll tell them not to get you any more gifts," Sam said. "No, no," Andrew said. "I don't want to be thought insulting." Andrew had wanted a Cartier tank watch like Sam's.

Eleanor insisted on a family dinner the night before Harry left for Princeton his freshman year. "No dispensations," she said at breakfast. "That includes everyone." Rupert nodded. "All hands on deck at 23:00 Zulu," he said. The boys groaned. "How does Zulu work with daylight saving time?" Sam asked, working the calculation in his head.

Dinner was all of Harry's favorite foods: strip steak, artichokes, skinny French fries, and chocolate mousse. Drinks were ginger beer shandies and Brunello. The three older boys were allowed to have wine that night. Harry, at eighteen, was legal in New York; he could drink as much as he wanted. Will and Sam, weighing over 130 pounds, were each given a glass. "I want you to learn to drink before you go to university," Rupert had said to the boys. He had spent a good deal of time at Cambridge snockered, a way of fitting in. "Was it worse at Cambridge," he had asked himself, "to be a Jew, the son of a butcher, or a foundling?"

At Longleat, Rupert had come up with a workable response to inquiries into his origins. He would say that he'd been orphaned as an infant and raised as the ward of the Reverend Henry Falkes, St. Pancras Church, Chichester. The shared name was reassuring to his interrogators, and Rupert regularly offered up silent thanks to the reverend for giving him his last name. The other orphans who'd arrived storklike at St. Pancras had last names from Dickens. "True," Rupert said. "I'm not pulling your leg." His infant schoolmates included a Copperfield, a Nickleby, a Dombey, a Harmon, a Jaggers, a Carstone, and a Trotwood. Reverend Falkes gave them the names of worthy if flawed characters, a kind of literary blessing on their heads. He liked naming and took it seriously; it was, after all, the first task God set Adam. He told Rupert his only regret was wasting Summerson on a small pockmarked bully. "I should have called him Murdstone."

Rupert never asked the reverend why he alone had his last name. He feared he would appear presumptuous or, worse, Heepish; he suspected Reverend Falkes would be acutely embarrassed. From his seat on the sidelines, Rupert observed that embarrassment or, more accurately, the avoidance of embarrassment was the chief moderator of English social arrangements among the upper middle classes. So many of the Englishmen he knew were embarrassed by the smallest things: wearing the wrong pair of shoes (brown in town instead of black), saying the wrong word ("wealthy" instead of "rich"), playing the wrong game (football instead of rugby). Rudeness was the antidote, injected into the conversation at the merest hint of encroaching embarrassment.

America cured Rupert of the last vestiges of embarrassment; it became superfluous. As far as he could tell, Americans were embarrassed only by public nakedness, a situation he felt he could easily avoid. His rudeness adapted to the New World, propagating, kudzu-like, into an instrument against stupidity, carelessness, laziness, and boredom, especially boredom. One of the other reasons Rupert married Eleanor was that she didn't prattle. He'd found that rare in a girl as beautiful as she, used to attention and admiration. His mother-in-law had been beautiful, he was told, which helped him understand his father-in-law, smote by forget-me-not blue eyes.

Dinner was roisterous on Harry's last night. He was excited and nervous for himself. He couldn't eat; he drank. His brothers were excited and nervous for him. They ate enormous amounts.

"It's Harry's last meal," Will said. Harry grinned like the Cheshire Cat and drew his index finger slit-like across his throat. Everyone laughed, except Sam.

Sam shook his head. "No, no," he said, his voice cracking, his eyes filling with tears. "This is serious. This is the end of normal life." Silence fell on the table.

At that moment, Harry decided that his brothers would follow him to Princeton. Normal life would continue, only shifting its center of gravity seasonally, between the Hotel des Artistes and Nassau Hall.

"I can't believe in ten years, you'll all be gone. Pfffft," Eleanor said. She looked at Rupert. "Short of a cricket side, but not a bad lot."

"No duffers," he said softly. She nodded.

"I should play taps, shouldn't I?" Jack said. He went to get his trumpet.

"Just a minute," Harry said. He poured himself another glass of wine. "To Mom and Dad."

"Hear, hear," the others replied.

Eleanor cleared her throat. Rupert covered her hand with his own. From the far end of the apartment, they heard the first melancholy notes of the bugle call. They looked at each other, then looked away, too happy to speak.

Rupert lingered for four months, three more than anyone expected. His doctors said it must have been the last powerful chemo combination and wanted to write him up. Eleanor wondered at their notion of success. He'd been dying the whole time. He died on a Saturday morning in April. The floor nurse called Eleanor at seven a.m. to say the end was near. Eleanor called all the boys. Harry and Sam went to the hospital with her. Eleanor said to Rupert, "I'm here. It's all right." Harry held his hand. Sam kissed his forehead. He died ten minutes later. Pulled under by a wave of grief, Eleanor wept.

Rupert did not die on the front page of

the *Times,* a private wish, but he was given a two-column obituary inside with a photo. He'd been a prominent lawyer and a good one, and he'd given away a lot of money to good causes. The death notice Eleanor submitted to run for a week was characteristically succinct. No lovings, no beloveds.

Rupert Falkes. Born February 2, 1934, Chichester, England, died April 14, 2000, New York, NY, of cancer. Graduate of the Prebendal School, Longleat College, Cambridge University, and Yale Law School. Senior Partner, Maynard, Tandy & Jordan. Trustee, Trinity School. Corporation Member, Yale University. Board Member, New York Public Library. Survived by his wife, Eleanor Deering Phipps; his sons, Henry, William, Samuel, John, and Thomas Falkes; their wives and partners, Lea Abrams, Frances Gore, Andrew Lanahan, Katherine Ellway, and Caroline Steinway; and two granddaughters, Alice and Elizabeth Falkes. Funeral Friday, April 18, 11 a.m., St. Thomas Church, Fifth Avenue at 53rd Street. No flowers. Donations in his name may be made to the Soup Kitchen, Holy Apostles Church.

"I see you've taken back your maiden

name," Harry commented when he read the notice. "Inspired by my daughters-in-law," Eleanor said. "I'm giving it a trial. I always disliked the awkward alliteration of Eleanor Phipps Falkes. Like a rude limerick." Harry stared at her. "We're all Phipps Falkes," he said. "Yes," she said.

Eleanor bought the coffin she wanted from Herbert Brothers Funerals, a plain cedar box, lined in white linen. Will came along to close the deal. She liked that Herbert's had the word "funerals" in their name and not "chapel," but when the salesman pointed her toward their collection of Chinese ginger jars, sized perfectly for her "loved one's cremains," she almost bolted. Will put his hand on her arm, as if to say, "I'll take care of this." Herbert's wanted to sell her one of their deluxe models, the Porsche of caskets, a spruce burl number, hand carved, silk-lined, and priced just below a Steinway grand. "It's wrong for my husband," Eleanor said. "He'd want something along the lines of a Jewish-type coffin, a simple wood box." When the salesman demurred — "Your husband was such a distinguished man, so many important people will be attending the service" — Will took over. "If you don't have what we want, Mr. Herbert, please tell us," he said. "We'll go somewhere else. This is tiring my mother out." His voice was even, almost pleasant, no trace of annoyance or irritation creeping in. Rupert would have done exactly the same thing, Eleanor thought, but sooner and with an edge of menace.

The funeral at St. Thomas was longer than Eleanor would have liked, but she wanted music, Bach's Passacaglia and Fugue in C Minor and, of course, "Jerusalem," and she knew the partners and parishioners expected orations on Rupert's passing, as they called it. Passing to what? she thought. Jim Cardozo showed up. Harry and Sam spoke, along with Rupert's closest friend, Dominic Byrne, a Cambridge don, and his oldest friend, John Earlham, a cricket buddy from his first years in New York. She had told them all they could speak no more than seven minutes each — twice the length of the Gettysburg Address seemed a generous allotment — and they obliged. Harry spoke humorously about sailing with his father and grandfather. "Both wanted to captain. They had this unintentionally comical Alphonse/Gaston routine. Too polite to seize the wheel, each waited for the other to defer. Sometimes, I'd just take over," he said. "Excessive good manners can provide an opening for a young brute." Sam was the most affecting. He had come out to his dad when he was fourteen. They were walking to church. "I'm gay," Sam had said, not looking at his father. "Yes," said Rupert, nodding. They kept walking.

Among the mourners, the most visibly bereft were the old Maynard associates who believed he'd made them into lawyers. He was cremated, according to his wishes, and his ashes cast upon the waters of Long Island Sound.

Two months after the funeral, Eleanor decided to refurbish the apartment. She laundered all of Rupert's clothes, then gave them away to Housing Works, along with his personal effects, except his watch, an antique Patek Philippe. None of the boys wanted her to sell it but none of them wanted to own it. "Too Dad," Harry said. "Too East Coast lawyer," Will said. "I'm not mature enough to wear it," Sam said. "I'll never be mature enough," Jack said. "I have a Timex," Tom said. They looked to their mother to decide. Eleanor shook her head. "I won't play Solomon," she said. Harry stepped up. "Sam should take it," he said. "Yes, Sam should take it," Tom said. Jack nodded. "Sam, by acclamation, then," Will said. Sam took it home and put it in his top dresser drawer. Andrew eyed it.

Eleanor bought a new bed and new linens. She had the apartment professionally cleaned by a housekeeping service. It took a team of four three weeks to bring it up to her standards; she had them wash down all the walls and woodwork. She took the posters and paintings to be reframed and sent the furniture out to be reupholstered. She trashed the heavy silk curtains and put up museum shades. She bought a Christopher Farr rug for the living room and gave the old Persian, freshly steamed, to Tom, her sentimental child. The other Persians she had cleaned and put in storage. When she was finished, five months later, the apartment, like a great face-lift, looked the same but better. Every sign of Rupert, except for books and family photographs, had been purged. It smelled different.

Rupert's will held no surprises. He left Eleanor his law firm pension and 401(k) plan. His investments, which were substantial, he left as a life interest to Eleanor and then in trust to "my sons or, if they do not survive me, their issue per stirpes."

Six months after Rupert's death, Eleanor received a letter from a woman living in Brooklyn.

October 8, 2000

Dear Mrs. Fawkes,
For some years, I had a relationship with
your husband, Rupert Fawkes. We met
in 1975 and had two children together,
Hugh, 24, and Iain, 23. Rupert always
said he would provide for them. I have
advised them to contact a lawyer. As
sons of your husband, they are entitled
to their share of his estate.

Yours very truly,
Vera Wolinski

The letter temporarily threw Eleanor off
stride. She didn't know what to think. After
two days of mulling it over, she decided she
couldn't know. She knew that "laughing
heirs" often appeared on the death of a rich
and prominent man. If this Wolinski woman
were a fraud, her army of Maynard lawyers
would beat her back.

Shortly after hearing from Vera Wolinski,
she received a letter from a lawyer in Brooklyn. He informed her he had filed a petition
in Probate Court on behalf of his clients,
"Hugh and Iain Wolinski Fawkes, the natural born sons of Rupert Fawkes."

Rupert's name did not appear on the birth
certificates of the Wolinski boys. Nor had he

acknowledged paternity. Vera said he had provided support of a thousand dollars a month for each boy and a thousand dollars for her until the younger one reached the age of twenty-three. Her account showed deposits for these funds but not from Rupert, not from anyone. The money, in a monthly lump sum of three thousand dollars, had been wired anonymously, directly into her account from a bank in the Caymans.

The only evidence Vera could produce was an old blurry sepia photograph of herself and a man in fisherman sandals, who might be Rupert, standing in front of Toffenetti Restaurant in Times Square. Vera had never told the boys who their father was until she told them to sue Rupert's estate.

A hearing was set to review the claims. Harry and Will went with their mother. The Wolinski boys were blond and fair, as Rupert had been, as was their mother. A disquieting aspect for Eleanor was Hugh's gait, which was like Rupert's, at once languid and athletic. Both young men had graduated from the US Coast Guard Academy and were serving in the Coast Guard.

The case was reported in the *Post* and Eleanor's friends rallied around her in indignation. Eleanor remained cool and

steady. The more she thought about the Wolinskis' claim, the more she thought it not
impossible that Rupert had fathered these
children. Vera's misspelling of his last name,
oddly, made the relationship more likely. So
did the fisherman sandals, so un-Rupert but
so English schoolboy. Then there were the
boys' very British names and the spelling of
Iain.

Maynard's lawyers swung into action, ac-
cusing the Wolinskis of fraud and threatening to countersue. They were ferocious in
their attack, bombarding the petitioners
with discovery requests for interrogatories,
depositions, mental examinations, tangible
evidence. Eleanor began to feel sorry for
Vera. She was so dogged in her pursuit of
what she considered her sons' rightful inheritance. The young men were ready to
withdraw. They found the experience humiliating. It was plain they were only doing it
for their mother. Rupert's sons would feel
that way, Eleanor thought.

Eleanor's sons were at first astonished,
then bemused, then upset. They couldn't
believe their father could have had a mistress
and a second family. He was so correct, so
reserved, so devoted to them all. The money
wasn't an issue for them. They all had
Phipps trust funds — Eleanor's father had

invested in McDonald's too — and whether they got one-fifth or one-seventh of their father's estate didn't matter to any of them; there was enough money for a slew of heirs. The blow was to the family amour propre, their idea of the five brothers. They saw it too as a betrayal of their mother, except for Jack, who thought it was cool. "Who knew Dad was a Romeo?" Will punched him hard in the arm. "What was that for?" Jack said. "What did I say wrong?" Harry saw a resemblance to his father in the older boy, in his blondness and high coloring. Sam didn't know what to think. "Could they be his?" he asked Harry. "I don't know," his older brother said. "They're more like him than any of us. We're a gaggle of mama's boys." He paused. "Maybe we're not his, and they are. Kidding. Sort of."

Vera asked for DNA testing. "Just give us a piece of his clothing, a sweater that hasn't been cleaned, a coat he wore, and we'll prove it," Vera said. The Maynard lawyers were outraged the way only a Wall Street firm can be. There was no justification at all for this request, they argued. There was not one iota of proof of a relationship. Eleanor asked her oldest: "Should we give them some money? I feel like a bully, even though they could be complete frauds."

"I'm not suggesting we oblige them," Harry said, "but just out of curiosity: is there anything of Dad's left to test?" He knew the answer. He had watched his mother, with awe and dismay, as she had obliterated all physical traces of his father from the apartment.

Eleanor shook her head.

The Surrogate denied the request. "I will not have the Falkeses' apartment turned into a crime scene."

Vera next asked for one of the sons to provide DNA.

The Maynard lawyers were dead against it, arguing once again with ringing indignation that there was no evidence, not one jot, to justify the request. Harry, the criminal lawyer, had an additional reason to turn them down — "You don't want that information in the wrong hands. And there are no right hands" — but he held off a decision, asking Sam to do some research on the likelihood of a definitive result. A colleague at the hospital provided a short answer: "Without your father's DNA, the results would be inconclusive: a matching Y-chromosome test would establish if the young men were half-siblings of the brother tested, but it would not establish your father's paternity, only that of a 'common ancestor.' " Jack — "Always Jack," Will said — had been willing to give "bodily fluids" for a DNA test. "What the hell," he'd said, "they sound like nice kids" — but he went along with his brothers when they insisted it would be insulting to their mother and the memory of their father to undergo a test that might impugn the integrity of their parents' marriage.

"You realize, of course," Sam said to Harry, "that none of us can prove that Dad was our biological dad."

"Ah, the vexing problem of paternity," Harry said, as if he were teaching a class. "It's interesting what science has wrought." Harry paused to collect his thoughts; Sam without sighing settled in for the tutorial. "It used to be that maternity was never in question and paternity always was." Harry looked to see that Sam was listening. "Now paternity can be settled with DNA testing, if the dad is around, but maternity can't. With mothers, DNA doesn't get you to second base. Who's the 'real' mother: the woman who provides the egg, the woman who gives birth, the woman who paid for the egg and 'hired' the surrogate, the wife of the sperm donor? Some very nice issues in family law."

"God," Sam said, "you lawyers are ruth-less. These are people's lives. I'll bet DNA testing has blown a lot of marriages apart."

"Wouldn't you want to know if your children weren't yours?" Harry asked.

"No, I wouldn't," Sam said. "Why would I want to break my heart? They're here; they're mine."

"You're not a father," Harry said, "and you probably won't be. You might think dif-ferently if you had children."

The Surrogate denied the request: "With-out the father's DNA, there can be no conclusive results."

Vera came back a third time, asking for Rupert's blood type. It was a straw-grasp, a last gasp.

Harry and Sam took their mother to lunch. They talked genetics with her. Sam told her that a blood test might rule out Rupert as a father, but it could never establish paternity. Harry's advice was to give it to them. "If we let them know his blood type, and there's no possibility of a match, we might be able to get rid of them, once and for all. Anyway, hundreds of people already have access to that informa-tion." Rupert, Eleanor, and the boys were all type O.

The Wolinskis gave a report of their blood

types. Vera's was A, Hugh was O, Iain was A. Against the advice of the Maynard lawyers, Harry, with his mother's permission, released a medical report to the Wolinskis with his father's blood type.

Vera asked the family doctor to analyze the results. He told her what any tenth-grade biology text would have told them: the results were inconclusive. At the next hearing, Vera turned on Eleanor. "You've cheated us," she said. "Look at my boys. Anyone can see the resemblance. He's their father." Her sons folded her into their arms and took her home. On April 25, 2002, the Surrogate dismissed the Wolinskis' petition, eighteen months after it was filed, two years after Rupert's death. Mourning can resume, Eleanor thought.

Eleanor couldn't put the Wolinskis out of her mind. She brought the subject up with Harry two months later over lunch at Café Luxembourg.

"I feel I should do something for them," she said to him. "What do you think?"

"Do you know something?" he asked. "Something you're not telling us?"

"I don't know if your father is their father, if that's your question, but I think there was some link between him and Vera Wolinski."

She paused. "I can't figure it out."

Harry looked more alert. "Is that why you stripped the apartment?" he asked. It was still a raw subject for all the boys, though they hadn't been altogether surprised. With the Phippses, mourning was purging.

"No," Eleanor replied, a hint of irritation in her voice. "I didn't know about them."

"Why weren't they in the will?" Harry asked. "Wouldn't Dad have looked out for them in some way if he had wanted to? A trust, a permanent Cayman account? He'd have known how."

"Yes, yes, if he had wanted to, but he didn't." She stopped.

"I don't understand," Harry said.

"Don't you see," Eleanor said. "The Wolinskis' claim makes no sense unless it's true. Why would Ms. Wolinski pick him as the father? How would she have settled on him unless she knew him? She's not a scam artist."

"How could he have abandoned them?" Harry asked. "He was an orphan. How could he leave them fatherless?"

"That makes it more likely, don't you see?" Eleanor said, wondering at Harry's slowness. He was usually so quick to see things. "Dad gave them a mother and provided her with the wherewithal to stick around and raise them. I don't think he ever thought of himself as fatherless, only motherless. All his life, men have looked out for him. Reverend Falkes. Dean Rostow. Granddad."

Harry thought about this. "But why should he leave us so much? We have so much. They have nothing."

"Not nothing. No inheritance. Whoever paid the support cut it off when the younger son turned twenty-three. He launched them. That seems like something Dad might do."

Harry looked sharply at his mother. For the first time in his life, he saw her as a person, and not his overly fond mother. He found himself growing angry.

"You didn't know about them until they appeared, is that right?" he asked.

"The Wolinskis? No."

"You've been thinking about this for a while, is that true?"

"Yes."

"You believe her, don't you?" He was the lawyer now, cross-examining a hostile witness.

"No," she said. "Maybe. Vera knew your father. He's the man in the photo." Eleanor cleared her throat.

Harry sat quietly for a few moments.

"Dad was a bigamist. Our family life was a lie," he said. He turned on his mother. "Two years, two children. You had to . . ." He stopped.

# CHAPTER 2
## SAM

They say the best men are moulded out of faults,/And for the most, become much more the better/For being a little bad.

WILLIAM SHAKESPEARE,
*MEASURE FOR MEASURE*

Harry put off calling Sam for ten days. He had been too rattled by the conversation with his mother to talk about it. All his life, he had trusted his instincts. The question he had asked Eleanor had come to him in a flash, a sudden, staggering insight, penetrating to the heart of the mystery that was his mother. He waited for the shock of recognition to pass between them.

Eleanor's response was white anger. He saw it in her tight mouth and narrowed eyes, the dagger look, not seen since Gran had died.

"Another woman may have had two children with your father," she said. "I don't

64

know more than that." She cleared her throat.

Harry sat back in his chair, jolted by the unexpected response. Looking up at the ceiling to avoid her eyes, he replayed the scene in his head. She was not telling the truth, not the whole truth. How could she not have known? Why else would she be bringing up the Wolinskis now? He lowered his eyes to meet hers, then looked sideways, out the window. She wants to throttle me, he thought. She had never hit him, or any of them.

Eleanor reached in her bag for her wallet. "I'm thinking of setting up a trust for the Wolinski boys," she said. "I've talked to the lawyers at Maynard. They haven't figured out how I can do it without reopening the Surrogate's case, but they will. They don't approve. Not their business."

She rose from the table. He turned his head to look at her. "You need to stop thinking you're always the smartest person in the room," she said. She put down a wad of twenties and left. Harry went home and took a Xanax.

When he finally talked to Sam, Harry stopped short of her parting remark.

Sam was enraged. "Do you know what you did? You accused Mom of covering up

65

for Dad, of allowing herself to be humili-
ated by him."

Harry felt his temper rise; he had been on
a quest for the truth. "I didn't make an accusation, I made an observation, an obvious
observation." He paused. "And she cleared
her throat, twice."

"What about Dad? Why aren't you mad at
him?" Sam asked.

"He's dead," Harry said. "I can't tell him
what I think."

"What is it you think?" Sam said.

"He betrayed us," Harry said.

"No," Sam said. "If he betrayed anyone, it
was our mother. How are you the injured
party?"

"He didn't care for us. He was never
there," Harry said.

"That's a lie," Sam said. "He was there, in
his way, and he loved us, in his way." Sam
wanted to punch Harry, something he
hadn't done in thirty years. "And we all
loved him."

"An affair is one thing," Harry said, "but
another family? And not one son, but two.
That's unacceptable."

"Where is this anger coming from?" Sam
said. "Why weren't you angry when the Wolinskis were suing us?"

"I thought they were cheats, frauds,"

66

Harry said. "I didn't believe them. I thought of it as a kind of joke. Ha-ha-ha, Dad's secret life."

"We still don't know," Sam said. Harry didn't say anything.

"Oh, I get it," Sam said. "Your masculine intuition."

"It makes sense, if you'd let yourself think about it," Harry said. "Why did she clean out the apartment and get rid of all Dad's stuff, making it impossible to test their DNA? Why wasn't she upset when they sued? Why does she want to pay them off? It's all clear now. Mom made fools of us in Surrogate's Court. She played a very deep game."

"You can't believe that," Sam said. "Have you ever seen Mom upset?"

"Why isn't anyone else angry, or at least upset? Dad was a bigamist."

"More like Schrödinger's father," Sam said. "With us and with Mrs. Wolinski at the same time."

"Always clever, Sam," Harry said. "No heart."

"You're all heart, Harry," Sam said. "Have you discussed this with your wife? What does Lea say?" His question was met with silence. He waited.

"I haven't said anything to Lea," Harry said.

"Have you spoken to Mom since then?" Sam asked. Silence again.

"No," Harry said.

"You've never gotten Mom right," Sam said. "You've always gotten her wrong."

"What if I am right?" Harry said.

"What if you're right? Should Mom have left him when she found out?" Sam asked. "If you keep on, you'll wreck the family. I won't forgive you."

"It has a life of its own," Harry said.

"Snuff it out," Sam said.

Harry couldn't keep his counsel, even when it was in his interest. Will called him "the Blurter." Jack was a blurter too, but his blurts seemed more in keeping with his genial egoism. He attached no value to secrets or confidences, no matter how painful or humiliating. "Who cares who knows?" Jack would say. He told his fourth-grade class that his grandmother had dropped dead sitting on the toilet. When Mrs. Mortimer, his teacher, reported this to Eleanor, Eleanor didn't blink.

"I thought Jack's third-grade teacher had spoken to you," Eleanor said. "You should get ready for more of the same. He's tactless, guileless. He says whatever comes into his head. I found it almost endearing when he was younger. There's no cure yet. He doesn't care what other people think except the musicians he admires."

"Is he ever scolded? Punished?" Mrs. Mortimer asked.

"Nothing works," Eleanor said. "We've tried everything short of confiscating his trumpet. We threatened once to take it away for a day. He held his breath until he passed out. He's better now with his brothers. They do not suffer under the same ethical constraints as his parents or his teachers."

Eleanor didn't tell Mrs. Mortimer that Harry and Will had beaten Jack until his nose bled after he told his third-grade class that they had wet their pants when they were mugged in Central Park by a man with a gun and tattoos on his face. They had tried first to humiliate him — Mikado justice — but already at eight, he was inured to humiliation.

"Your wiener is smaller than my little toe," Harry said.

"Tom's wiener is bigger than yours," Will said.

"I'm only a kid," Jack said. "Wait until I'm grown. Mine'll be bigger than your foot. Trumpet players have the biggest pickles.

Everyone knows that." Will pushed him to the floor; Harry put him in a headlock.

Will said Jack was the Dark Side of the Golden Rule. "He does unto others as he would have them do unto him, and the others want to kill him."

Harry's blurts were different. They fell into two categories. The first kind were excited utterances, spontaneous and thoughtless spoilers, admissible as hearsay. If Harry brought a gift, he'd announce the contents as the recipient was unwrapping. "It's a Swiss Army knife, the big fancy one." If he recommended a movie or a book, he'd tell the ending. "Ewell, the guy who killed Tom Robinson, tries to kill Scout and Jem. Boo Radley saves them and kills him." If he was planning a surprise, he couldn't keep it under wraps longer than a week. He told Lea he was going to propose a month before the actual event. "I think I'm engaged to be engaged," she told her mother. Harry's egoism was less pervasive than Jack's but also less genial.

The second kind of blurts were unwelcome truths — hard, unpleasant facts he thought other people ought to know. It was an old story for Eleanor, but until Café Luxembourg, she had never been a blurt victim, only a witness. When he was fifteen,

70

he told seven-year-old Tom there was no Santa Claus. Tom was furious with Eleanor. "Why didn't you tell me? I look like a baby." He was crying. Eleanor knelt down. "I believed in Santa Claus until I was eight," she said. Tom wiped his eyes with his sleeve. "Really?" he said. She nodded. Tom put his arms around her neck and cried with relief. Eleanor was not telling the truth. Her awakening had come much earlier. She knew her mother would never let a fat man who smoked a pipe and trailed soot into their apartment. "I buy you all the things you need," Mrs. Phipps had said when Eleanor, age four, had asked if Santa was coming. "Don't be greedy."

"Harry is mean," Tom said. Eleanor considered her reply. "He can't help himself," she said.

When Eleanor asked Harry why he did it, he said, "It was time he knew. It was embarrassing that he still believed."

"Who was embarrassed?" Eleanor said. "Tom or you? You're too old to be embarrassed by another person's behavior. Look to your own." Harry flushed. He never again let someone else embarrass him. His brothers were the chief beneficiaries of this new policy, though Eleanor too benefited; she no longer had to mop up after him.

Eleanor's Santa intervention worked only in cases of displaced embarrassment. Harry kept telling people things they didn't want to know. When he was in his late thirties, Harry told a good friend his wife was having an affair; he'd seen the adulterous couple kissing on a street in the East Village. The good friend stopped speaking to him. Harry couldn't understand why, when he was only telling the truth. "It's killing the messenger," he said to Sam.

"The messenger here is not innocent," Sam said. "You're not Western Union. There's a difference between the person who writes the telegram and the person who delivers it." Sam laughed. "Then again, you may have saved the marriage," he said. "Your friend could get mad at you instead of his wife. One of the relationships had to go."

Harry might have kept his friend if he had been willing to apologize, but he wasn't. Apologies weren't in his repertoire. "The two are related, the blurting and the not-apologizing," Sam said to his mother. "He's never wrong."

Sam taught himself to read when he was four. "I had to," he told his father, "I needed to read my Superman comics. No one will read them to me." Harry and Will would be in the park throwing a ball, catching a ball, hitting a ball. Sam would be in his bedroom archiving his comics or building LEGO. As he worked, he would hum to himself, snatches of melodies he'd heard on the radio or in church. Sitting with Sam one evening shortly before his sixth birthday, Rupert realized the boy was humming a section from "Im Abendrot," the last of Strauss's "Four Last Songs."

"Do you think you'd like to sing in the St. Thomas Choir?" Rupert asked.

Sam looked up from the instructions. "No, thank you," he said.

"Do you sing at school?" Rupert asked.

"No," Sam said. "I don't like to sing. I listen to songs in my head. They sound better. The songs at school are rubbish."

Sam was the only one of Rupert's sons who'd picked up his Anglicisms. He'd use them when he was alone with Rupert, as if they shared a secret language. Sam liked especially the British English words that meant something else in American English: trainers, flat, bonnet, braces, dust, fringe, flannel, jumper. He kept a list in a strongbox. Sam was a collector and archivist, not only of comics. He never wanted to throw anything out.

"Can't we at least toss the Duplo," Eleanor asked him when he was six. On most days his room looked as if it had exploded. "What about the Lincoln Logs?"

"No, no," Sam said. "I'm saving them for Tom."

"What about storing them in Limbo?" Eleanor asked. Limbo, a large closet off the pantry, was where Eleanor stored old toys and athletic equipment the boys had outgrown but weren't ready to part with. After three months in Limbo, an item was passed on to another brother, thrown in the garbage, or taken to a thrift shop. Eleanor's mother disapproved, seeing it as "coddling Collyering." She thought they should use things until they wore out. "I counted eight tennis racquets in that closet," she said to Eleanor the year Sam went into middle school. Eleanor refused the bait. "I think you missed two behind the door," she said. The boys had mixed feelings about Limbo. Sometimes, months later, one of the boys would spot a discarded toy or racquet in one of his brothers' rooms and express regret at its loss. He'd complain to his mother. "Why don't you share?" she'd suggest. Harry and Sam didn't like sharing. Tom insisted he never got anything new, not even new underwear. "Everything I have came out of Limbo," he'd complain. Years later, Tom came to think of Princeton as one more Limbo pass-along.

"I might change my mind after three months," Sam said, already hedging his offer.

Shortly before his eighth birthday, Sam gave all his LEGO to Tom. He announced the handover at dinner. "I'm through with LEGO."

"Just like that?" Eleanor asked.

"It's all the same. I'd like a microscope for my next birthday."

"Yes," Rupert said.

"Can I have a horn for mine?" Jack asked, only six but already possessed. "A real one, not plastic." Eleanor nodded. "Any other requests?" she asked.

"I'd like one of those steel tennis racquets," Harry said.

"Me too," said Will.

"Since when?" said Harry.

"Since Jimmy Connors," Will said.

"Right," said Harry.

"It's true," said Will.

"Next up," Rupert said.

Eleanor smiled at Tom. "And you, Tomahawk?" she said. The others all turned to look at him, bibbed in his booster seat. He froze, stricken, then covered his eyes with his hands, silently, hopelessly willing his mother to pick him up and hold him in her lap. She wouldn't, not at dinner.

"I don't know what a tennis rocket is," he said, looking up at the ceiling, blinking back tears. "I might want one. I like rockets."

Everyone laughed, Jack loudest. Tom put his head on the table.

"I like rockets too," Sam said.

Tom lifted his head.

"Give me five," Sam said.

All his life, Tom loved Sam with the passionate feelings of a little boy. "I could do without the others," he told his wife, Caroline. "Will's OK." Caroline shook her head. "You love them all, even Jack." Tom grunted.

That year, Sam's scientific career began in earnest. He looked at everything under his microscope: hot dogs, French fries, oysters, LEGO, sand, acorns, dead worms, living worms, mice, moles, lady birds, flies, sticks. He wrote down his observations in three notebooks: Things, Living Things, and Dead Things.

"Is a leaf I just picked living or dead?" he asked his father.

"Dying, I would think," Rupert said. "So, living."

Sam was quiet. "Living is dying," he said.

He was quiet again. "I'm going to be a doc-tor."

"Yes," Rupert said.

Sam had dreaded the move to the upper school. His father wanted him to play a sport. Over the years, he had joined and quit Little League, Soccer League, and Hockey League. He liked playing games; he hated being on a team. "The coaches are always yelling," he told his mother. "And they make fun of the fat kids." He was not a team player, not in athletics, not in life. He had his family, Team Falkes; that was the only team he wanted to play on. Rupert believed in playing sports the way he be-lieved in churchgoing: it was character-building. But I have character, Sam thought, just a different kind. He wished he had Jack's character. Jack got himself kicked off every team for poor sportsmanship. "I am a soloist," Jack said.

Everyone at Trinity played sports. It looked good on college applications: Honor Society, Soup Kitchen, Varsity Soccer. Trinity expected it: *labore et virtute.*

In ninth grade, Sam went out for squash. He played for the team intermittently and listlessly. His game was a tennis player's game. He attacked the ball with a wide swing that enraged his opponents. "Do I have to play on a team?" Sam asked his father as the next school year began. They were listening to music in the library, Schubert's songs.

"What about running?" Rupert said. "You're fast."

"I always come in second," Sam said. "It makes me cross. I get like Harry. I hate losing."

The next weekend, Rupert took Sam to see *Chariots of Fire* at Lincoln Plaza, around the corner from their apartment.

That summer, Sam joined Road Runners. He got stronger, faster. Junior and senior years, he competed in the 400- and the 800-meter. "Tailor-made for neurotics," he said to his father. Sam was built like a distance runner, as were all the boys when they were young. Legs and lungs, Eleanor thought, like me. At Princeton, Sam took up squash again. He paid attention to the coaches and learned to whip his racquet. Exploiting the runner's advantage, he regularly beat Harry.

Eleanor never listened to music. It made her anxious. When Rupert proposed, she told him, as a warning, that she couldn't be made to attend concerts. "I'd rather listen to news radio," she said. She knew music was important to him. He had told her it had saved his life.

"We don't have to like the same things," he said. "I can go by myself."

In middle school, Eleanor had been made to suffer through Saturday-afternoon concerts at the New York Philharmonic. She had a subscription, a birthday gift from her mother. In the beginning, her nanny went with her. "I expect you to appreciate what I'm doing to cultivate your musical taste," her mother said. "I pay for Nanny's tickets too."

Sitting in her stiff, scratchy taffeta dress, not knowing what to do with her face, Eleanor found the concerts more boring than church. Music made no sense to her. She couldn't remember melodies unless they had words. She never knew when to clap. When she was twelve, she was allowed to go by herself. Realizing that a good portion of the audience stayed only for the first half of the concert, Eleanor started leaving at the interval and going to movies, taking the concert program to show her mother. The year 1950 was a spectacular one for movies, a lucky break for a good girl on the lam. She saw: *Sunset Boulevard, All About Eve, Born Yesterday, A Streetcar Named Desire, Strangers on a Train, Rashomon.* She also

79

saw duds: *Father of the Bride, Cheaper by the Dozen, Cinderella, King Solomon's Mines, Quo Vadis, Harvey. Harvey* almost put her permanently off Jimmy Stewart. The others confirmed her early prejudices against Technicolor, toga sagas, domestic comedies, and Disney. Dud or hit, she always stayed till the end, as a rebuke to the Philharmonic, a "counterpoint of honor."

The boys, musically, ran the gamut. Harry and Will liked the Stones, Patti Smith, James Brown, Jimi Hendrix, the Police, Dylan, Springsteen. Mostly, they listened; occasionally, they went to concerts. Tom liked country, the Doors, the Stones, Motown, and the Beatles. He took guitar lessons for two years but gave it up. "I'm no good," he said, comparing himself with Jack. Jack heard the album *Bird and Diz* when he was five, at a friend's. He came home and said to his mother, "I need you to buy me all of Dizzy's records. And all of Bird's. I also need a record player and a horn." At six, he started lessons. He played the trumpet, he later explained, because he loved Coltrane and Parker too much to play the saxophone. "I cry when I hear a great sax. It's like a human voice," he said. "Chet, Dizzy, Miles, Louis, they make me glad to be alive." Sam was the only one who loved classical music.

It started early. He would toddle unevenly into the library, where his father was reading, and point to the stereo. Rupert would put on a record. As the music filled the room, Sam would sit on the floor leaning against his father's legs. He never fell asleep. Songs and chamber music were his favorites. His father bought him a Cambridge Soundworks radio for his sixth birthday and tuned it to WQXR. Unlike Harry, Will, and Tom, Sam couldn't listen to music and read or do homework. He was like Jack that way. "Music invades my brain," he said. He hated background music. All music was foreground. When he hummed, as he often did while working on some project, he didn't notice he was doing it. "My brain does it by itself," he told his mother.

For his eleventh birthday, Sam asked his father if he could have a subscription to the opera. He had heard *Carmen* on the radio and was transported. Over a late dinner at his in-laws' a week later, Rupert mentioned it.

"I got tickets for us both to *Rigoletto, Traviata, Madame Butterfly, Billy Budd.*"

"Sam's a little fairy, isn't he?" Mrs. Phipps said. "Too bad. I wonder where it came from." She looked at Eleanor.

Rupert turned to his father-in-law. "You'll

excuse me, Edward," he said.

Rupert then turned to his mother-in-law. "You stupid cunt."

The Falkes boys all had a wide streak of single-mindedness; it made them successful and, to varying extents, self-absorbed. Jack's single-mindedness was extreme, crossing over to obsession. Unable to think about anything other than jazz, he talked about little else. No family occasion passed without Eleanor's mother remarking in his hearing, "All play and no work makes Jack a dull boy." She would laugh as she said it, pleased with her joke. "Is it worth a Granny slapdown?" Rupert said. "Do you mind when Granny says that?" Eleanor asked Jack. "Granny is not nice. We all know that," Jack said. "She picks on Sam more than she picks on me. It's OK."

In their single-mindedness, the boys were like their father. Rupert could do multiple things: litigate, negotiate, sail, sing, read, but he could only do one of them at a time. If he was interrupted in the middle of a task, even an unpleasant one, like bill paying, he grew testy. "Is it important?" he'd ask. Father and sons thought that multitasking was for the butterfly-minded. They made a permanent running joke of it. Harry said he could eat and read at the same time, but not pie and economics. Will said he could breathe and argue. Sam could hum and titrate. Jack said he could fart and chew gum. Tom said he could barely do one thing at a time, let alone two.

Eleanor could make a sandwich and do LEGO, sing and drive, push a stroller and settle a quarrel, listen and wipe a nose. Testiness wasn't an option. Is constant and instant availability to the needs of boys the same thing as multitasking? she thought.

In eleventh grade, Harry read Isaiah Berlin's *The Hedgehog and the Fox*. For his class project, he devised a ten-point scale, running from 1 (hedgehog: knowing one big thing) to 10 (fox: knowing many things), as a test of the two categories. The night before his project was due, he did a pilot study on his family, plotting them along the axis: he was a 5; Will a 4; Sam a 3; Jack a 1; Tom, hypothetically, then only eight, a 5. He presented his results at dinner.

"This is very interesting," Rupert said. "Where do your mother and I go?"

"You're a 5, I think, like me. We don't like interruptions, but we cope," Harry said. "Mom's an 8, maybe a 9. A fox."

"Is that your way of telling me I'm a multitasker?" Eleanor asked, always aware she had been raised to be good at nothing.

"It's not an insult," Harry said. "You're always doing at least two things at a time. You don't mind being interrupted."

"How do you know I don't mind?" she asked.

The boys stared at her. Rupert stared at her.

"No," she said. "I'm not an 8 or a 9. I'm a 1, a purebred hedgehog, Mrs. Tiggy-Winkle herself. All I do is all of you. That's what I know. One big thing. Boys."

Harry considered her objection. "The extremes meet. Is that it?" he asked.

"No," Eleanor said. "Synecdoche."

"I don't understand," Harry said.

"All the things I do are simply parts of the whole," Eleanor said.

Later that evening, catching her alone, Sam asked his mother whether she ever wished she were something other than a mother. Eleanor winced inwardly. None of the others would have asked that question; none of the others would even have thought of it. She felt her old sense of guilt about Sam rising. Breathing slowly to tamp it down — what use was guilt, after all? — she unexpectedly felt a wave of irritation with his brothers.

"Not 'other' than a mother. Never. Perhaps 'in addition,' " she said to Sam.

"What would you do?" he asked.

"I don't know. I'm almost forty," she said. "I've never worked."

"Is that why you had five children?" he asked.

"I had five children because I was lucky. I could afford five children. I had household help. I thought it was a good idea. Dad thought it was a good idea. I was an only child; he was an orphan. We like having all of you around. Dad would have had more. I think his fantasy was eleven, a cricket side."

"What do you do during the day when we're not home?" Sam asked.

Eleanor didn't answer at once. Sam waited.

"I go to movies," she said.

"I thought you shopped," Sam said. "I thought you were bored."

"Mothers are often a mystery to their children," Eleanor said.

"Do you go to movies alone?" Sam asked.

"Sometimes I go by myself, sometimes I go with a friend," Eleanor said.

"Do you have a favorite movie?" Sam asked.

*"Smiles of a Summer Night, The Third Man, Casablanca, The Sorrow and the Pity,"* Elea-

nor said. "I don't run to favorites. In any-thing."

"Not even Harry?" Sam said. In a family of five boys, there was a lot of jockeying for attention, and Harry had a way of elbowing to the front.

"Cheeky boy," Eleanor said, ruffling his hair. "Only his first two years."

"You're not a pure hedgehog, are you?" Sam said.

Eleanor shook her head.

"My favorite movie is *Close Encounters of the Third Kind,*" Sam said.

"Not *Star Wars*?"

" 'He says the sun came out last night. He says it sang to him,' " Sam said.

Lea called Sam. "What do we do about Harry?" she asked. "He's stuck on being right. As if that mattered more than being decent. What did you say to him? He won't tell me."

"I said if he didn't pull himself together, he'd wreck the family, and I'd never forgive him. I was very angry. I'm still very angry," Sam said.

"I'm sorry," Lea said.

"I loved my father," Sam said. "He never for one minute wanted me to be straight. He wanted me to be me. In the world of parents of gays, that is so rare. Andrew says he was the snow leopard of dads."

"Is this only about your father, not your mother?" Lea said.

"Both. I don't understand why he's so mad at her. He wasn't close to Dad but he loves Mom," Sam said. "He's always believed he was her favorite. He's always acted as though the rest of us were superfluous. Case in point."

"He's trapped himself. It's reached a state of imminent mortification with him, backing down, that is. He was expecting Lana Turner; she gave him Bette Davis. He was sure she would confess; he still can't believe she didn't."

"I don't understand how he could have done it. He led the charge against the Wolinskis because their lawsuit was an insult to our parents. But he can insult them, is that it?"

"What do we do?" Lea said.

"He needs to apologize to Mom — a clean apology, or as clean as he can manage," Sam said. "He can think whatever he wants, but he can't talk about it to her. Or anyone. If he keeps on, there will be civil war, with Jack the only one on speakers with him."

"Could he be right?" Lea said.

"Oh, Lea," Sam said, "don't go there.

Don't join him."

"I love him. It's been hard," she said.

"Is something else going on with him?" Sam asked.

"I don't know," she said. She was silent for a few moments. Sam waited. "Freud for dummies. All this displaced anger. Is he going to blame me for something he's done, something he's doing? It's always the woman's fault, isn't it, ever since Eve?"

"I'm sorry," Sam said.

"Unlike him, I can't ask," she said. "I might have to leave him."

"Dad dies, and we fall apart," Sam said.

Sam had never seen his parents fight. When he was nine, he asked Harry and Will if they had. They hadn't. "They don't fight and they don't hug or kiss," Harry said. "They're WASPs." "Do they love each other?" Sam asked. "Of course," Harry said. "They're married." Watching them sitting side by side on the library sofa, reading the paper or looking at TV, Sam longed for his mother to rest her head on his father's shoulder, his father to lay his hand on her knee. He offered up his comic-book collection. Neither moved, though his father looked at his mother in a way that Sam thought was like an invisible hand on her knee. There were

88

other signs too. They went to bed at the same hour and locked their bedroom door. He knew; he had tried the handle.

Sam had never seen his grandparents fight either, but he didn't need to consult Harry. Their politeness to each other was guerrilla warfare. Every "please," every "thank you" bristled with hostility. They couldn't stand each other. It was a secret everyone knew and no one mentioned. At the holidays, Eleanor served buffet dinners so her father could sit in the living room, her mother in the dining room. At the end of an evening, Granddad would send Gran home alone in the car. He liked to stay on to smoke a cigar, an activity forbidden at home. The driver would come back later for him. No one liked Eleanor's mother, but no one except Rupert was allowed to be rude to her.

Sam loved his grandfather the way he loved no one else ever; it was undefended love, love without boundaries. "There's a meeting of the minds with me and Poppa," he told his mother. For Sam's tenth birthday, Mr. Phipps bought him a dissection kit and a fetal pig marinated in formaldehyde. Sam was over the moon. The next week, Mr. Phipps asked him two questions; they would become his standard greeting: "What did you observe today?" and "What did you think about what you observed?"

"Is this about my pig, Poppa?" Sam asked. "Are you training me to be a scientist?"

"Partly," said his grandfather. "Mostly, I'm training you to be a person."

"Sometimes I see things that make me sad, things I'd like to fix but can't," Sam said.

"Ah," Poppa said.

"Do you have to live with Granny?" Sam asked.

"Yes," Poppa said. "It's my duty. Old-fashioned, isn't it?"

"I don't think I have a sense of duty," Sam said.

"Good," Poppa said. "It can hobble your life."

When Eleanor's mother died a year and a half later, only her father and Rupert went to the graveyard. The funeral service had been impersonal: readings, hymns, prayers. The priest gave a canned eulogy. Eleanor remembered him saying, "She was a remarkable woman." The day was rainy and cold. "No one need go to the interment," Mr. Phipps told the mourners. "We'll meet you back at Eleanor's." At lunch, out of the presence of their parents, the boys speculated:

"Pops and Dad went to the graveyard to make sure she was dead," Jack said.

"I didn't cry. Nobody cried," Tom said.

"Will anyone miss her?" Sam asked.

"Did anyone love her?" Harry asked.

"Did she love anyone?" Will asked.

Sam knew she didn't love him. When he was four, he had asked his grandmother if she knew how to wipe a little boy. There was some urgency to the question. His grandparents were looking after the boys while Eleanor went out briefly to do an errand. "Are you saying you can't wipe yourself?" she said. "Are you a baby?" Mr. Phipps rose from the sofa. "This is between us men," he said. He took Sam to the bathroom. "Was Granny ever a little girl?" Sam asked his grandfather. Sam would not miss her.

After the guests had left, Mr. Phipps took a walk over to Lincoln Center with Eleanor. "She was very beautiful, your mother, as a young woman, and I knew nothing of young women," he said. "I can't regret the marriage. There's you. I'm sorry we stopped you from marrying Jim Cardozo."

"No need to apologize," Eleanor said. "I married the right man." She gave a small laugh. "You kept me from making your mistake."

"Well, well," Mr. Phipps said. "I'll take the credit." He patted her hand. "I love

Rupert," Mr. Phipps said.

"Why don't you give up the apartment and move to the West Side," Eleanor asked.

A month later, he put the apartment on the market. It sold in two months, with all its furnishings. He gave Eleanor the family silver. There were generations of it, including a huge set of Christofle Cluny, enough for four brides and a groom. Her father bought a two-bedroom, two-floor artist's studio on West Sixty-Seventh, down the block from the Hotel des Artistes. He filled the bookshelves with books. He and Sam had a Philharmonic subscription. The boys all had keys and strict instructions to drop in anytime. "Anytime," Poppa said. "Night or day."

Sam took him at his word. A week after move-in day, he dropped by on his way home from school. He stayed five minutes.

"I saw Poppa today," he said as he slid into his seat at dinner that evening. He spoke slowly in a hushed voice, leaving spaces between the words. Everyone looked at him, even Tom. "He has —" Sam trailed off and looked around the circle, making sure all eyes were on him. "— a girlfriend." The boys squinted sideways at their mother. Granny had been dead less than six months. "How do you know?" Eleanor asked. She hadn't known. "I have eyes," Sam said, opening his own very wide, for punctuation.

"What did they see?" Eleanor said.

"I interrupted," Sam said. Jack snickered.

"Do we have to beat this story out of you?" Harry said.

Exploiting the momentousness of his intelligence, Sam stood up. "I went into the apartment with my key. Poppa and this lady were sitting next to each other on the big sofa, very close, drinking Champagne. They were surprised to see me. Poppa burst out laughing. She looked cross." Sam suppressed a laugh. "She said, 'Who's this intruder? Is he armed?' She was trying to be funny." Sam grinned like a maniacal clown. "Poppa got up and brought me over to meet her. He said, 'This is my grandson Sam, number three, out of five. They all visit me. They have keys and can come whenever they want. Sam comes the most.' Then he said, 'Sam, this is my friend, Mrs. Cantwell. Mrs. Cantwell visits too.' I told Poppa I just stopped by to say hello. I shook hands with the lady and left." Sam made a bow. His brothers pounded the table. Jack reached under his chair for his trumpet and blasted the racetrack salute.

The next day, Mr. Phipps called Eleanor.

"Sam met a friend of mine last evening," he said.

"Yes, he told us all. Mrs. Cantwell."

"She's an old friend. We met again recently. She's a widow," Mr. Phipps said.

"You don't owe me an explanation. Do you still want the boys coming and going whenever they want to? I think Sam was embarrassed. Also thrilled."

"They must come anytime when they want to. They come first, I told Marina that. My family comes first. Any friends come second, third, ninety-ninth."

"Maybe you want to have some kind of schedule. If the boys feel awkward, they won't drop by," Eleanor said.

"I'll work it out," he said. "You must meet her. Wonderful woman. Almost as beautiful as when she was young."

Eleanor laughed. "No use warning you, I suppose, against beautiful women."

"Touché, touché," he said, laughing. "She's beautiful and generous."

"Good work," Eleanor said.

"We'll have dinner, the four of us, one day in the next few weeks."

Two months later, Eleanor, Rupert, Eleanor's father, and Mrs. Cantwell met for dinner at Côte Basque. It was a success of sorts. Everyone was courteous. Mrs.

Cantwell's daughter Louisa, a sophomore at Smith, joined them. A pale blonde with a snub nose and bow mouth, she was pretty, like Sandra Dee. She wore an expensive suit — bespoke, Eleanor thought — and elegant jewelry. Eleanor admired her necklace, an intricate gold chain. Louisa preened. "Isn't it the loveliest necklace ever?" she said. "My boyfriend, Carter, gave it to me, for my twentieth birthday. Harry Winston." She paused for a moment, then with more warmth added, "It's amazing. I can wear it with everything, a swimsuit, blue jeans, a ball gown." She gave Eleanor a wide smile. "I came out last year at the Waldorf. It was so much fun. You meet the best young men. Did you come out?" Eleanor thought back on her debutante years. "I liked the rough-and-tumble of weddings for meeting men," she said. "You never knew who might have been invited."

"My friends aren't getting married. Only engaged. I hope to get married a year after I graduate. I want to work a year, to see what it's like."

"Do you like being at a woman's college?" Eleanor said. "I went to Vassar, but that was in the '50s. I don't think I'd do it again."

Louisa looked slyly at her mother, who smiled blandly at her. "My father died when

I was nine. He wanted me to go there."

"My mother went to Smith," Eleanor said. "A rigorous education."

For the rest of the evening the Cantwell women held the floor, occasionally talking over each other. Louisa talked gowns, parties, and jewelry. Mrs. Cantwell, in full throat, gossiped about people the Falkeses didn't know. "Did you hear?" she'd ask. "Would you believe?" Mr. Phipps chuckled at everything she said. She smiled back flirtatiously, as though she was still the prettiest girl at the cotillion. The Falkeses tried to open up the conversation. Rupert brought up the Iran hostage crisis, Eleanor, *Apocalypse Now.* Mrs. Cantwell closed them down. "You're both too clever for me," she said. "I don't understand those things." She gave all her attention to Mr. Phipps. "I could listen to him all day," she said. She gazed at him with Nancy Reagan eyes.

"I don't think mother and daughter have much to say for themselves," Rupert said to Eleanor as they crossed the park in a cab. He stopped, remembering his late mother-in-law. "It's good for your father. Mrs. Cantwell is so very fond of him. The way she looks at him must give him happiness."

Mrs. Cantwell lived on the Upper East Side and didn't like crossing the park. "Why

96

did you move to the West Side?" she said to him. "You should move back. There's so much crime where you are." Her prejudice worked in Edward's favor. Because she didn't like coming to his place, he went to hers. He got to decide when he went and when he didn't. The boys could always drop by his apartment. He might not be there, but neither would she. Sam ran into her only one other time. He was seventeen, a senior at Trinity. "I suppose you'll go to Princeton too," she said. "Yes," Sam said, "we Falkeses move in phalanx formation." She gave a quiet hmmph. "They're very smart boys," Poppa said. "I'm lucky to have them in my life." Mrs. Cantwell smiled at Mr. Phipps. "You are a lucky man," she said. "Lucky to have you too," he said.

The Falkeses and the Cantwells spent little time together. Once a year at most, Eleanor and Rupert would have dinner with her father and Marina. Eleanor and Rupert, but not the boys, were invited to Louisa's wedding, a large affair, at the Plaza. They sent, as their wedding gift, six of her Tiffany china settings. Louisa's note came three weeks later. "Dear Eleanor and Rupert (I hope I may call you that), Thank you for the six table settings. How very generous of you. We shall think of you at our Sunday dinners. Yours, Louisa."

"I thought Smith could do better than that," Rupert said as he read the note.

"What can you say about a gift that came from the registry? 'It's such a beautiful pattern.' "

"No, Louisa meant to be rude," Rupert said. "She's envious. She has a grievance against you or us."

Eleanor looked startled. "Should we have sent all twelve place settings?"

"If we had, the note would have been shorter, ruder," Rupert said. "We should have sent one setting. The meanness of the gift would have pleased her. She'd have gushed in her note."

"So long as Marina makes my father happy," Eleanor said. "So long as she doesn't turn him against Sam."

Sam waited a week after talking to Lea to call Harry. "When are you going to stop licking your wounds and call Mom? You can think about it all you want after that."

"I will," Harry said. "Lea's very worried about me. I think she thinks I'm having an affair. She can't understand why I said what I said."

"I can't either," Sam said.

"I'm right, but I'll stop now," Harry said.

"For the record, Dad was a bigamist."

"Are you having an affair?" Sam asked.

"Where did you get that idea?" Harry said.

"Susanna said she saw you with a woman downtown, in my neighborhood. Good-looking, red hair, high heels."

"Did she?" Harry said. "A friend. A colleague really."

Susanna Goffe was Sam's best friend, and he was hers. "We lost each other climbing Mount Olympus," Sam would say. "And found each other at Princeton." They met during freshman orientation. Their attraction to each other was immediate and intense; within days of meeting, they were spending all their free time together.

Sam arrived at college a virgin. He knew he was gay from the time he was thirteen — "awareness and hormones arrived on the same afternoon," he said to Susanna — but Trinity was too small a village for experimentation. He didn't want to be the butt of "Gay Falkes Day" jokes, even though he knew his big brothers would beat up anyone who picked on him. Older boys and men, strangers, often made passes at him on the street; he stared ahead, ignoring them, curious but afraid. They made him feel like quarry. Sometimes they got belligerent, yelling after him, "You too good?" He wondered at that as a come-on line. Did it ever work?

Knowing Sam was gay didn't keep Susanna from falling in love with him. "I don't want to be in love with you," she said, "and I won't let it get in the way of our friendship. I just wanted to let you know. You're my favorite person in the world."

Sam met Andrew in the spring of freshman year. Andrew was a first-year graduate student in history. Andrew knew from the very beginning that Sam was what he wanted. He pursued him the whole time Sam was at Princeton. Sam hung back, making excuses.

"I'm too young to get seriously involved," he said. "I have years of education ahead of me."

"You're afraid of losing Susanna," Andrew said.

"Yes," Sam said.

"You don't have to give her up," Andrew said. "Just don't sleep with her."

"No fear," Sam said.

Sam stayed in Princeton the year after he graduated, doing research for one of his professors, waiting for Andrew to finish his coursework. The following year, they moved to New Haven. Sam started medical school. Andrew worked on his dissertation, on "the

Troubles." When he finished, he got a position at NYU as an assistant professor. He commuted until Sam finished both degrees. Sam did his residency at New York Hospital, then stayed on, doing research.

In theory, Andrew liked Susanna and Susanna liked Andrew but they were jealous of each other and competed for Sam's attention when they were all together. Sam took to seeing Susanna alone. Susanna worked for NPR, producing shows out of New York and waiting to fall in love with someone who wasn't Sam.

Older relatives sometimes asked Eleanor if Sam was going to marry Susanna; she was around so much. "Of course not," Eleanor would answer, "he's gay." They'd persist. "But wouldn't you like it, if he did?" Eleanor always answered the same way. "I like him just the way he is." To the boys, she always delivered a similar message: "We're package deals. All or nothing." It was intended as a caution against wishful thinking and envy.

When Sam was no more than eleven, he asked her why she was always polite to her mother, but never minded when Dad delivered one of his Granny slap-downs.

"Package deal," Eleanor said. "Dad is who he is."

Sam shook his head. "I think you like it," he said.

"Yes," said Eleanor. " 'All or nothing' occasionally works to one's advantage."

Eleanor and Rupert met Susanna on Parents' Weekend freshman year.

"Are you a Goffe Goffe?" Rupert asked.

"That's me, bona fide regicide stock. We did it. We killed Charles I. You don't mind, do you?" she said, picking up on Rupert's accent.

"No, I'm a republican, small *r*," he said.

"Big *R* too," Sam said. "We don't mind, do we?"

"Not in the family, only the White House," Susanna said. "No one in my family has done anything revolutionary since. And William Goffe died in his bed. Still, we're treated better in Ireland than in England. Ancient grievance keepers, your tribe."

"I'm a thoroughgoing American these days," Rupert said. "No sense of history anymore."

Susanna's parents didn't come for Parents' Weekend, not that year or any year. They had divorced when she was an infant. She lived with her father and stepmother.

"I can't tell if my father is nice, or only pleasant," she said to Sam. "He's completely under the thumb of my stepmother, who is a self-pitying pit bull."

"Is she better or worse than your mother?" he asked.

"I'd put the odds in favor of my mother as 6 to 5," Susanna said.

Susanna's mother had three children with three husbands. "She was misnamed Prudence," Susanna said to Eleanor and Rupert. "Her mother, Granny Bowles, gave all her children allegorical names. Prudence was the most ironic, Patience second most." Prudence paid the bills for her children's private schools and college but otherwise ignored them. Susanna's father came to her graduation, the only time he stepped onto the Princeton campus. Her mother sent a check. Susanna graduated magna and won the English prize. "How come you're not nuts?" Sam asked her. "Granny Bowles," she said.

Sam brought Susanna home for Thanksgiving that first year, then for Christmas, then for spring break. In June, she went on holiday with all of them to Spain. By sophomore year, she had achieved the status of a beloved cousin. I'm becoming Sonya in *War and Peace,* she thought, with chill foreboding. She had full kitchen privileges. She answered the phone and, unlike the boys, took messages. She looked like a member of the family: dark-haired, dark-eyed, long and lean. People took her for Eleanor's daughter, to the pleasure of both.

"It's narcissism, Mom," Sam said. Andrew was also dark and long and lean. "Except for Dad, I'm used to loving people who look like me," Sam said.

"Ditto," Eleanor said.

In Susanna, Rupert felt both the loss and pleasure of a daughter. Until she came into their lives, he never thought he had missed anything by not having a girl. He had liked their all-of-a-kind family. "I don't know which one I'd give up," he said to Eleanor, "but I think now I'd like to have had a daughter." Eleanor was past wishing for a daughter. She had wanted one in the beginning, to make up for everything she had missed, but after Sam, she wanted only more boys. She knew the routines and rituals of boys. "Oh, I know which one I'd give up," she said. Even after twenty-five years, Rupert was not sure Eleanor was joking.

Harry made up with Eleanor in his way. He said that her willingness to recognize the Wolinskis' claim had thrown him. How could she be so understanding and accepting unless she had known? He got carried away.

"I'm glad," Sam said, eager now to move on.

"You do know," Harry said, "the woman Susanna saw me with, she was just a friend."

"Do you want to play squash Saturday morning?" Sam said.

Eleanor invited Susanna to dinner. She was worried about her. Susanna was already thirty-six. When I was Susanna's age, Eleanor thought, I had five children, ages five to thirteen, and no career. Eleanor made the meal festive: rack of lamb, asparagus, salad, Chaumes, Barolo. Eleanor always drank Italian or Spanish red wines. French and Californian gave her headaches. White wine tasted like organic mouthwash when it didn't taste like peat moss.

"Let's open another bottle," Eleanor said. "For the cheese."

"If I drink too much more," Susanna said, "I'll get weepy and self-pitying. Or vice versa."

"I'll risk it," Eleanor said.

"Work's fine. Satisfying," Susanna said. "But I have no one in my life. I've never been in love with anyone who was in love with me."

"It's more important to like your husband than to be in love with him," Eleanor said. "Liking lasts longer."

"I was so stupid to fall in love with a gay man," Susanna said.

"Unlucky, not stupid."

"I am pathetic," Susanna said.

"Do you want children?" Eleanor asked.

"More than a husband."

"Then do it without one. We couldn't in my day, but you can."

"No. I want to give my children a fighting chance. Two parents," Susanna said.

"You didn't have any parents. One would be a major advance. And one good parent is all a child needs, so long as there's enough money."

"You've thought about this," Susanna said.

"In a lot of Mom-and-Pop families, there's often a superfluous parent. I was very lucky. Rupert was a good father. My own father was not a presence in my childhood. I'm glad he lived a long time. We became close after I married."

"What was your mother like?" Susanna asked. "Sam loved your father but never has a good word for your mother."

"Boring and mean. Rupert protected me from her."

"You and Rupert were my ideal couple,"

Susanna said.

"Were we?" Eleanor said.

"You were so kind to each other and to the boys," Susanna said. "The boys being boys are of course cutthroat competitive, but in any other family of five boys, all so smart and talented, all so close in age, it would have been Old Testament, Cain and Abel."

"I think my mother would have preferred not to have had a child" — she paused — "or sex."

"You missed the jinx. I'm afraid I'll be a bad mother," Susanna said.

"Will you abandon your children?" Eleanor said.

"No."

"Will you beat them?"

"No."

"Will you browbeat them?"

"No."

"What are you afraid of then?" Eleanor said.

"Not loving them, not liking them, not wanting them once they're here." Susanna started to cry.

Eleanor put her hand on Susanna's arm.

"Not possible," Eleanor said.

Sam wanted children, or at least a child. It

had been a long time coming, this feeling. His father's death was a great blow, much worse than he'd imagined. It cemented the feeling. He had loved growing up in his family, the only team he'd ever wanted to play on. He wanted a team of his own.

Sam called Will to congratulate him on his big news: Francie was pregnant. He could hear the happiness in Will's voice. He felt a spasm of envy.

"I've been thinking about Dad," Will said. "Becoming a father does that. I hope I'm as good a dad. He always made me feel I was fine just the way I was. Like Mr. Rogers. Did he ever yell at you? He never yelled at me. He never criticized me. He never said he was 'disappointed' in me. When I didn't go to law school, which might have been a mistake: when I didn't finish my PhD, which wasn't a mistake: when I quit publishing to become an agent and moved to L.A., so far so good: he never was anything but encouraging. His advice to me was always the same: 'Jack knows the secret: his work is his play, his play is his work.' "

"What was Mom's advice to you?" Sam asked. "Or was she her sphinxlike self?"

"Mom's advice was similar but more bracing," Will said. " 'Not everyone has a calling. Jack is a rare bird. Aim for being interested, or at least not bored — and never boring. Vote Democrat.' "

"They had confidence in us," Sam said.

"I miss him, even two years on," Will said. "I didn't know I would. Stealth Dad."

Andrew was dead set against having a child for all the usual reasons: their work, their travel, their friends, their sleep. He liked their life the way it was.

"If we had a baby," he said, "we'd need a live-in nanny, what you and your brothers had."

"We can afford a nanny," Sam said.

"That's not the point," Andrew said. "I don't want to have a baby. I don't want to be a parent. One of the prerogatives of being gay, I always thought, was childlessness without guilt."

Sam and Andrew had been together more than fourteen years, time for the second seven-year itch. The ardor of their early years had faded, but their attachment to each other, their history together, their common interests, "the en-durables," Andrew called them, made the relationship still the center of their lives. Life without the other was if not an unthinkable event then one they avoided speaking about. Until Sam wanted a baby, their only other serious bone of contention, the only heated arguments they ever had, had been over Susanna. Andrew never said outright to Sam he didn't want him to see her; he wanted Sam on his own to give her up. He didn't understand the relationship; he felt it excluded him. Sam never mentioned to Andrew when he had been to see her. He kept her out of their conversations.

"You never spend time with Harry's girls," Andrew said. "Do you even like them?"

"I don't want Harry's children. I want my own," Sam said.

"Does Susanna want a baby?" Andrew asked.

"Why do you ask that? What has that to do with us?" Sam said.

"Does she?" Andrew asked.

"Yes," Sam said.

"Don't do that," Andrew said.

Andrew wondered if their relationship would survive. He had drawn the line: no children. He hadn't liked his parents. His parents hadn't liked him. They hated his homosexuality. They thought it was an accusation against them: they hadn't brought him up right.

"Didn't they know the domineering mother/rejecting father theory had been thrown out?" Sam had asked the first time

110

they talked about Andrew's family.

"No," Andrew said. "They're Catholic. Your parents were practically Jewish in their acceptance."

Sam shook his head. "It wasn't Jewish, it was echt WASP. There was no struggle to understand, no discussion of feelings, no looking for causes, no guilt or shame. They never thought they were responsible for our characters or our conduct; we were who we were." He laughed. "They ignored a lot. I suspect expediency had a part. They were outnumbered. Both of them knew parents could ruin children, by putting cigarettes out on their arms, insulting and belittling them, hovering and undermining confidence, that sort of thing. Beyond that, they didn't think parents had much influence. I asked my mother, when I was fifteen, 'Why was I gay, only me, not the others?' 'Why not?' she said. 'Genetic roulette. Package deal. You're also the only scientist. Don't worry. It will work out. Everyone has an awful adolescence.' I believed her."

"My parents are of the lifestyle school," Andrew said. " 'Your choice,' my father said when I told him I was moving to New Haven to be with you. 'You'll never get tenure, either of you.' I couldn't tell if he was prophesying or placing a curse."

Andrew had been and remained in love with Sam. Sam wasn't sure what he felt anymore but he knew he had never loved Andrew with the same intensity. Sam was used to being loved. And then there was Susanna. Andrew knew that Sam wasn't sexually interested in her, but she offered a compelling alternative narrative, the possibility of traditional married life.

"I don't mind your old boyfriends at all," Andrew said to Sam during one of their talks about having a child, "or even your new ones." Sam knew he meant Joe, but said nothing. "Only Susanna," Andrew said. "What is it with her?"

"She's the Other," Sam said.

"Are you going hetero?" Andrew said.

"Don't be an ass," Sam said. "We're not lovers, Susanna and I. We have less at stake. We let things ride. She's like a sister."

"Another member of Team Falkes," Andrew said.

"Women's Auxiliary," Sam said, wanting to end the argument.

"I don't want to lose you," Andrew said. "But I couldn't stay if you had a child with Susanna."

Sam didn't tell Andrew about Harry's blowup with his mother. Andrew's interest would verge on the prurient, another blot,

after the Wolinskis, on the Falkeses' escutch-
eon. Only fair, I suppose, Sam thought.
We've been too lucky. He told Susanna, but
only months later, after he had cooled off a
bit. He had thought she would be angry at
Harry, and Sam was angry enough at him;
he didn't need backup. He could have
spoken to Lea, but that would be feeding
the maw. Lea was loyal. For all he knew, she
might have come around to Harry's position. Harry was a fierce partisan, which
made him a first-rate litigator but a second-
rate husband. Lea regularly gave in to him
because she didn't have his thirst for combat. It was only because her parents were
outraged that their daughters weren't baptized.

"If you marry Jewish," she said to Harry,
"you have to make accommodations."

"I could say the same thing," he said.

"Isn't it enough that they won't be bat
mitzvahed?" she said. "Don't be greedy."

Harry wanted to replicate his childhood.
Church was a part of it, along with Trinity,
tennis and, one day, he anticipated, Princeton. He was incredulous, almost indignant,
when he learned that Lea was pregnant with
a girl. He had assumed he'd have sons.
"Watch it," Lea said, as his face fell. "Fait
accompli. And, it's your fault." When the

second child was also a girl, he wondered out loud to Sam if it was divine retribution, payback for all his good luck.

"You have been lucky, we all have been," Sam told him, "but this is about sperm. God isn't tinkering in your scrotum; he's off helping college basketball players make their free throws."

Susanna called Sam. "This is it," she said. "My birthday is in a month. I'll be thirty-seven. I've reached the 'now or never' point. I want a baby and I can't wait any longer. My eggs are decaying as we speak."

"Andrew is adamant. I feel stuck," Sam said.

"I know. You were on a fool's errand thinking it would work out," Susanna said. "It can't work out. He doesn't like me. I don't like him."

"Give me six months," Sam said.

"No. If you and Andrew break up, you'll never forgive me. We've been pretending these last months," Susanna said.

"I want a baby too," Sam said.

"We don't get everything we want," Susanna said.

"No," Sam said.

"Have you said anything to your mother?" Susanna asked.

"Sort of. I was embarrassingly indirect, but she caught my drift," Sam said. "She said I had to choose. She said that she had had to make a choice not so different from mine. I asked her what her choice was, what she had chosen. She laughed and said, 'Don't you know?' "

"Don't you?" Susanna asked.

"I don't want to think about it," Sam said. "I don't want either of my parents to have had a life of their own, separate from us, separate from each other. They belong entirely to us."

"Well, then, you know," Susanna said.

"Yes," Sam said.

Sam had spent the morning feeling agitated. The day was hot and humid; his research wasn't going well; he and Andrew were fighting. He was still cross with Harry even though they'd made up. He needed a break, from work, from Andrew, from himself. A Sam Mendes film was playing at Lincoln Plaza. Like his mother, he was a moviegoer. Most of the time he went alone; now and then, he invited Susanna. His favorite time was after lunch, instead of a nap. He caught the crosstown bus. He hated riding with New York cabbies. Most of them drove like drunks.

He found *Road to Perdition* creepy and perverse, a disappointment after *American Beauty.* I must be ready to be a father, he thought as the credits rolled, looking forward to the next Pixar. Standing up to leave, Sam saw his mother at the back of the theater, moving toward the exit. She was with a man he didn't recognize. When he got outside, his mother and her companion were gone.

Sam called her that evening.

"Is there a man in your life?" Sam asked. "Other than Carlo?" Even when their father was alive, the boys teased their mother about her old boyfriend, Carlo Benedetti. He had a dashing, piratical quality they admired and he clearly admired Eleanor. "Do you wish you were married to my mom?" Jack asked him at a summer luncheon party. He was seven; his older brothers had egged him on. "You always hang around her at our parties." Carlo laughed. "I think she's *meravigliosa,*" he said.

"A man? Other than you and your brothers?" Eleanor said.

"I saw you at Lincoln Plaza today, at *Road to Perdition,* with a tall, dark stranger. I couldn't see him, but I don't think I know him."

"Jim Cardozo," she said, "an old acquaintance. I ran into him at the theater."

"Is he a romantic interest?" Sam said.

"No," Eleanor said. "Children. Friends. Grandchildren. That's enough. Wonderful news about Will. They were trying for a long time. Another girl. All-of-a-kind grand-children."

"What does he do, this Jim Cardozo?" Sam asked. Eleanor didn't answer.

"I'm sorry," Sam said. "Childish question."

"Has Harry been talking to you?" Eleanor asked.

"Yes," Sam said. "I told him he was wrong. I was very angry with him. He said he apologized."

"A Harry apology," Eleanor said. "It was my fault he thought what he thought, and he would now stop thinking it. I don't believe the word 'sorry' crossed his lips."

"Are you still mad at him?" Sam asked.

"At the moment, I prefer the Wolinski boys," she said.

# CHAPTER 3
## ANNE

The Heart wants what it wants — or else
it does not care —

EMILY DICKINSON,
LETTER TO MARY BOWLES, 1862

Anne Lehman fell in love with Jim Cardozo when she was a freshman at the Spence School. She was fourteen; he was twenty, a junior at Yale. She was walking down Madison Avenue with her mother. Jim was walking up, his arm around a girl. They were so beautiful, the pair of them, she had to turn away, not to be caught gaping. They looked so much alike they might have been sister and brother, except they couldn't be, not the way they were together, their bodies magnetically entwined. Later, Anne would wonder if it was Jim's happiness as much as his beauty that had ensnared her.

Anne saw him again the following September, at Rosh Hashanah services at Temple

Emanu-El. He was sitting with a man and a woman — his parents, she decided, plain versions of him — the beautiful girl was not there. Anne followed him around at the reception until she learned his name. She went home and practiced writing "Mrs. James Cardozo." On her wedding day, Anne confessed to her mother that she had been in love with Jim for sixteen years, long before she met him. "I saw him on the street and I knew he was it. I would have him or no one." She didn't mention the girl. Her mother, a practical woman, argued with her. "You don't fall in love with strangers," Mrs. Lehman said. "Love at first sight is chump's love, not worthy of the name. So many things can make your heart beat faster. Almost anything at fourteen." When Anne insisted it was love, her mother said, "Oh, my dear, I must feel sorry for you, then. 'When the gods wish to punish us, they answer our prayers.' Oscar Wilde." Anne didn't think her mother was wrong. She had no sense of triumph, only one of ill-fated inevitability. Jewish tribalism and Christian anti-Semitism had made the match.

Mrs. Lehman, née Ethel Lewisohn, had gone to Vassar. Devoted as she was to her alma mater — she endowed a chair in her grandmother's name and sent her three daughters there — she had resisted its efforts to educate her. She had read only to fill her commonplace book. Her head was stuffed with epigrams, which she would summon, as she had on Anne's wedding day, to end a conversation she thought had drifted off track. They were her "trouncing bon mots," in family parlance, and she had a gift for calling up the right quote at the right time. Generally, she won her point, touché without irony. At bedtime, her preferred reading was Bartlett's. She was still, at sixty, collecting quotations. The night after the wedding, she browsed in the marriage section. "Happiness in marriage is entirely a matter of chance." Jane Austen. "Marriage is an adventure, like going to war." G. K. Chesterton. "Marriage is the triumph of imagination over intelligence." Oscar Wilde. She sighed as she read the last: if only she'd had it at hand when she was speaking with Anne. Too late, she thought, closing the book, years too late.

Mrs. Lehman preferred English sources; they were wittier than the Americans. The French were mean, which some occasions called for. All her wit was borrowed. She couldn't tell a joke, she often confused a cliché with a witticism, and she collected only those sayings and quotes that confirmed her stout good sense. But she was so good-natured and cheerful that her family and close friends never minded, and her trove was, after forty years, impressive: Nietzsche, Tolstoy, Montaigne, Thackeray, Machiavelli — writers and thinkers she'd never think of reading. There were some in her crowd who thought she was the cliché, a character out of a Restoration comedy or Jane Austen, like Mrs. Malaprop or Sir Walter Elliot, his nose in the Baronetage; but there was nothing ridiculous about Ethel Lehman despite her highbrow illiteracy. She had a kind of Will Rogers shrewdness about people and a generosity of spirit. She believed the rich should pay taxes; she thought the state should support the poor; she marched against the Vietnam War; she supported the NAACP Legal Defense Fund. She was contented in her own marriage and wished her children the same estate. She had tried to talk Anne out of marrying Jim Cardozo, if not out of loving him. She liked Jim, the whole family did, but the relationship seemed so one-sided. Hopelessly smitten, Anne didn't argue. "You're right," she said to her mother. "I can't help myself. No exit."

Anne, unlike her mother, had been educated

by Vassar. She studied biology, chemistry, and physics along with the literature of hopeless love: *Villette, The Age of Innocence, The Scarlet Letter, Great Expectations, The Spoils of Poynton.* After graduation, she got a PhD in neurobiology at Columbia. She met Jim finally when she was twenty-seven and he was thirty-three. She was working at Presbyterian Hospital, doing research on the brain's limbic system. He was finishing a cardiology fellowship. A friend introduced them. At last, karma, she thought. They got along. They went out. They were almost a couple. Jim didn't say he loved her, but he liked her immensely and he liked her company. She knew from Jim's friends there had been an early love affair that ended badly, shattering Jim — the girl wasn't Jewish, no more needed to be said — but by the time they met, he would speak of it only as his "Romeo and Juliet moment"; he seemed recovered. They had been dating for two years when she proposed the first time. "I don't want children," he said. Anne went home and wept. In proposing, she had cast herself as Leah, the unloved, wrongfully supplanting Rachel, but finding consolation in her "open womb." She had anticipated her marital happiness lying with their children, three of them, dark and beautiful like their father, Rebecca, Simon, and Benjamin named for the Justice. She retreated for three months, then came back and proposed again. "No children," he said. She submitted. I am the beater and the beaten, she thought.

Jim bought Anne a beautiful ring, a large, good, square-cut diamond. After their engagement party, she asked him why he agreed to marry her. "We have nice times together. We have friends in common, interests in common. You understand my work, I understand yours. And no more holidays with my parents." He laughed when he said this. He referred to his parents as Clytemnestra and Agamemnon, "but less loving." He was genuinely fond of the Lehmans, "not a rotten one in the bunch," he would say. "The real question," he said, "is why you want to marry me. You could do so much better." She shrugged. "Sheep love," she said, looking up at him with tender eyes. He tousled her hair. "I forget to mention," he said, leaning down to whisper in her ear, "you've got wonderful breasts." It was the only compliment he regularly gave her about her looks. She saw the two of them as a *New Yorker* cartoon of a couple, the lump of lignite coal standing on the wedding cake with the Koh-i-Noor diamond.

Jim had had a vasectomy when he was thirty-five, not long after he met Anne. Starting in college, he'd always taken precautions, carrying condoms in his wallet, a gesture that passed for gallantry. When women asked him whether he minded using a rubber — most of the men they knew did — he'd shake his head. "Look, it's not as good as sex without one," he'd say, "but don't let anyone tell you it's bad." Pre-pill, he didn't want to rely on ill-fitting diaphragms or coitus interruptus. Post-pill, in his prowling years, he didn't want to rely on the women he slept with.

Jim told Anne about his vasectomy only weeks before the wedding. He'd always insisted on using condoms. Anne was stunned and hurt by his deception. He didn't apologize, he explained. "It's not about you. I made this decision before we decided to get married. The condoms were for protecting you against possible diseases." Anne hadn't reckoned on a vasectomy, but on the usual, less reliable methods of birth control, the kinds that failed. She had wondered, before Jim had boxed her in, or out, whether down the road, had the responsibility been hers, she would have lied to him about taking the pill. He would be angry if she had gotten pregnant, she knew, but she'd have the baby. "A vasectomy was the only fair way," he said with an air of magnanimity. "The burden shouldn't fall on you." Anne's temper flared, the only time in three years. "Will you still use a condom after we're married?" she asked. "No," he said, "I was tested for STDs. I'm clean."

Anne didn't recognize Eleanor at the wedding. The reception line moved with breathtaking alacrity. "There are six hundred hands to shake," Mrs. Lehman said as the bride and groom came into the Harmonie Club's great hall. "Let's keep things moving. No kissing except relatives of the first degree." She had hired twice the usual number of waiters and they were everywhere, carrying trays of Veuve Clicquot and Perrier. Along the walls, she had placed four well-stocked bar tables and four lavish hors d'oeuvres tables, mostly trafe. She knew her crowd. Half the guests went for the shrimp over the line, knowing that the bride and groom would circulate during dinner. Rupert insisted they go through the line. His good manners were often more annoying to Eleanor than his bad manners. He knew in some way that Jim was an old boyfriend but he didn't mind. Who was going to run off on his wedding day with the mother of five young boys, the oldest thirteen and deep into sarcasm, the youngest still occasionally wetting his bed?

Eleanor had been surprised when Rupert had indicated interest in attending the wedding. She had planned to send their regrets. "No, no," he said. "I've never been to a posh Jewish wedding." More than a cross-cultural experience, he wanted to know people in "Our Crowd." His firm was a white-shoe firm, with only two Jewish partners out of fifty. He wanted more Jewish lawyers; he wanted more Jewish business. He hadn't known Jews until he came to America and his relationships with the two who launched his career, Dean Rostow and Judge Friendly, made him think anti-Semitism was rooted in envy and insecurity. He never joined a club that discriminated against blacks or Jews; he thought it bad behavior and bad business, and he led the charge for the Century Club to admit women. When women were finally admitted in 1989, Eleanor was one of the first women invited to join, along with Jackie Onassis, Brooke Astor, and the dean of Columbia Law School. The Phippses had been members since the club's founding and Eleanor assumed she was proposed as a "legacy" candidate. She turned them down, politely. "Rupert deserves a club of his own," she wrote.

The year after he made partner, Rupert began advocating for hiring Jews, blacks, and women at Maynard, Tandy. He never appealed to the better angels of his partners' natures, only to their business interests. Moving in their limos between the Upper East Side and Wall Street, most of them hadn't noticed the changes the '60s were bringing, except for the demonstrations. Nixon's election in 1968 reassured them. Rupert, alert to the shifting zeitgeist, took it upon himself to rouse them out of their complacency. He made a list for them: A Jewish pitcher threw a perfect game; a month later, he refused to pitch the first game of the World Series because it fell on Yom Kippur. A black man was appointed to the Supreme Court. Actors let down their hair and took off their clothes on Broadway. Boston's Cardinal Cushing had stopped eating grapes in support of farm workers. Yale College had voted to admit women, with only one faculty member dissenting. "Listen to Dylan," he told his partners, "listen to what your children are listening to." When he was forty-two, he was elected to the management committee, the youngest member in the firm's history. Eight years later, he was made managing partner. Rupert was a first-rate lawyer but he had no illusions about his partners' barometers; he owed his success within the firm to his English badges, the accent primarily, so irresistible to even the bluest bloods in the firm. His ability to speak in well-formed sentences also served him, though he knew, as his colleagues didn't, that in England, his very articulateness would be held against him, the telltale sign of upstart origins. Upper-class Englishmen stammered like Hugh Grant, or said *w* for *r,* like Elmer Fudd or his old pal John Earlham. It fell to parvenus like him to speak like Olivier. Then there was his rudeness, which was widely admired in the firm. "If only I could get away with it," old Mr. Maynard said. "It" came back to the accent, a kind of get-out-of-jail-free card for every occasion.

Eleanor watched Jim and Rupert shake hands. Rupert looked the happier of the two. Jim introduced them as Rupert Falkes and Eleanor Phipps. Anne smiled at them. "Thank you for coming," she said, then turned to kiss a first cousin. To Eleanor's surprise and relief, Jim's parents were not in the receiving line. Mrs. Lehman had banished them. "We're keeping it to Jim and Anne and my husband and me," she told the in-laws. "Too many people to move through." She had refused to accept any money from the Cardozos; they had offered five thousand dollars, an amount so paltry, she'd found it insulting.

Eleanor hadn't seen Jim's parents in fifteen years, not since the breakup in 1960, when they approached her. She was standing alone. Rupert had gone to the hors d'oeuvres table to investigate; the orphan in him was always drawn to food excesses. "How nice to see you again," Mrs. Cardozo said. "Yes," Eleanor said. "Now, please excuse me, won't you?" She turned and walked away. It was an electrifying moment. She had never been so rude to anyone in her life. I must be careful, she thought. I could get used to this. She found Rupert gazing admiringly at a mountain of shrimp. "Not a cucumber sandwich in sight," he said with satisfaction. "I think I'd like a gin and tonic," she said. Rupert nodded. "I was thinking of having a scotch," he said. Fortified with shrimp and scotch, Rupert began circulating, introducing himself to strangers, saying, "Ah, yes, of course. So glad finally to meet you." Eleanor tagged along, as much as the other guests, seduced by his charm offensive. At their table, he sat next to Mrs. Lehman's sister, Pauline Straus. On her way out, Mrs. Straus took Eleanor aside.

"I think you may be the luckiest woman at this wedding," she said, "luckier than the bride." A week later, Mr. Straus called Rupert to talk about problems his company was having with IBM.

Anne and Jim bought an apartment on East Eighty-Eighth, between Fifth and Madison. "Convenient to the Guggenheim," Jim said, his idea of a joke. They hadn't lived together before their marriage, and the two or three nights a week they had spent together had been spent at Anne's place on Seventy-Eighth, off Lexington. Anne had wanted to stay in that neighborhood. It was lively, with good restaurants and shopping. "There's nothing nearby on Madison except E.A.T.," Anne said when Jim said he wanted to be closer to Central Park. "And it's dead at night," she said. "Yes," Jim said, "like Paris." Anne gave in. They split the down payment 50-50. They split everything 50-50, their mortgage payments, their vacation expenses, their food bills, their car loan, everything except devotion; that was 80-20. They had separate bank accounts, separate credit cards, separate savings. Am I the beneficiary of his life insurance? Anne wondered. Not knowing, she made her niece Caroline the beneficiary of hers.

Jim kept his old apartment as a study. Anne had seen it only once. He showed it to her early on in their relationship, evidence of why they should always stay at her place. It was on West 106th between Broadway and Amsterdam, a 250-square-foot studio, spare and elegant, with bookshelves, a fireplace, a sisal rug, a refectory table, a chair, and a daybed. The kitchen had a half-size refrigerator, like a college student's, with a tiny stove that looked like a Fisher-Price toy sitting on top. The bathroom could not have been more than 16 square feet.

"Do I get a key," Anne asked Jim, "now that we're married?"

"Of course," he said, "just call before stopping by." Two months after this conversation, she called him on a Saturday morning, asking if she could drop by the studio. She was in the neighborhood, finishing up a long coffee break with a friend at the Hungarian Pastry Shop.

"I'm working against a deadline, honey," he said. "Another time. See you at dinner." She tried again two months later, in the early evening. She had been meeting with a colleague at Columbia's Morningside campus.

"I'm sorry, honey," he said. "I've got to finish my article. I was going to call you. I'll

131

be home late. Don't wait up."

"Honey" is shorthand for no, she thought.

Anne took to visiting the studio when Jim was out of town, at a conference or convention. She would move around the room, touching the furniture, taking a book from the shelves, never sitting. If she used the toilet, she would lift the seat before she left. Once she saw a note on his desk: "Do you want me to wash the sheets? It's been a while. Doreen." Another time she saw a riot of pink and magenta peonies in a crystal vase sitting on the mantel. Sometimes, there were tulips — red, purple, and orange — gorgeously tangled together in a silver pitcher on his desk.

Nine months into their marriage, Anne discovered that Jim had changed the lock to the studio. She wanted to call a disreputable locksmith but hadn't the spirit. Snooping was shameful enough. The following Sunday, as he dozed between first downs, she took his keys to the local locksmith and had them all copied. None of them worked on the studio door. Locked out, she started calling the studio from pay phones. If he answered, she stayed on the phone, not saying anything. The fifth time she called, Jim asked, "Who is this? What do you want?" What *do* I want? she asked herself. The next time she called, she found the phone had been disconnected. She waited three weeks before saying anything to Jim.

"Your telephone at the studio has been disconnected," she said.

"I was getting obscene calls," he said. "I don't need a phone there. Call me at work if you want to talk."

The next morning, when Jim was showering, she went through his wallet, looking for receipts. There were lunches at the Madison Deli and E.A.T. and one at the Four Seasons. After he left for work, she rifled through his desk, looking for his American Express bills. When she couldn't find them, she decided they still went to his studio address. I'm like a woman in a Russian soap opera, she thought.

She joined the 92nd Street Y and started exercising: weights, rowing machines, step machines, stationary bikes. She got a trainer, Ted. She had always liked games — she had played softball for Vassar — but she'd never liked gym workouts. They made her feel like a hamster on a wheel. Ted changed all that. He was very encouraging. Soon, she was seeing him five times a week, early in the morning. These sessions were the best part of her days. Jim noticed.

"You're looking thinner, stronger. What's

up?" he asked.

"Decathlon prep," she said.

He stared at her, then tousled her hair. "Don't lose too much weight," he said. "I'd miss your breasts."

Ted made a pass at her. "Not yet," she said.

Ted was dark-haired and dark-eyed like Jim, but shorter, sturdier. She had never known a man so comfortable in his body. He likes himself, Anne said to herself. He'd look at his body sideways in the mirror, and if she caught him, he'd smile and say, "C'mon. Feel my muscle." He never made the self-deprecating remarks that Jim and his buddies made about their bodies, looking to their women to reassure them: "I need to lose this belly." "My backhand's going to hell." "I gave Greg a good game for an old guy, losing only by two points." Ted's interests were narrow — cross-training, fiber, Pink Floyd, and the *Godfather* movies — but his conversation was effective, mostly movie lines. " 'In Sicily, women are more dangerous than shotguns,' " he said in a gravelly voice that made her feel she might be dangerous. It was a new and startling feeling. Has there been a dangerous Jewish girl since Judith? she thought. In the locker room, she looked at herself in the mirror.

Her underwear, which her mother ordered specially from France, was made of heavy white silk and lace. It looked like the underwear nuns, schoolgirls, and grand-mothers wore; it covered her navel and hid her cleavage. I'm thirty-one years old, she thought. Why am I wearing Nana's under-garments? That afternoon, she bought herself bikini underpants and push-up bras to wear to the gym, beige and pink and lav-ender lace. Ted picked up on the change. A hint of danger, Anne thought, feeling almost happy. "Let me know when 'yet' arrives," Ted said.

Jim sent Anne twenty-four pale yellow long-stem roses for their first anniversary, and took her to dinner at La Grenouille. No peonies, Anne said to herself, no tulips. The next week, she began following him. She would call him around two thirty in the afternoon to check on dinner plans. If he said he might be late, she'd make her way to the lobby of his building at five p.m. and take up a post of discreet surveillance. She wore a brown knit hat with a visor that hid her face; she buried her head in the *Post*. She wasn't hiding from Jim, but from the staff. Jim, on his way out, wouldn't notice her — or anyone else in the waiting room.

Like most doctors, he avoided eye contact in waiting rooms, fearing he'd be accosted by a patient or, worse, a patient's relative.

The first three weeks were uneventful. Jim came home on time, stayed late working, or went to dinner with colleagues. Twice he stopped by his studio in the early evening, but both times he stayed only a half hour or so. "Pay dirt," as she dismally called it, came in the fourth week.

Jim called Anne at one thirty in the afternoon to say he would be home late. "Don't hold supper for me." She immediately left the lab and took up her position in the lobby. At two forty-five, she saw Jim leaving the hospital. She followed him out, giving him a ten-second lead. He got into a cab. She got into the one behind. "Follow that cab," she said. "You're kidding, lady," the cabbie said. "I never kid," she said. "If you don't lose it, I'll give you an extra ten dollars." Jim's cab took off down St. Nicholas Avenue; Anne's raced after it.

At Broadway and Fifty-Eighth, Jim got out. Anne had her driver pull over and gave him twenty dollars. Jim walked slowly across Fifty-Eighth, on the south side of the street; Anne followed on the north side, five feet behind, clutching the *Post*. At Sixth Avenue, as he waited for the light to change, Jim started whistling. Above the traffic, Anne heard the wistful strains of "These Foolish Things." Jim often whistled as he walked down the street, but not love songs, not with her; with her, he whistled jaunty airs, marches, anthems, snappy show tunes from *Oklahoma!* or *Guys & Dolls.* Is this madness? Anne wondered as she skulked past the Plaza Hotel. "Am I going off the rails?" Jim stopped under the marquee of the Paris Theatre. He looked around expectantly. Anne lurked at the edge of the fountain across the street. Jim looked at his watch. She looked at her watch. It was three fifteen. They waited.

At three twenty-five, a woman came up to Jim. They didn't kiss or shake hands but stood facing each other. Even at a distance, Anne could see he was excited and happy to see her. His body leaned toward hers, his face alive with emotion. Anne turned from Jim to the woman and recognized her as the girl on Madison Avenue, all those years ago, less beautiful but still beautiful. She felt tears rising. Jim bought tickets and they went in. Anne crossed the street. *The Story of Adele H.* was playing at three forty. She waited a few minutes for Jim and the woman to settle, then followed them in. They were sitting on the first floor, in the middle section, toward the back of the theater. Anne went upstairs to the balcony and took a seat in the front row. She could see them clearly from this perch. The woman wasn't less beautiful. She is the peonies, Anne thought, she is the tulips.

The movie, a story of hopeless, desperate, unrequited love, ending in madness, was wrenching for Anne. As she watched, she felt tricked and exposed, as if Jim and the woman, knowing she had followed them, had picked this movie with the pitiless intention of humiliating her. It was the last foreign movie she would see for years. They're too smart, she thought. Years later, watching *Fatal Attraction,* a thoroughly American movie of mad passion, she found its violent ending satisfying, reassuring. She told herself it was the husband's fault, all of it, not the crazy girlfriend's. He was craven, guilty, egoistical. Of course, the wife would be the one to kill the girlfriend, she thought. They're all Dimmesdale. I would have had to do it for Jim too. She caught herself. Unless, of course, I was the one to be killed. She laughed dully. Even then.

The movie let out at five thirty. On the street, Jim and his companion talked briefly, then parted. The woman walked west; Jim looked after her receding back for a good minute before turning east, toward home. Anne followed the woman, keeping thirty feet between them. They walked across Fifty-Eighth, then up Central Park West. At Sixty-Seventh, the woman went into the Hotel des Artistes. Anne followed her into the building's lobby, as if she were going to Café des Artistes, the restaurant on the ground floor. She heard the elevator operator greet the woman. "The boys are home, Mrs. Falkes. I heard Jack playing." Anne walked to the café door, then stopped, as if she'd thought of something. She shook her head and turned around to go. "Can I help you, ma'am," the switchboard operator asked. "I had the time wrong," Anne said.

Anne caught a cab to East Eightieth Street and stopped at E.A.T. to pick up takeout. She got home at seven. She showed surprise at seeing Jim. "I thought you'd be late," she said. "I have food for me, but not for you."

"Let's go out," Jim said.

"Only if the food is better than E.A.T.," Anne said. "How about Caravelle?"

Jim looked at her. "It's very expensive," he said.

"On the Lehmans," Anne said. "My father has a house account."

"I didn't mean that," Jim said.

Anne didn't say anything.

"Let's go there," Jim said. It was very expensive. He paid.

Anne stayed up late reading the Manhattan phone book. She started with "FA." She tried "FAW" and "FAU," before she thought of Lieutenant Columbo. "Falkes, Rupert, 1 West 67th Street." The name sounded familiar, as if it belonged to someone she should know but didn't. She got out the wedding list. There it was: "Mr. and Mrs. Rupert Falkes (Eleanor Phipps)." Anne thought about Jim's movie date with Mrs. Falkes. There had been nothing in Eleanor's behavior that gave off any scent of romance. There had been no kissing, no touching, no intimate smiles. They might have been third cousins. She's going to break his heart again, Anne thought, what's left of it.

Anne got up at six the next morning. She called the Y to reschedule her session with Ted until the evening. At seven, she made her way crosstown to the Hotel des Artistes. At seven fifty, Eleanor emerged with five boys. They all looked like Jim, especially the oldest, who she guessed was thirteen or fourteen. He and the next oldest took off on foot toward CPW. "We've got practice till five, Mom," he called out. Eleanor hurried the other three into a waiting black car.

Anne couldn't move. Rooted to the ground, she watched the car drive away. She was unsure what to do next. She felt light-headed. She knew she couldn't tell a cabbie to follow a car filled with children. She'd look like a stalker, a pervert.

The next morning, Anne rented a car and drove across the park to West Sixty-Seventh Street. At seven fifty, Eleanor and her sons came out of their building. As the two oldest boys walked toward CPW, Eleanor called after them, "Harry, Will, don't forget the dentist." "Harry, Will," Anne said to herself. "English kings." Anne followed the cab with the younger boys up Amsterdam to the Trinity School. Watching them walk in, she felt a rush of blood to her head. I am a pervert, she thought. I am a stalker.

Over the next week, Anne staked out Trinity at the start and end of each day, trying without success to catch the younger boys' names. She saw that the two oldest boys carried tennis racquets. JV, she guessed. She looked up the schedule.

All fall, Anne spied. She hung around the Hotel des Artistes in the mornings; she watched Trinity JV tennis games in the afternoons; she scoped out Jim's studio in early evenings. JV tennis was hands down her favorite. Often, she went to practices.

She traveled to away games, to Riverdale and Brooklyn. There were few regular spectators, a handful of mothers, a nanny or two, one old man. At first, she felt conspicuous, but no one seemed to pay her any mind. She didn't talk to anyone. She watched the Falkes boys closely but never cheered or clapped. After a month, she gave up on West Sixty-Seventh Street and Jim's studio. She'd lost interest in everyone but the two boys.

When spying had begun to take over her afternoons, she took unpaid leave from her job. She said nothing to Jim and didn't change her phone message. "Health reasons," she said to her chairman, who thought it was female trouble and didn't want to know more. "Of course," he said. "But don't forsake us." To encourage her return, he put in a promotion for her from associate research scientist to research scientist. She was very useful to him; she had drafted his last two successful grant proposals.

At the last away game of the season, the old man, the only person she recognized, approached her.

"I've seen you at all the games," he said, sitting down next to her. Anne froze. "You come to watch my grandsons, don't you?"

142

He nodded toward Harry and Will.

"I'd never hurt them," Anne said quickly.

"No," he said. "Of course not."

They sat silently side by side for several minutes, not looking at each other, watching the game. The boys were playing doubles, against each other. Will aced Harry.

"Harry won't like that," Anne said, giving herself up.

"No," the man said. They resumed their silence.

"I'm Edward Phipps," the man said.

For a split second, Anne thought of lying.

"Anne Cardozo," she said.

"Jim's wife?" Mr. Phipps said, looking directly at her for the first time.

"Yes," she said.

"You have no children of your own," Mr. Phipps said. Anne couldn't tell whether he was telling her or asking her.

"No," Anne said. She sat still, not wanting to disturb the molecules between them. She felt a sense not exactly of relief, more like release in the old man's company, in his knowing who she was and what she was doing.

"Do Harry and Will suspect anything?" she asked. Her heart seized as she waited for his answer. She had refused until now to think about what they might think.

"I don't think so," he said. "They've never said anything, and they're boys who say what they're thinking. So far."

When the game finished, she stood up. "I won't come to any more games. I'll leave your family alone."

"I'm sorry for your unhappiness," Mr. Phipps said.

"Thank you," she said. "Thank you for talking to me. Thank you for not calling the police."

Edward Phipps had a life full of regrets, beginning with his parents. His parents didn't care for him and, isolated by their remoteness and indifference, he grew not to care for them. By the time he was seven, he gave up the wish that they would change, that they would talk with him, eat dinner with him, tuck him in at night. The one good deed his parents did him, inadvertently, was to send him to Bovee. It was cheaper than St. Bernard's. Bovee was for its day a progressive school. It admitted Jews and forbade hazing, a linkage Edward would make for the rest of his life. It was also traditional. Operating under Gradgrindian principles, it believed in drills and recitation. Edward's lessons in mathematics, Latin, and geography stayed with him all his life. On his death-bed, he recited the rivers of northern Europe, including the Volga. "Moscow is Europe, barely, but still," he said to Sam, who, with his archival tendencies, appreciated more than his brothers his grandfather's recall. "What did you like best about Bovee?" Sam asked. "The Bergdahls," his grandfather said, his mind drifting with the Volga. As early as first grade, Edward saw that some boys had much better parents than his, attentive, kind, even affectionate; he decided to shop for a new set. He found them in the third grade, the parents of his friend John Bergdahl. Starting that year and until he went to prep school, he spent more time at the Bergdahls' than at home. They were warm, funny, generous, intellectual. Rumor had it Mrs. Bergdahl was "Jewish, or part Jewish, or Russian, or maybe Czech," but she was so charming and rich, no one who knew her cared. Years later, Edward saw Eleanor's relationship with Clarissa Van Vliet's family as a replay of his relationship with the Bergdahls. He knew it was not to his credit.

After Bovee, Edward went to Andover and then to Yale. He met Virginia Porter Deering at a Christmas ball. He was twenty-one, a senior; she was nineteen, home for the holidays from Smith. She was breathtakingly lovely, with black hair, pale skin, and dark blue eyes. Later, in his own defense, he would say, "Vivien Leigh hadn't a patch on Virginia." Still, he knew he had been Lydgated into marriage. After six months of seeing her only in groups, he recklessly pursued her one evening, down a dark hall in her house, and clasped her tightly to him, kissing her neck, her lips, her shoulders, her bosom. She submitted rag-doll-like until he finished, then said in a bright, clear voice, "Are we engaged?" He stammered, "Yes," and threw away all possibility of marital happiness. For the next twenty-five years, he submitted to her will, rising up only when Eleanor brought Rupert home. He would think of that hour as "the changing of the guard." He saw that Rupert would protect Eleanor from Virginia, where he had failed.

Edward didn't think to object when Eleanor at twenty had fallen in love with a Jewish boy from Yale. He had had Jewish friends at Bovee and Yale and he worked with Jews at his bank. He knew Jim couldn't join his clubs but he didn't think that mattered to Eleanor. His wife disabused him of his complacency, clubbing him with the marriage's impracticalities. "We may not mind, but our friends and relations will, and Eleanor will find herself moving in entirely different circles from us. We couldn't have them for holidays, no more Christmas or Easter. Her children will be thought of as Jewish by our side, and gentiles by Jim's. According to Hebraic law," Virginia said, "the mother must be Jewish for the children to be Jewish." She then struck with her deadliest blow. "His parents are also dead set against it. His family will never accept her. They've threatened to disown him. They will be outcasts. Bohemians. They'll be poor too. We couldn't support them under the circumstances." Edward persuaded Eleanor to give Jim up. In later years, he would come to think of that conversation as his most cowardly act, made more shameful, more exploitative, by the benefits subsequently accruing to him from Eleanor's marriage. He loved Rupert and his grandsons more than he could ever have imagined. In her marriage to Rupert, his daughter gave him the family he had longed for.

Edward first met Marina Cantwell on his forty-first birthday, at a dull party in his own home. She was then the very young wife of a colleague at the bank. She asked his opinion and laughed at his jokes. In her easy laugh and enthusiasms, she reminded him of Mrs. Bergdahl. He fell in love. They had an affair for a year, the happiest of his marriage. When he couldn't bring himself to leave his wife, Marina gave him up. After Virginia's death, Edward could only marvel at the hollowness of his life: he had forsaken himself, his daughter, and his lover, but kept faith with Virginia. The Bergdahlian fantasy resolved itself into dew. He had not escaped his blighted childhood; he had perpetuated it. Struck by this insight, he had to face a second, more complicating, one: perhaps his parents hadn't so much disliked him as each other. A feeling of sympathy for fellow sufferers stirred in him. He wished he could steel himself against this insidious thought, knowing it would allow him to forgive himself, but he could not. He was a self-forgiving man and if a quieted conscience required forgiving his parents, he knew he would do it, regretfully perhaps, but inescapably.

As he watched Anne Cardozo leave the playing field, he thought of Jim and, for the first time, the unhappiness he had inflicted on him as well as Eleanor. He had liked Jim, and Eleanor had been madly in love. He had thought they were having sex. After they broke up, he hoped he was right; he wished them that happiness. He didn't like to think of the reasons propelling Anne to stalk his grandsons. He knew he was implicated. He turned his attention back to the game. Harry hit a scorching backhand neither of his opponents could get a racquet on. Edward stood up and cheered. Harry gave his grandfather a quick nod. Edward wished he had a cigar, to make the moment perfect.

Anne stopped spying on Harry and Will. She went back to work. She threw herself into her exercise regimen. Ted said he'd teach her squash. "You were built for squash," he said, laying emphasis on the verb, making her feel she was built for danger. She began seeing him seven hours a week, five mornings for weights and machines, two evenings of squash. Cheaper than therapy, Anne told herself, and more acceptable. Often after squash, they'd grab a sandwich at the Madison Deli. He made her eat whole wheat bread. "Your body is a temple," he told her.

"What's going on?" Jim asked. "You've become this demon exerciser."

"I'm getting ready," she said.

"Ready for what?" he said.

"Anything," she said.

One morning after her workout, Ted met her at the front door of the gym. "Don't go to work yet," he said, breathing into her neck. "Come home with me."

For three months, Anne went home with Ted almost every weekday morning. Often, they skipped the workout and met at his apartment. "One workout a day is sometimes all I can manage," Anne said. It was the best sex of her life: illicit, secret, athletic. Ted was new, experienced, generous, and tireless. Every time she left his apartment, a sense of sorrow settled on her; their mornings together were numbered. She tried to have sex with Jim every time she had sex with Ted, to allay her happiness, but she couldn't always keep up. Jim warmed to her new openness and availability. He had liked her French silk underwear. He had liked removing it. It had given her a youthful, virginal quality that had aroused him. But he liked the new underwear more. It played to darker fantasies. He liked it half on, half off.

"Who are you?" Jim asked one night as he lay beside her, spent.

"Would you like to tie me up?" she said. "Or down? I'm never sure of the right locution."

Anne told Ted she couldn't see him anymore outside the gym. He wasn't surprised or disappointed. "You don't have to give me up entirely," he said. "We'll stay friends. We'll play squash. And every now and again, you'll come over to my place. It will be good for you."

She cut back on her training sessions. Another woman, short, athletic, and blond, took her hours. Anne liked that she was Ted's type. This is a very well-run gym, she thought.

Anne and Jim had dinner with her parents on most Sundays. Her sisters and brother and their families came also. Anne wondered if parents without wealth could regularly summon their children to a weekly weekend dinner. She loved her parents; they were good parents, affectionate and kind, but still she wished she could spend Sunday after-noons wasting time her own way. Her childlessness had metamorphosed after two years of marriage from a matter of interest among the family to a matter of concern. She was regularly scanned walking into the house, and her intense exercise regimen, which had thinned her out, had them all talking. "She's no spring chicken," her mother told her father. "She better get on with it. I had all four children by the time I was her age." Mr. Lehman told his wife not to say anything to Anne, and Mrs. Lehman held off; his demands on her were so few, perhaps two a year, she believed it her wifely duty to submit. Her demands on him were many; those he didn't care for, he ignored. "My batting average with your father is almost as good as Ted Williams's," she announced during one of the Sunday dinners. All the children immediately understood.

When Anne showed up in late fall rounder and glowing, everyone noticed. There were murmurings during cocktails but no one said anything to Anne or Jim; they waited for them to share their happy news. Throughout dinner, the conversation stalled, no one wishing to miss the announcement. When dessert had come and gone and nothing had been said, Mrs. Lehman lost patience.

"Anne," she said. "Why haven't you told us you're pregnant?"

Everyone looked at Anne. She flushed at the attention.

"I'm not," she said. "I've stopped exercising so vigorously and gained weight. My muscles must have turned to fat."

Mrs. Lehman didn't like to apologize; she saw it as a sign of weak-mindedness.

" 'Three things can not hide for long: the Moon, the Sun and the Truth.' The Buddha," she said. "I'd take the test, if I were you," she said.

Jim didn't say anything to Anne until they got home.

"Are you pregnant?" he asked. He hadn't noticed before Mrs. Lehman had spoken but once she had, he too knew she was.

"You can leave," Anne said.

"Why didn't you tell me?" he asked.

"I didn't want to have an abortion unless I had to. I was waiting for the amniocentesis."

"Why did you do this?" he asked.

"I didn't do this. It happened."

"Who's the father?"

"You are," she said. Jim looked at her for a long time without saying anything. She met his gaze.

"I can't have children. You know that," he finally said.

"Vasectomies fail," Anne said, "and we've been having lots of sex." She kept his gaze. "I think it was the bikini panties."

"Who are you?" he said. "You're a different person."

"Yes," she said. Jim was silent for several seconds.

"I'm not angry," he said. "I would have thought I would have been — if I had thought this could happen, which I never did." He stopped. "I'm stunned."

"I expected you to be angry and then gone."

"I'd look a cad if I left you pregnant," he said. "I'd be a cad."

"We can say we had agreed not to have children and I decided on my own to get pregnant. I'll do the explaining. I'll say we were having trouble before I got pregnant."

"I've never seen you look lovelier," he said. "How far along are you?"

"Twelve weeks."

"And it's my baby?" he said.

"Your baby," she said.

"Let's go to bed," he said. "I'm not thinking straight."

"There's no reason we can't have sex," Anne said.

He took her hand. "Your breasts are even more wonderful," he said.

# CHAPTER 4
## WILL

Not knowing how he lost himself, or how he recovered himself, he may never feel certain of not losing himself again.

CHARLES DICKENS, *A TALE OF TWO CITIES*

Will was the family pundit. "Granny slap-down" was one of his jibes. Harry briefly claimed ownership but no one believed him. "You don't have a sense of humor," Sam told him, speaking for the family.

Will gave all his brothers nicknames, mostly as a cover for giving Harry nicknames. Harry was most famously "the Blurter," but also "First Brother" or "First." Will had numbered all the boys, after *The Five Chinese Brothers,* and they often called one another by their numbers. For two years, Jack was known almost exclusively as Fourth Brother, or, when his brothers were feeling more kindly toward him, Perfect Fourth Brother. Tom was in heaven; he

155

wasn't the butt. Sam refused to play along. "You have no respect for numbers," he said to Will. "You don't know the difference between an irrational number and an imaginary number." Rupert occasionally called them out by their numbers, to quiet them down, in the manner of Mr. Darling in *Peter Pan.* "A little less noise there, First and Second, a little less noise." He didn't tease. Eleanor never used the numbers. "No way," she said. "I'd only get in trouble calling you by numbers. Another example of Refrigerator Mom when you came to write your memoirs."

Will had worshipped Harry when he was little, following him everywhere, doing whatever he did, setting the pattern for his younger brothers, who came to worship him too. Harry accepted their homage with princely condescension and ruthlessness. He was harder on Will than the younger ones, but with all of them he shouldered his responsibilities as the oldest. He might goad or punch or bully or tease them, but no one outside the family could do it. He instilled in his younger brothers a sense of their specialness; they were the Five Famous, Fierce, Forceful, Faithful, Fabled, Fortunate, Fearless Falkeses. He left off "fantastic." "We're not comic-book heroes," he said to Eleanor.

He was ten. Well into his teenage years, Will was under Harry's thrall, safe and surly in his thralldom. The mocking nicknames were the earliest signs of revolt. Will wondered if he hadn't gone to law school because Harry had.

Will came east for the Fourth of July. It was only his second time back since his father's death, more than two years earlier. He felt bad about that, but also relieved. He'd only had to deal with the Wolinskis secondhand. Francie stayed in L.A. The first trimester had been rough. "All I want to do is sleep for a week without throwing up," she said. "Off with you." The second day there, Will went through the family photos. Eleanor had them in boxes, by decade. She had photos of everyone dotting the apartment, on tables, mantels, and bookshelves, but she'd never made up albums. Her mother made albums. In an ancient, tattered, straw suitcase with a luggage tag marked "R. H. Falkes, The Rectory, St Pancras, Chichester," Will found relics of his father's early life: his English driver's license from 1954; a photo of him, age twenty or so, punting on the Cam; another photo of him at the same age, standing next to an aged priest; a clipping from the *Chichester Observer*,

August 3, 1940, with a photo of five small boys in V-neck sweaters, shorts, high socks, and sandals, under the headline "St. Pancras Home for Orphaned Boys Collects 200 Tins for War Effort"; a faded baby blanket and bonnet. The blanket and bonnet had never been laundered. Eleanor picked them up. "They smell stale, like old books," she said. "There's no baby smell left." She laid them back in the suitcase.

"What does the *H* stand for?" Will asked. "Dad never used it."

"Henry. Reverend Falkes gave Dad his first and last names, fronted by 'Rupert,' for Rupert Brooke or Prince Rupert, Dad was never sure which," Eleanor said. "The name was the making of Dad. Without saying it, he and the Reverend took it as a special relationship, a claiming. And Dad could call him Father."

"Is that Reverend Falkes in this photo, with the collar?" Will asked. "He looks so proud of Dad." He laughed. "Dad looks so serious."

Eleanor picked up another photo. "That's Dad in the orphans' photo, second from right," she said. "No smile. He never smiled to please anyone."

"I remember Dad smiling," Will said. "Where are the wedding photos? I'll bet he's smiling there." Eleanor pulled them off the shelf. Will was right; in photo after photo, Rupert was smiling at Eleanor. "My mother wanted us to face the photographer. Dad wouldn't. 'Why should I look at him?' he said. 'Who is he to me?' Then he turned to me and said, 'Look at me.' And I did. I think this is the photo. Look at us. We were so young."

"This is my favorite," Will said, pointing to a photo of his parents dancing. They were laughing, as if they had a secret.

"You look so in love," Will said.

"Do we?" Eleanor said.

Will nodded. "You know how kids, when they're seven or eight, never think or want to think their parents had sex? Most of our friends had only one or two siblings, which meant their parents only had sex two or three times, max." Will laughed. "I punched out Trip Fitzgerald for saying, 'Yuck, your parents had sex five times.' I felt I was standing up for the family honor."

"It's mutual, you know, or reciprocal, one or other of those," Eleanor said. "Children don't want their parents to have sex and parents don't want their children to have sex. At least, they don't want to think about it; the mind recoils."

Will looked sideways at his mother. "I

159

thought you and Dad had a good sex life," he said. "Not when I beat up Trip. Later. You were so undemonstrative in public. I took that as proof. I've always distrusted public displays."

"Are we ready for this?" Eleanor said. "What we talk about when we talk about sex."

"Did I put my foot in it?" Will asked.

Eleanor shook her head.

"Those earrings you're wearing," Will said, pointing to a wedding photo, "you're wearing them now."

"Dad gave them to me. His wedding present. I wear them all the time."

"I bought a pair like them for Francie last year."

"Did you?" Eleanor said.

"She doesn't wear them," Will said. "Occasionally she does. She said they were beautiful."

"Ah," Eleanor said. "The old spousal gift fallacy."

Will laughed. "What fallacy?" he said. "It would have helped if we had a sister or two. Susanna came too late to civilize us."

Eleanor smiled. "Not all men but most, when they're buying their wives a gift — a necklace, a nightgown, a handbag, it doesn't matter — are buying their mothers a gift.

160

And when their wives show their disappointment, by returning it or burying it in the back of the closet, the men are baffled, hurt. 'What woman wouldn't want a Tiffany tennis bracelet?' they ask. Wrong question. 'What woman *would* want it?' Dear old Mom. Dad didn't fall into that trap. A benefit of being an orphan." Eleanor looked at Will. "You look abashed. We can talk about sex instead, if you like."

"Francie admired the earrings on you," he said.

"On me, yes," Eleanor said.

"Are we all buying our wives gifts you would like?" Will asked.

"Not Jack and Sam," Eleanor said. "Jack buys his wife gifts he would like. A laptop, a big-screen TV, a BMW, a turntable. I'm surprised he never bought Kate a trumpet mouthpiece. Sam and Andrew don't buy each other gifts. But the rest of you, yes."

"Mama's boys, that's what we always say we are," Will said. "A bevy of mama's boys."

Eleanor didn't say anything.

Will looked again at the photo of his parents dancing.

"You were a baby," he said. "And the next year, you had a baby."

"We were the old young," Eleanor said. "We liked it. Your generation wants to be the young old."

"We want to be the beautiful young," he said, "and the forever young."

"You're holding up very well," Eleanor said.

"Holding up is the word. Gravity has kicked in. I'm past my prime in L.A. I'm thirty-eight, no chicken. Everyone is too good-looking in L.A., until they turn thirty-two, except the nanny. Too risky. Then, one day, they're too old, and only good-looking for someone their age. The feverish regimen begins: fasting, hydrating, lifting, running, cleansing. They see a trainer four days a week. They eat nuts and tofu. No drinking at lunch. Cocaine only on weekends. The men wear weaves and cowboy boots. The women have mouths like duckbills. As for their gravity-defying boobs . . ." He stopped.

"Are the women looking for husbands?" Eleanor said.

Will nodded. "L.A. is Noah's Ark. A divorce means you're on the market for your next husband — or wife. Men too need to be married. The unmarried ones are too expensive to insure."

"I'm not marrying again. I won't risk my luck. And I'm not going to have 'work.' It's too late anyway. I've been told you have to lay a foundation in your thirties."

"I'll bet there are men who'd like to marry you, even with your crow's-feet." Will leaned in, as if to examine her face. "What about Carlo Benedetti?"

"I can't imagine the gauntlet a suitor would have to run with the five of you."

"We'd have a hard time," Will said. "We'd give you a hard time."

"Do you remember proposing to me when you were five?"

"I hope you accepted," Will said.

"I was torn. You all proposed."

"Oedipus run amok," Will said.

"Dad began locking the bedroom door," Eleanor said. " 'Too much night traffic,' he said."

"New York isn't Noah's Ark, is it? You haven't been 'dropped' now you're on your own?" Will said.

"No, not yet," Eleanor said, "but I am very careful at dinner parties. No gin or vodka. No flirting. Only married people are allowed to flirt. It makes no sense. A widow is much less dangerous than an unhappy wife. A female acquaintance, divorced for several years, was almost salivating at Dad's funeral, like one of Job's comforters: 'Just you wait, the invitations will dry up. All your friends will think you're after their husbands.' As if."

"Bill Macy?" Will said. "Gag me with a spoon."

Eleanor told Will about her conversation with Harry at Café Luxembourg. Will groaned.

"Jesus, one for the Guinness book of blurts," he said.

"He was awful," Eleanor said. "I had just told him I wanted to give some money to the Wolinski boys and he accuses me of a lifetime of deception. He sounded like an injured wife."

"I don't think he believed it. He was angry, he thought it, boom," Will said. "If he says he believes it now, he's talked himself into believing it. Harry's like Jack that way. Their editing functions are screwy. I don't know where that comes from. You don't shoot your mouth off; Dad didn't."

"Oh, no, Dad did," Eleanor said. "He said stinging things all the time, not at home, not with us, except of course his Granny slap-downs, but with almost everyone else, everywhere else. He was famously rude. I was always expecting New York magazine to write him up as 'The Rudest Man in New York.' People would complain to me all the time. He lashed the associates in the firm and even some of the partners. He told poor old Gosford he was a 'useful idiot.' Gosford called me in tears."

"Are you still planning to give money to the Wolinski boys?" Will asked.

"Probably. I don't know," Eleanor said. "It's become so fraught, all of it. Harry is still angry, calling Dad a bigamist, rewriting his childhood."

"You should think about it some more," Will said. "I've been wanting to say something, looking for the right moment. I didn't know if you wanted to talk about it." He looked at his mother, trying to read her face. "What a mess," he said. She was silent, unreadable. Will continued, "Vera was disingenuous. Not the boys."

"What's this?" Eleanor said.

"Did you look carefully at the photograph of her and Dad, her and Alleged Dad?"

"Only to see if it was Dad," she said. "It didn't seem to matter."

"I took it with me," Will said. "There was something about it that seemed off. I couldn't put my finger on it. Not the sandals, the whole thing. It kept bugging me. Last week, planning this visit, I looked at it under a magnifying glass. It might be Dad; it might be Viggo Mortensen. I assume it is Vera, yes?" Eleanor nodded. Will continued, "I asked a photographer friend to enlarge it. The faces got blurrier but the rest got clearer. Eureka. The cars were all from the '50s rounded with a kind of Deco look. There were four of them. I don't think any of them was later than 1954. No pointed fins. Vera and Alleged Dad are standing in front of a restaurant, Toffenetti's. It was rounded too, with glass bricks and metal trim. Toffenetti's closed in 1968. I called the New York Public Library's reference line. Nathan's Famous took over the site. At Forty-Third and Broadway. I remember eating at Nathan's."

"It didn't hold a candle to Gray's Papaya."

"I think I bought a hot dog at Gray's Papaya every day after school for ten years."

"Do you remember when Sam preserved one in formaldehyde, in the same jar as his fetal pig?" Eleanor said. "The pig life cycle. It made me queasy."

Eleanor picked up the photo. "It's Dad," she said. "I knew it the minute I saw it."

"In her letter to you, Vera said she'd had a relationship with Dad in the mid-'70s. This photo is twenty years earlier."

Eleanor was silent. The lost year, she thought.

"Are you all right, Mom?" Will said.

"I'm taking this all in, or trying. You're saying Vera knew Dad in the mid-'50s."

166

Eleanor cleared her throat. "I thought Dad, the young Dad, looked like the young Max von Sydow. He had wolf's eyes. You all have them."

"Sheep in wolves' clothing then," Will said. "We're an uxorious clan."

"Are you?" Eleanor said.

Will stared at his mother. "We're not?" he asked.

Eleanor didn't answer. Will started to ask, "Who?" but changed his mind. He didn't want to know.

"Dad, Viggo, Max, sheep, wolf," he said, "the photo wasn't taken in '75."

Eleanor thought back to 1975. She and Rupert had visited England for the first time since he'd left; they had celebrated their fourteenth anniversary, double seven; they had gone to Jim's wedding. Though never unkind to her, Rupert was seriously out of sorts all that year, distracted and irritated, as the English would have it; anxious and depressed, in the American vernacular.

"I think it odd, don't you," Will said, persisting in the face of her inscrutability, "that Vera's only evidence is so old, long before the years she claimed she had a relationship with Dad? Why didn't she say she'd known him in the '50s? Wouldn't that have strengthened her case?"

167

"I lie sometimes," Eleanor said. "Don't you? I never told you boys to always tell the truth. We don't owe the truth to everyone."

"Do you really think Dad is the father of the Wolinski boys?" he said.

"They're so blond; you're all dark," she said. She was silent for a few seconds. "Why didn't Harry notice this? He's a lawyer, paid to pay attention. Or Tom? Or Sam, for that matter? He's a scientist. He should have noticed."

"We took our lead from the Maynard lawyers. They said the photo proved nothing. Don't you remember Gosford intoning to the Surrogate: 'If a photo of a man and a woman standing next to each other was proof of paternity, I am the father of George W. Bush.'"

"Harry's going to be cross when he finds out you've deconstructed the photo," Eleanor said.

"Not to worry," Will said. "After a while, he'll begin thinking he was the one who figured it out."

"I don't know what's going on with him," Eleanor said. "Is it turning forty?"

"It's Dad dying," Will said, "and the Wolinskis. It's thrown all of us. And we didn't expect it to." Eleanor was silent.

"I understand why Harry got so mad at

you," Will said. "He should have behaved better, but the feeling, I understand."

"Why?"

"Who else do you get mad at when things go wrong?" Will paused. "You seemed so untroubled by the Wolinskis." He paused again. "Why did you clean out the apartment?"

"Are you mad at me too?" Eleanor said.

Will didn't answer.

After a long silence, Eleanor spoke. "There was too much of the five of you. Every time I asked any of you if I could, once and for all, clean out Limbo, you howled. You were never going to be ready." Eleanor picked up Rupert's baby bonnet. "Finally, I just threw it all out. The only things I kept were your stuffed animals. They're still here, sitting on the top shelf, bereft: Nins, George, Bup, Lump, Bama." Eleanor gestured toward Limbo. "You're the only one who gave your animal a proper name. From the beginning, you spoke in sentences. You had no baby words. Wouldn't you like to take George, for your baby?" Eleanor paused for several seconds, weighing her words. At what point, she wondered, would her sons stop thinking their parents existed only for them? "There was too much of Dad in the apartment. I

couldn't get on with life. Can you understand?"

"We were sore," Will said. "It seemed so
soon."

"I didn't sell it," Eleanor said. "I thought
of it. It's so big. There are rooms I never go
into. I don't need seven bedrooms."

"We talked about that," Will said. "Harry
was going to buy it. Over Lea's dead body."

"I knew Dad was dying from the first
diagnosis. You all thought he'd get better.
It's no surprise you were thrown." Eleanor
cleared her throat. "Götterdämmerung on
West Sixty-Seventh."

Rupert, once he'd settled in America,
showed no interest in returning to England.
It took almost twenty years for him to make
his first trip back, and he went in 1975 only
because Eleanor insisted. "It's time to visit
England," she said. "You need to go back."
Rupert continued to resist. "Only if you
come with me," he said. Eleanor agreed.
Tom was just five, old enough, she thought,
to be left for a week without sinking into
despair. He was her most dramatic child,
the most emotional of them, the most
responsive to suffering, his own and others'.
All through high school and college, when
he wasn't playing tennis, he devoted his free

time to the homeless and tempest tossed: mothers with three jobs, children with fetal alcohol syndrome, cons, ex-cons, gang members, prostitutes, drug addicts, SRO tenants. His Princeton was Trenton, where he tutored, worked in soup kitchens, registered voters, urban homesteaded, and campaigned to elect the city's first black mayor. His heroes were the Berrigans. He cursed his ill luck for having grown up post-Selma, post-Vietnam, post-Nixon, post-Attica, with no reason to sit in at lunch counters, burn the American flag, chain himself to a prison fence, steal FBI files, go underground. "All we can do now is sue the bastards," he told his parents. "I don't have a sense of justice, only injustice."

Tom wept his way through his first week away from his mother. His brothers rallied. Sam let him sleep in his room. Will took him to school on the public bus, like a big boy. Harry read to him at bedtime. Even Jack stepped up. When Tom cried at dinner or bedtime, he'd cry too. As she tucked Jack into bed her first night back, Eleanor asked, "Were you sad when we were away?"

"It's OK, Mom," Jack said. "I wasn't very sad, not like Tom. I'm bigger. I didn't want Tom to cry alone. He always cried first." Jack's face got serious. "I'll tell you a secret.

When I cried with him, he stopped crying sooner." He lowered his voice to a whisper. "I have another secret. Harry gave me a quarter every time I cried. I did it ten times. That's two dollars and fifty cents. It's in a jar over there." He turned to point to his bookshelf, then looked back at Eleanor. "Could I sleep in your bed tonight?" he said.

Eleanor found Tom in Sam's room, begging his older brother to let him sleep there. Sam refused. "Now that Mom's home, you have to sleep in your own room." Tom started to whimper. "If you cry, I'll call you a cry-baby," Sam said. "Sam," Eleanor said, startled by his ruthlessness. Sam threw her a look of aggravation. "We've all looked after him and we're tired of it. Please put him away." Tom turned his face to the wall.

"Time to go to bed, Tomahawk," Eleanor said. She picked him up and threw him over her shoulder in a fireman's carry. He clung to her back, laughing and shouting. In his room, she dropped him with a thump on his bed.

"Are you going to go away again?" he asked.

"Not for a while," Eleanor said.

"Jack cried every night," Tom said. "Harry read me *Charlotte's Web*."

Eleanor reckoned the trip a partial success; Rupert said he'd go again. Before leaving for America, Rupert had spent no more than ten days in London. He felt almost as much an alien there as Eleanor. During their visit, they stayed at Claridge's, went to museums and the theatre, ate dark gray roast beef and pale gray Brussels sprouts, attended evensong at St. Paul's, and explored the neighborhoods rich American tourists preferred. As always, with Eleanor, Rupert behaved well but she saw he was out of sorts, listless and tired, as if he were coming down with the flu.

"What's wrong?" Eleanor asked the fourth day.

"It hasn't changed enough. Or I haven't," he said.

"Let's leave. Let's go to the Cotswolds or Salisbury or Bath," she said. She knew not to suggest Chichester or Longleat or Cambridge.

"Maybe next time," he said.

When Tom was seven, they took the boys to London for the first time. They went to the Tower, Hyde Park Corner, Madame Tussauds, the Mews at Buckingham Palace, and the Royal Observatory at Greenwich. They had high tea at the Dorchester, fish and chips at Arthur Treacher's, and bangers and mash at Wimpy's. They saw *The Mouse-*

*trap* in its twenty-fourth year. The boys thought Cornish pasties the worst things they ever ate, after English ice cream, which didn't melt. They saw England play Australia at Lords and Chelsea play Aston Villa at Stamford Bridge. Rupert bought them each a cricket bat and ball and they played in Hyde Park, drawing a small audience attracted by their loud voices and colonial accents.

The boys declared it a great vacation, and Rupert seemed reconciled to England, almost taking pride in his homeland as he explained the rules of cricket and the War of the Roses. Tom acquired an English accent that passed on the plane for the real thing. "An English cousin," Eleanor said to the stewardess. Sam added to his list of Anglicisms. "What's a bugger?" he asked his father. "There are two equivalents," Rupert said. "As a throwaway insult, 'asshole' pretty much covers it. More literally, a bugger is a butt fucker." Sam stared at his dad. He had never heard him use bad language. This must be English Dad speaking, he thought. "I wouldn't use it around adults, if I were you," Rupert said. Jack had brought his trumpet, smuggled like contraband in his backpack, a violation of Eleanor's packing rules. "There will be no place to play it," Eleanor had said to him before they left. He carried it with him at all times. During their scratch cricket match, he played "God Save the Queen." The audience applauded. Harry called him a suck-up. "It's 'My Country 'Tis of Thee' I was playing," Jack said, kicking at Harry's shin. "I was fooling them." Will asked his dad why no one in America played soccer. "Your children will play soccer," Rupert said. "Americans think a World Series is Detroit against Cincinnati."

Rupert visited Will at Cambridge in 1989, during Will's second year there. He went alone. Eleanor insisted. "It means something special to both of you. Off you go." It was his tenth return trip but the first time he had left London's environs. He rented a car, a Peugeot. He liked driving in England. The transition to left-hand drive was easy and he liked shifting. It gave him a false but comforting sense of belonging. He turned the radio on. Melvyn Bragg was interviewing Penelope Fitzgerald. He fiddled with the knob, searching for music. He could feel the blood rushing in his ears as he drove east.

Will was at King's, where Rupert had been. They spent their first day walking around the college, pointing things out to each other. Will introduced his father to his tutor, Dominic Byrne, a shambling, humorous, heavy-drinking ex-Jesuit with a Derry accent and an Irish appetite for irony.

"A lot has changed since you've been here," Byrne said. "And a lot hasn't. Your boy, a chip off the old block."

"He's a chip off his mother's block," Rupert said. "I was a scholarship boy."

"Will said you went to Longleat," Byrne said.

"Scholarship boy," Rupert said.

"Before that?" Byrne said.

"The Prebendal School. Chorister. Scholarship boy."

"Before that?"

"St. Pancras Primary School, Chichester. It was attached to the orphanage I grew up in," Rupert said.

Byrne rocked back on his heels.

"Yes, I know," Rupert said, "I could almost pass for a gentleman."

"Would you be my guest at high table tomorrow?" Byrne said. "I know Will will want to have dinner with you tonight, but by tomorrow the two of you could no doubt use a break."

"Are you setting me up? Will the provost ask me for money?" Rupert asked.

"We've got a scholarship fund," Byrne said. "Just up your alley." He paused. "Though we're short of orphans these days."

Rupert endowed a scholarship at King's in the name of the Reverend Henry Falkes, orphans preferred but not required. He and Byrne became good friends, close friends, as close as both were able. Byrne visited Rupert six months before he died, a last visit when Rupert was still himself. He came back to speak at Rupert's funeral. Eleanor wanted to pay his fare. He refused. "My pocket can sustain the loss, dear heart," he said. "It's my heart that can't."

"I was right to wait to go back to Cambridge," Rupert said to Eleanor when he was back in New York. "It's almost a different place. I could breathe there for the first time." He looked away from Eleanor as he often did when emotion caught up with him. "It was effortless for Will. He felt as comfortable there as at Princeton." He turned toward her. "He has a beautiful English girlfriend, Frances, Francie," he said. "Blond."

Rupert's visit to Longleat that year was unsettling, more like what he'd been expecting from Cambridge. He had been at

Longleat just after World War II, when no one had money or servants or heating or meat or electricity. What had survived the war were the titles and bloodlines, the great houses and families. Rupert had felt his disinheritance and dispossession; there were other orphans, war orphans, but they knew their fathers' names. By the end of his first week, he knew where he stood in the social rankings. As a scholar and the ward of an Anglican minister, his status was just respectable. An earl's son, thick as a post, might stumble his way through Longleat on his way to Teddy Hall without a hint of self-doubt troubling his sleep. Rupert saw that he would have to succeed. Longleat was an indelible lesson on money and class. England in 1946 was not far removed from Trollope. A gentleman might inherit money, spend money, borrow money, marry money; he would not work for money. He would take up a profession, one of a limited number — the bar, the church, government and politics, the Army or Navy, public school or university teaching. Salary never determined his choice. City men worked for money; so did Americans, unabashedly, unapologetically. Rupert determined to go where the money was to be made.

Rupert stopped in at the Headmaster's

Office to introduce himself. He didn't want to be discovered lurking on the grounds by a porter and taken for a pervert or stalker. In his day, the school had been down-at-heel but beautiful, with its ancient stone buildings, some going back to the fourteenth century, and its swaths of green lawn. Now it was only beautiful. Rupert had not been happy at Longleat; he'd been lucky. Seeing the place again reminded him again of the great debt owed his guardian. As a very young man, he hadn't acknowledged all that Reverend Falkes had done for him. He was only twenty when the reverend died, too young to bear thinking of himself as a charity case. If I'd had to be grateful, he thought, I would have been deformed by it. At twenty, Rupert had wanted to think the reverend didn't expect his gratitude or even desire it, but only looked to him to fulfill his early promise. Thirty-five years on, he felt sadness and regret, even as he absolved his younger self. All the unasked questions, the ones he had avoided, came with a rush: Why did he pick me out of the dust heap? Why do I have his name? What did I owe him? Did I thank him? Did he know I . . . ? Rupert stanched the flow. The words "loved him" hung in the air. Rupert walked toward the chapel, Lear's curse ringing in his ears:

179

"How sharper than a serpent's tooth it is / To have a thankless child." Evensong would start at five thirty. Rupert gave up God early, about the time Eleanor gave up Santa Claus, but he held to the Anglican rituals, his inheritance. God save the Queen, God help the poor.

When Harry was thirteen, he asked his parents whether he should go to boarding schools. They were all at dinner. Friends of his wanted to go away, to Andover, Exeter, Milton. "What do you think?" he asked his parents and brothers. Rupert was, to everyone's surprise, against it. "Boarding schools are for orphans," he said. "Children who have parents should stay home until university."

The boys stared at their father. He had never before said anything to them so revealing. No one said anything.

Later that evening when they were alone, Eleanor followed up with Rupert.

"What is your grievance against boarding schools?" she said.

"They're sexual cesspits, like prisons," he said.

Eleanor stared at him. "What happened?" she said.

"You don't want him to go away. Do you want him to go away?" Rupert said.

Eleanor reached out and touched his cheek. "No," she said, dropping her query, knowing she'd never get an answer. "I am still attached to him. And I'm not finished with him." She paused. "Neither are his brothers. He can't leave home until one of them takes him down a peg. I'm betting on Sam. The others haven't the stomach for it." She was too optimistic. To her frustration and admiration, Harry resisted all takedowns, bouncing back like a punching bag. As he forgave his own trespasses, he mostly forgave others theirs, never offering a proper apology, never expecting one.

"I underestimated him, his resilience, his self-confidence, his willed blindness," she said to Rupert years later. "Where did he get that from?"

"My side," Rupert said.

"It's my mother, isn't it?" Eleanor said. "Or maybe my father."

Rupert invited Will to go with him to Chichester. "We'll walk around. No knocking on doors." Rupert knew no one from his St. Pancras days. He had left the orphanage at seven, when he went to the Prebendal, and he had never returned to it. During holidays, he stayed in the rectory, in a small room in the staff quarters. The church was still there, looking like its old flint self on the outside but so much smaller than Rupert remembered. Inside, the changes distressed him. Renovations in the early 1980s — adding on a large recreation room, replacing the pews with chairs, taking down the altar — gave the sanctuary the look of a middle school auditorium. "It's Low Church, practically Methodist," Rupert said to Will. "Father Falkes wore a cassock. I used to wonder if he had grown up a Catholic and changed the spelling of his name, dropping the *w*, adding the *l*, when he took Anglican orders. I think he would have liked to shrive his parishioners. He would have hated the guitars." The orphanage was now the Parish Hall. A brochure said it had closed in 1958. "Father started it during the Depression," Rupert said, "after several infants had been left on the steps of the church. I don't know what happened to the girls."

"Did you ever think about your parents?" Will asked.

"No, not then," Rupert said. "When your whole world as a small boy is made up of orphans, you think you're normal. When I went off to the Prebendal, Father explained that the children there would likely have parents, a mother and father. 'Tell them what you want,' he said. 'Don't lie if you can help it.' I said I had been orphaned. I hated the word 'orphan.' I don't know why Father Falkes singled me out. He wasn't my father. I've read *Great Expectations*."

"What was it like to be at a boarding school at seven?" Will asked. "You were so little."

"Being an orphan provided me with an early advantage," Rupert said. "I didn't miss my mother. 'How come you don't cry?' a classmate asked. I told him I never cried. This was true." He laughed. "Another child asked me why I called my dad 'Father Falkes' and not Daddy, or Papà or even plain Father. 'Your parents must be very polite people,' he said. I said, 'Yes, Father Falkes is very polite. Very proper too. I haven't got a mother.' I looked down as if I were sad. I almost said 'My mother is dead.' That might have been a lie."

"Were you ever interested in looking for your parents or their children?" Will asked. "Their other children?"

"No," Rupert said. "Sometimes I imagine being contacted by a lost relation. 'Rupert, how are you, old man? Sorry we had to give you up. Depression.' That sort of thing. The thought fills me with suspicion and rage. What could any one of them be now but a cadger."

"I'm sorry," Will said.

"No, don't be," Rupert said. "Coming to America, I felt cast into Eden. I can't imagine that any brothers or sisters I might have had are better off than I. I'm not talking about money, though it plays its part. I'm talking about Father Falkes, Cambridge, your mother, you five, Granddad, Yale, my work, West Sixty-Seventh Street, our life. I've no illusions about my origins. No family romance. Gypsies didn't kidnap me. I'm not a Fitzroy or a Moses. I was the straw that broke the camel's back."

Francie had gone to St. Paul's Girls' School, London, where she had been educated within an inch of her life. Will said St. Paul's was Brearley squared. Both parents taught there. She was a scholarship girl. At Cambridge, she was also a scholarship girl. It was a bond between Rupert and his daughter-in-law, though Francie said it was much easier in the '80s and '90s to be poor at King's. "Very little tipping. We made our own beds." Their immigrant status was also a bond but they felt differently about it. Rupert had come to America, fleeing England, wanting a better life. He did not look back or hold back. He gave everything he had to America and America gave back. His success was complete; he became a Republican. The first time he voted after becoming a US citizen, he voted for Nixon. Over time, he moved slightly leftward, " 'correcting' toward the center," he said. He deplored Reagan's trickledown economics. He remembered the humiliation of being poor at Longleat and Cambridge; he knew what it was to be the resentful recipient of rich men's largesse. Government benefits didn't have the sting of private cap-in-hand charity.

Francie came as a bride, confident and assured, knowing and loving her parents, thinking of going back someday, ambivalent about America. She was Labour until Tony Blair, whom she called Thatcher's Pussy, then George Bush's. "Always someone's pussy," she said, "including Cherie's." She said she and Rupert were Churchillians, he Winston, she Caryl. She became an American when she got pregnant, registering as a Democrat but keeping her British passport. "In case the country goes berserk and elects Cheney president." She often used bad language, which Rupert, to his sons' surprise, found funny. *Nostalgie de la boue,*" he said at a family gathering to celebrate Will and Francie's seventh anniversary in 1999, not long after he had shared his grim diagnosis with his sons. The conversation had been circling around Bill Clinton and Monica Lewinsky. Francie, an English rose with a pukka accent, asked: "Would you call Clinton a cocksuckee?" Will, who loved Francie's dirty mouth, laughed. So did Rupert and Eleanor. The others weren't sure what to do. "I don't remember table talk like that," Harry said. "What happened?" Eleanor looked around the table. "We were waiting until you all grew up." Jack thumped the table.

"We had foul mouths at the orphanage, every last little bugger," Rupert said. "I didn't know the correct word for a woman's private parts until I went to Cambridge." The boys shifted in their seats. Rupert went on. "I knew it only as 'cunt,' which we called each other at the orphanage." All the boys, except Sam, stared at their father in astonishment. Rupert continued, "Americans don't use it much. A shame." Eleanor shot him a look. "Americans take it so seriously; they'd rather be called an asshole." Harry fiddled with his flatware. Tom put his head in his hands. Francie shook her head, as if in commiseration: "I've known so many, I can't count. England is cunt-try." Lea looked at Harry: "I didn't know I was allowed to say it. This is very interesting."

"Do you miss England?" Rupert asked Francie after dinner. They were sitting together in the living room, away from the others. Francie had brought along her wineglass. Rupert was drinking scotch. The cancer had spread to his bones and whiskey helped with the pain. "I'm more lucid with scotch than morphine," he had said to Eleanor. Eleanor ordered four cases of Black Label. "Optimistic, are you?" Rupert said when he saw the boxes in the pantry. "Thank you."

"All the time, but it's all right," Francie said. "Your family is so offbeat, I feel at home. I feel I can say anything to you and Eleanor. And Sam. Jack is his horn. Tom shies, like an Arab horse. I'm never quite sure of him. Harry is, well, Harry. Wonderful and maddening. He's like Kip, my old dog, our border collie. There were five of us in the house then, my parents, my sisters and me. In the evening, when we had all gone to our rooms, Kip would spend ten minutes, more sometimes, trying to find a place to lie down. It was her job to lie equal distance from all of us. In case of wolves. We were her sheep. Harry's like Kip. He's always looking out for his brothers, not perhaps the way they'd want it, but the way he sees it. I find his devotion, his protective

187

impulses, moving. I think his fundamental identity is as the oldest of five brothers."

"I missed out on a lot when the boys were growing up," Rupert said. "I wonder if that's it with Harry, making up for the missing dad."

"I don't think so. Harry took on the responsibility of the Oldest, the First. What are they, the five famous, fierce, fearsome Falkeses?" Francie laughed. "Will can recite the whole series. They all can."

Rupert poured himself another scotch.

"Do you miss England?" Francie asked.

"Never. I have no nostalgia for it. I wish Father Falkes had lived longer. He was a decade younger than I when he died."

"Do you think about your parents ever? Will said you hadn't wanted to know. Is that still true now? You might be able to find them with the Internet."

"Good God, no," Rupert said. "The Internet is a curse. I'm so glad I came up before everyone could find everyone else, before everyone knew what everyone else was doing. The thought of English relations crowding around my hospital bed, looking for my bank accounts and will . . ." Rupert stopped, overcome by visceral disgust.

"Are you dying?" Francie asked. "Everyone's afraid to ask."

He nodded. " 'Most things may never happen; this one will.' Eleanor knows, of course. She says the boys, the men, are not afraid to ask; they don't want to know."

"Are you afraid?" Francie said.

"Cross. Too soon."

"Are you still getting treated?" Francie asked.

"Yes, experimental protocols. I'm being kept alive by poison. Eleanor wants the end to be as good as it can be. I want it to be as long as it can be. She's right, of course, but I can't let go. I want a scientific breakthrough, a miracle."

"Not very English of you," Francie said. "We still 'go gentle into that good night.' 'So sorry to bother you, Sister, but I think the liver transplant has failed. Eyes awfully yellow. My fault I'm sure,' Old World fatalism." She shook her head. "Americans think they can beat the reaper with bench pressing and cod liver oil. Maybe that's only L.A. Midwesterners must know they're going to die. They're farmers. *Charlotte's Web.* Will had me read it. 'When Charlotte died, she died all alone.' Heartbreaker." She shot Rupert a sly smile. " 'When Charlotte passed, she passed all alone.' Not the same."

"Eleanor's bugbear," Rupert said. " 'Passing be not proud though some have called thee/ Mighty and dreadful . . .' " He smiled at Francie, then took a swallow of scotch. "I maintain the English disdain of euphemism, but I've been Americanized on the medical front." He paused. "Almost all fronts. I love America."

"I take it the doctors are willing to cooperate," Francie said.

"With unseemly enthusiasm," Rupert said. "They haven't tried arsenic or mercury or Drano, but almost everything else."

"I shall miss you so," Francie said. "When I met you the first time, in 1989, when you came to visit Will at King's, I thought, All right, I might be able to marry this young American, with his English father. I won't stop being English. I won't become American, or Americanized. You're still very English, you know. Not all fronts. You walk like an Englishman, a cricketer. You've got that English athlete's slouch."

"Do I?" he said. He smiled at her.

"And then, you were so open with everyone there, about being an orphan and being poor. It knocked me for a loop," she said.

"I wasn't like that when I was a student. When I was at Longleat, I played on the cricket first eleven. I'd been given a bat by a master but I didn't have any of the other equipment or any of the clothes. The headmaster asked an old boy if he would buy them for me. He did. I was instructed to write him a thank-you note."

"Christ," Francie said, then stopped. "I'm sorry. No blasphemy," she said. "Only profanity. Like the Restoration."

Rupert waved his hand. "I'm past that distinction these days," he said.

"Did you play cricket at Cambridge?" she asked.

"Yes. For King's, not for Cambridge. This time, I asked Father Falkes if he could help. I couldn't ask the provost. It would have been too humiliating. And the thought I might have to write a letter of thanks was stomach-churning. I've never supported the named scholarships that have the student recipients write the donors. Exacting gratitude. Father sent me money. He must have taken it from the collection plate. My paltry pocket money probably came from the collection plate. I didn't think about it." He paused. "I have a tendency to avoid thinking about personally unpleasant things. All my life. Close the door and move on."

Rupert gazed at his lovely daughter-in-law, realizing he had never had a conversation so personal, so unguarded with an Englishwoman. He understood why Will had fallen in love with her. He felt half in love with her too. Cambridge in his day was a man's world. There had been so few women when he was there, fewer than ten percent, and the university had shunted them to the women's colleges on the out-outskirts. He had never spoken to a female student. He wouldn't have known what to say. It was as if girls spoke a foreign language. He had known no girls or women growing up, except school matrons and housekeepers. If he had seen a girl like Francie, he wouldn't have approached her. It wasn't until America, until Vera, that he ever talked to a woman. He knew he was lucky to have married Eleanor, as elusive as she was, and until he met Dominic, she was the only person he spoke frankly to and with. Still, he was a man of his generation. It wasn't so much that he preferred the company of men as that he found them so much easier to be with. "How about those Yankees?" Until Susanna, he was grateful he'd had only boys. Now there was Francie too.

Rupert cast back his thoughts to Cambridge. His memory was fragmenting, whether from the cancer or the chemo or the scotch, he couldn't say. He had not been happy at Cambridge, but not unhappy either. It was his ticket. He took advantage of his opportunities. At Longleat, he had kept mostly to himself, the fear always lurking in the back of his mind that he'd be exposed, despite his last name, as a parish child, "to be cuffed and buffeted through the world, despised by all, and pitied by none." That fear receded at Cambridge. As a bona fide Leater, he'd moved up in the world, becoming even an object of envy. There were boys at Cambridge from lower castes, boys who went to grammar schools and minor public schools, boys with regional accents, boys who weren't Church of England. He saw there was currency other than money and ancestry: accent, education, Latin, cricket, most of all the aura of effortless superiority. He knew what he needed to do.

"Being poor in my day was still thought to be a personal failing, as being rich was regarded as a personal virtue," Rupert said. "Americans still feel that way. The English seem to have moderated their views. The landed rich are deserving; the rest just got in at the right time." He paused. "Partners at my firm used to point to me as the American Dream incarnate, the orphaned immigrant who came from nowhere." He laughed. "There are Americans who never heard of Cambridge, only Oxford."

"Why Cambridge?" Francie said. "I'd have taken you for an Oxford man, so worldly."

"Reverend Falkes had gone to King's, right after World War I. 'So many dead young men,' he said. 'They took me because I applied and could pay the fees.' "

"I'm no different from your partners. I had never heard of Princeton, only Harvard and Columbia," Francie said. "Will felt slighted. I told him I was London provincial. I had never before met anyone who'd gone to Princeton."

"Eating clubs. Princeton is famous for its eating clubs," Rupert said.

"Will said you'd say that," Francie said, laughing. "He said you've always regretted that none of them went to Harvard."

"I've never understood why Harry picked Princeton," Rupert said.

"I asked him once, a few years ago, when I first realized that the whole pack had gone there. He said, 'I think I knew it would take even Jack.' Harry rounding up his sheep."

Rupert poured himself another scotch. "Sweet old Harry," he said. They sat quietly for a few minutes, Rupert sipping his drink the whole time. "Tell me," Rupert said. "What's going on with you?"

"Will may have told you. We're trying in

vitro fertilization, a test-tube baby. It fills me with hope and dread. I want a baby so much but I worry that I'll get someone else's baby and someone else will get ours. I'm half-mad with worry. Will says I'm completely mad. It must be the hormones, I'm on the verge of tears all the time and I obsess about everything, not only *Rosemary's Baby.* How will I know if it's ours, both of us in that tube? People are so careless, so sloppy." She stopped. "I'm sorry about what I said, not wanting someone else's baby. I can be so stupid."

Rupert shook his head. "No, no. Science is doing miracles, as it ought," he said. He reached over and touched Francie's hand. "Don't get sentimental. Don't name a boy for me. I never liked Rupert — better than Cyril, but just." Francie nodded. Rupert sat back. "If we had had a girl, we were going to call her Mary, after Father Falkes's mother."

"My granny was Mary," Francie said, wiping away tears with her sleeve. "Don't mind them," she said. "Hormonal."

"I'm sad I won't get to meet your baby," Rupert said.

# CHAPTER 5
## SUSANNA

As far as she could see, her life was ordained to be lonely, and she must subdue her nature to her life, and, if possible, bring the two into harmony.

ELIZABETH GASKELL,
*THE LIFE OF CHARLOTTE BRONTË*

Susanna and Sam had sex once, in their sophomore year at Princeton. Both were drunk, though not as drunk as they afterward remembered. The mechanics had worked but for both it was a mortifying experience. Sam had no interest in foreplay; a quick ejaculation was the most he wished for. Susanna felt abandoned, stranded with wrenching emotions she couldn't express. They hadn't even gotten fully undressed. Minutes after they'd finished, Susanna slunk back to her dorm room.

The next morning at breakfast, Susanna moved quickly to restore law and order.

"Let's never do that again," she said. They were facing each other across the table in the Mathey dining room.

"I'm sorry," Sam said. "I was drunk."

"It wasn't your fault," Susanna said. "It was a bad idea and a worse experience, and it won't ever be repeated." She paused. "Or talked about."

"Can't I tease you about it?" Sam asked.

"No, not yet, maybe not ever," Susanna said. "I'm too embarrassed."

"In my family, that's the time to start making fun," Sam said. "It speeds recovery."

"How did your mother stand the five of you?" Susanna said.

"She drew the line at blood. And if an older brother picked on a younger brother, she might call him out, except if it was Jack being picked on. The Teflon Kid." Sam shook his head. "He's amazing. He's a genius. He's a dickhead."

"There should be a book about the five of you," Susanna said.

"We have the title: The Five Famous, Fierce, Forceful, Faithful, Fabled, Fortunate, Fearless Falkeses. Harry made it up when he was ten, in the spirit of *Alexander and the Terrible, Horrible, No Good, Very Bad Day,* but out-adjectiving it. Mom praised Harry for including 'fortunate.' "

"Self-fulfilling title, I'd say," Susanna said. "You are famous, famous for Princeton."

"Harry left off 'fruity,' " Sam said. "He didn't know then. I didn't know then."

"Stop that," Susanna said.

"You aren't entering into the spirit of things," Sam said. "I can't keep bringing you home with me if you're too well behaved."

"Where's all that 'He ain't heavy, he's my brother' stuff?" Susanna said.

"Harry believes that. 'We few, we happy, we band of brothers.' Only marines feel that way. Real brothers have the long knives out. The first murder was fratricide, and it only took one generation. Whoever wrote the Bible knew his onions. Mom said her goal was getting Tom to twenty-one with the rest of us still alive."

"Will I ever be able to joke about last night?" Susanna asked.

"Yes," Sam said. "It's our lavender moment. September 18, 1985. Next year we'll celebrate our first anniversary. I'll buy you a lavender bouquet. You'll buy me a lavender tie."

"For a gay man, you're horribly insensitive, and mean too," Susanna said.

"It's time to explode the myth of the sensitive gay man, once and for all," Sam said.

"I'm the middle of five boys. I wouldn't have survived if I'd been sensitive. The baby, Tom, is sensitive. Straight and sensitive. It's been rough for him." He smiled. "Anyway, you weren't looking for sensitive in me."

"No," Susanna said. "You're a beast a lot of the time. I like the guyness of you. I think that's what confused me last night — in my drunken stupor."

"I was curious," Sam said. "That's settled."

Sam didn't want Susanna to have a baby with someone else. He thought it should be his baby. The idea of a sperm donor, "some anonymous, muscled-up onanist," as he put it, "with decent college boards and blond wavy hair," enraged him. He told Susanna she shouldn't go the donor route.

"But I'm not," she said. "A friend has offered."

"Is he gay?" he asked.

"No, straight," she said. "You don't know him. He's a friend from work. Charles. Blond, tall, a bit nerdy, very smart. Stanford. He's younger than I am, thirty-two."

"Will he be the dad, on the birth certificate?" Sam asked.

"We're talking about that."

"I don't like it," Sam said.

"You can be the godfather," she said.

"How are you doing it? Turkey baster?" he said.

"None of your business," she said.

Sam insisted on celebrating September 18 every year. He and Susanna would go out to dinner. He'd bring her a lavender rose for each year. Susanna went along in bad humor, not seeing the original event as a night to remember. "It's like America celebrating the Bay of Pigs," she said.

On their seventeenth anniversary, Sam took her to Balthazar. She had had her fill; she gave him a box of monogrammed lavender stationery from Mrs. John L. Strong, one hundred cards and envelopes. "They cost four hundred and ninety-five dollars," she said. "OK," he said. "We won't do this again." Susanna ordered steak au poivre, the most expensive dish on the menu. "I'd like a Barolo," she said. "You might like the crow."

Sam took a deep breath. "Crow may be just the thing," he said. "More than you know. We should order a bottle of Barolo." He then told her about Harry's clash with his mother over the Wolinskis.

Susanna didn't get angry, as Sam had thought; she was quiet. "What?" he said.

Susanna shook her head.

"If you'd told me this earlier, I'd have wanted to put a hit on Harry as well as Vera. Now I don't know what to think. I think Harry's onto something. I think your father knew Vera at some point but . . ." Susanna stopped.

"But what?" Sam said.

Susanna shook her head again. "I can't believe he would have two babies with another woman. Maybe one, an accident. Even that's hard to believe. It must be awful for everyone." She stopped again. Sam waited this time. "Harry shouldn't have said that to your mom, that she knew. Even if he thought she did, even if she did. He must be a mess."

"We're all pretty much a mess, except Jack and Mom, though you can't tell with Mom. She never lets on, not to us, at least."

"What do you expect? You're all blaming her, if not as savagely as Harry. You all still act like babies with her and with each other," Susanna said. "Me too."

Sam ordered a second bottle of Barolo.

"So," Sam said, "where are you in your baby-making plans?"

"Moving along," Susanna said.

"Would you marry me if I were free?" Sam said.

"No," Susanna said. "Why would I do that?"

"You love me," Sam said.

"I see," she said. "A Rock Hudson husband."

"Would you let me be the baby's father?" he asked.

"No," she said. "Andrew."

"I'm going to split with him anyway," Sam said. "I want a baby and I'm going to have one, one way or another."

"We can raise them together. They can be friends," Susanna said.

"You don't believe me," Sam said. "Wait and see."

"I've waited, I've seen," Susanna said.

"How can you be so coldhearted," he said. "You know we should be having a baby together."

"I woke up one day and realized I wanted a baby more than I wanted your baby," she said.

"Are you mad at me?" Sam asked.

"Oh, Sam," Susanna said. "I'm thirty-six and eleven-twelfths years old. We've been talking about this for two years. I can't wait for you any longer. You've had a life with Andrew for fourteen years. I've been alone. I've given up on a husband, but not a family."

Sam complained to his mother. "I think Susanna's going to have a baby," he said. "Without me."

"Yes," Eleanor said.

"Aren't you sad? Disappointed?" he asked.

"Are you?" Eleanor said.

"Yes," he said. "She won't wait for me to work things out."

"Sam," Eleanor said in a voice that made him sit up straighter. "What is the matter with you? You're married, or the next closest thing, and Andrew doesn't want a baby."

"I didn't know I wanted a baby," he said.

"That's your problem, not Susanna's."

"She could wait a bit longer," he said.

"No, she can't. She's almost thirty-seven."

"There's IVF," he said.

"When did you become so egoistical? I don't remember you like this," she said.

"I was always like this. I seemed a bit nicer than the others because I got my way most of the time. All the time, really," Sam said. "Oh, I paid attention and I listened without taking sides, but I think that was the gay boy's wary watchfulness and ingratiating posturing. It also helped me get my way." He paused. "Ask Andrew. He knows the darker side. He thinks I'm a narcissist and an egoist. So there."

"And here, we all thought it was Harry

taking up all the oxygen in the room," she said.

"Harry's got a big personality. All his emotions are big. But he's really a better, kinder man than I." Sam laughed. "He's like Freud, a grandiose inductionist. He thinks everyone thinks the way he does. But he doesn't hold a grudge."

"Not so fast there," Eleanor said. "Lately, he's been less awful to me but he can't forgive Dad. He's rewriting his entire life up until yesterday." Eleanor paused. "How come the rest of you aren't mad at Dad?"

"Why should we be, when we can be mad at you?" Sam said. "Kidding. Sort of." He shook his head. "We don't know what to believe. We're all behaving according to script. Will says it doesn't make a difference to his life. I know Dad loved me. Jack thinks it's cool Dad had another family. Tom wishes he'd grown up with the Wolinski boys so he wouldn't have been the youngest. Kidding. Tom refuses to believe it. Harry, of course, is enraged. He didn't plan it that way."

"I never thought I'd say this," Eleanor said. "It was much easier when you all were small."

Sam moved out two weeks later. Without

saying anything to Andrew, he paid off the mortgage on the apartment, three hundred and twenty-five thousand dollars, and had his lawyer make over his interest to Andrew. It was a large two-bedroom on West Sixteenth. "If you need support," he said to Andrew, handing him the deed, "let me know." To Andrew and almost everyone they knew, Sam had moved with eye-popping speed. Sam didn't care. If he acted now, he might still persuade Susanna to let him be her baby's father. His mother and brothers were stunned. Andrew was stunned, wounded, and furious.

"Who are you?" he asked Sam, as Sam was packing his suitcases. "Henry the Eighth?"

"Don't tell me you didn't see this coming," Sam said. "You've made it difficult for me to see Susanna for the last dozen years, turning me into a liar and a sneak. We've been arguing about a baby for months. You gave me an ultimatum. You said I had to choose. I'm choosing. I want a baby."

"You're giving me no warning," Andrew said.

"It's no use, Andrew," Sam said. "I can't stay. The apartment's yours. The furniture's yours, and the books, plants, pots, everything. You can have the friends too. I'm done here."

"Where are you going?" Andrew asked. "West Sixty-Seventh?"

"I've taken a place on East Twenty-Second, Gramercy, a rental," Sam said.

"I see," Andrew said. "A better neighborhood."

"If you don't want the apartment," Sam said, "you can sell it."

"You're a bastard, a complete bastard," Andrew said. "I don't know you anymore."

Sam called everyone in the family, resisting the siren song of email.

The first divorce, Eleanor thought. "Just like that?" she said to him.

"Not 'just,' " he said. "You must have seen it coming."

"I'm surprised," she said.

Eleanor, Will, and Tom called Andrew to say how sorry they were. Harry was indignant.

"We don't do divorce," he said to Sam. "We stick it out; we work it out. We fight it out if we have to. We don't leave."

"Do you hear my eyes rolling?" Sam said. "You've basically disowned Dad, ex-postmortem, making a huge family rift, bigger than the one I'm making. I want a baby and I'm not going to sneak around."

"You can't have everything," Harry said.

"I know," Sam said. "I made a choice. You don't like it. I thought maybe you'd especially understand, with your feelings about family. Can't you understand why I might want children?"

"This is all because of Dad and the Wolinskis," Harry said.

Eleanor wondered if she'd ever see Andrew again. She realized she didn't care. She wouldn't miss him. She had little feeling toward him that wasn't derivative. Sam had seemed happy with him, or happy enough, until he wasn't. That was her bottom line with in-laws, and with Andrew, it had been her top line too. She shared the general family feeling that Susanna and not Andrew belonged at family gatherings. Everyone loved Susanna; no one, except Sam, loved Andrew, and even Sam's attachment to Andrew seemed tepid compared with his love for Susanna. From the beginning, Andrew knew their preference and blamed Susanna. At the family parties they both went to, he would become aggressively withdrawn, flattening everyone's pleasure, reminding Eleanor of holidays with her parents. She thought he had bad manners. She wished Sam would speak to him. Sam would make excuses for him. "Package deal," he'd remind his mother. I don't like anything in that package, she thought. She did not stop inviting Susanna but Susanna often made excuses. When she didn't show up, they all blamed Andrew.

Andrew hadn't gone to Princeton for his undergraduate education, only for his PhD. He'd gone to Penn State. He was lucky to have gone to any college. His parents didn't believe in college any more than they believed in homosexuality. In their minds, the two were linked and they believed Andrew would have been straight if he had stayed home in Pittsburgh and worked construction or some other manly job. At Princeton, Andrew had a chip on his shoulder. Quick to take offense, he gave it even more quickly, setting people right. "I don't have wingtips. I don't own a tuxedo. I can't afford a computer." He was sensitive to the slightest slights.

"I'd never have gotten into an eating club," he told Sam.

"Would you have wanted to?" Sam asked.

"That's beside the point," Andrew said.

"Well, it's all speculative. You didn't go here as an undergraduate."

"I know that. Why do you keep saying that?"

In the beginning, Sam had thought Andrew was like his father, coming from nowhere. He even found Andrew's anger attractive. It had none of Harry's self-righteousness but bristled with working-class resentment. As the years went on, these charms waned. Andrew was nothing like Rupert and he was no longer poor, but upper middle class, complaining about co-op prices, like everyone else who lived in Chelsea. Sam was tired of hearing how indulged and spoiled he and his brothers had been.

"Andrew likes my money," Sam said to his mother. "And he likes insulting me about my money."

"I think you're rewriting your past," Eleanor said. "You loved him. Now you don't."

"I thought I maybe loved him, in the beginning. He loved me. He probably still does. He's a romantic. He thought I was the most wonderful person he'd ever met. It was irresistible, once upon a time," Sam said. "You know the feeling. Dad adored you — I saw it in the way he looked at you."

"It's so interesting hearing my sons' view of my marriage," Eleanor said.

"We're still not willing to see you and Dad as people who exist separate from us. We all had this fantasy of our family life — until the Wolinskis. Now we're trying to reclaim it."

"Why don't you start with Bup? Take him back to your new apartment." Eleanor nodded toward Limbo. "Would you like a case of Black Label?"

Sam began to court Susanna. He started by not apologizing. "I've been selfish. I am selfish. That's not going to change. But I love you and I think we'd be good parents."

"I used to think so, but not anymore. And the way you dumped Andrew was chilling," she said. "Gone in sixty seconds."

"No, no," Sam said. "It was at least a year in the making. You know that. I kept thinking I could bring him around to a baby."

"I knew he'd never want a baby, especially my baby. He wanted you all to himself."

"I was used to getting my way," he said.

"How do I know you won't dump me and the baby? You might meet some cute guy at a bar one night and decide the two of you should live in San Francisco. On the water. You have too much money." She shook her head. "If Charles piked off, it would be OK. He's first-rate genetic material and a decent person but not someone I care for especially."

Sam was slow to answer. Susanna's scenario was not so outlandish it couldn't happen. "I think I'd love the baby and want to

210

stick around to see him grow up."

"What if the kid turns into a thirteen-year-old goth with violent tendencies? Where will you be? It's not enough to pay for Austen Riggs. Are you going to stick around then?"

"My mother and brothers would never speak to me again," Sam said. "I'd be leaving their grandchild, their niece or nephew."

"You're so attached to Team Falkes. They're the only ones who ever really matter. A baby is not going to make up for your dad's . . ." Susanna trailed off, not knowing how to say what she thought. "Be a better son, a better brother."

"I didn't know you had such a low opinion of me," he said.

"I love you, Sam. I always will, but I don't think that I can count on you for the next twenty-five years." She looked at him, then away, blinking back tears. The thought she might cry made her angry.

"Have I let you down?" he asked.

"Yes. You sidelined me. Andrew always came before me, between us. We had our dinners, our movies, but I could never drop by, I could never call you spontaneously to go for a drink or meal. You never came to any party I gave, not one." She shrugged. "And now you're telling me you're always going to be selfish. Not exactly a selling line.

A Darcy proposal."

Sam went home to his empty apartment on Gramercy Park. There was no one to call. His mother and brothers would only jump in where Susanna left off. When had he become just a cad, not a charming cad? He loved Susanna but not with the same devotion he loved his mother, his brothers, his grandfather, his father. Andrew had said the same thing. "Team Falkes. Always Team Falkes."

Sam poured himself a tumbler of Black Label and sank into an ancient armchair that had once been his father's, the only piece of furniture in his living room, rescued from the West Sixty-Seventh Street purge. How had it come to pass, he asked himself, that at thirty-seven, he was fatherless, husbandless, childless, homeless, friendless? A wave of self-pity swept over him, followed almost immediately by a tide of indignation. He took a swig of scotch. It was Andrew's fault he hadn't grown up. He was only twenty-one when they moved in together; Andrew was thirty. Back then, unlike now, being thirty was being an adult. Andrew had taken advantage of him, robbed him of his youth. He'd been old young, like his mother. His mother too was to blame. Swamped by three boys under four, she had shunted him off to his father and grand-father. He'd never known a mother's love, not the way his brothers had. His brothers too were to blame. Harry and Will had op-pressed him. Tom was needy, Jack obnox-ious. What were Andrew and Susanna talk-ing about? Team Falkes was nothing to him, not anymore. He took another swig of scotch. The tumbler was half-empty. Or was it half-full? He couldn't remember which he was, a half-empty or a half-full type. Tom was half-empty, no question, and Jack was half-full. Harry could go either way, depend-ing on the circumstances. Will liked to refill his glass before it got too low. "Topping up, keeping it full," he'd say.

Will might understand, Sam thought. He wondered if he should call him. He looked at his watch. It was only five thirty in L.A., too early to whine. Will would still be at work, brusque and efficient. Sam sat back, imagining his conversation with Will.

*Jesus,* Will would say. *You're not even drunk yet and already you've thrown every-one overboard. . . .* Will would then pause, the Hollywood touch. *Except Dad,* he'd say softly. *What about Dad?* Sam tried to think what Dad would think. He could almost hear him say, *Susanna's a great girl. You're lucky to have her in your life.* That would be it.

What is wrong with me? Sam thought, I used to be a decent fellow, more decent than not. People used to like me, people relied on me. I'm worse than Harry. It's Dad's fault, dying before we were ready. It's the Wolinskis. They've ruined everything. Sam emptied the glass and went to bed.

Sam was home nursing a scotch when Eleanor called. He hadn't heard from her or Susanna in a week, though he'd called both. Eleanor told him Susanna had had a miscarriage that morning. She had been nine weeks pregnant. Eleanor had spent the day with her. "She's heartbroken," Eleanor said. "She has a D and C scheduled for tomorrow afternoon, three thirty. I said I'd go."

"No, I will," Sam said.

Sam caught a cab to the Vinegar Factory. He had the driver wait, promising an extra ten dollars. He bought two bottles of Arneis, eight ounces of smoked salmon, brown bread, poached salmon with green sauce, mixed greens, an avocado, a baguette, a fruit tart, bagels, and cream cheese. Flush with provender, he had the cab take him crosstown to Susanna's at Ninety-Second and West End.

He gave his name to the doorman, adding, "She may not answer. She's ill. I'm worried about her." The doorman called up. No one answered. "Let's go up and check on her," Sam said. He sounded like his father. The doorman nodded.

The doorman locked the front door and went up with Sam to Susanna's apartment. They knocked, then knocked again. No one answered. "Maybe she's out," the doorman said. "She's ill. She's at home," Sam said, again sounding like Rupert. "I think you should get the key." When the doorman had gone off to find the super, Sam called loudly through the door. "Susanna, it's me, Sam. I've asked the doorman to get the key. I'll make a scene if you don't open up."

After a minute, the door opened. Susanna stood there, the saddest person Sam had ever seen. He put down his groceries and clasped her to him. She burst into tears, burying her head in his shoulder. He was still holding her, by the door, when the super arrived. "I'll take care of things," Sam said. The super nodded. With his arm around her shoulders, Sam edged Susanna into the apartment.

Susanna's crying ebbed. "Do you have a tissue?" she said, catching her breath.

"We need to talk," Sam said, handing her

his handkerchief. "And we need to eat."

Andrew had called Susanna the day after Sam moved out. Susanna couldn't tell if he was looking for sympathy, for someone to blame, or for Sam. Probably all three, she decided. Susanna was kinder than she wanted to be. Almost against her will, she found herself murmuring words of support. "It's very sad. I'm so sorry." He was in pain. He even cried at one point. What a schmuck, she thought. Andrew wanted to know if Susanna knew anything about the breakup. "No," Susanna said. "I haven't seen or spoken to Sam in a few weeks." She went on, leaking irritation, "No doubt he wanted to wrestle with this decision by himself." Susanna never heard from or saw Andrew again. Some weeks later, she asked Sam how Andrew was doing, out of curiosity tinged with politeness. "I don't know how he is," Sam said, "or where he is." Susanna winced. Sam's cruelty had at one time come as a surprise; lately, it came only as disappointment. Had he really been like that all along, the result of growing up the middle of five boys? Or was it peculiar to his relationship with Andrew?

Andrew disappeared from all their lives, like a drowning man beneath the waters.

Every so often one of them might ask Sam how he was doing. Sam would shrug and shake his head. Eleanor almost expected him to say "Andrew who?" It troubled her, as it troubled Susanna.

"If you don't want to talk about it," Eleanor said, "I understand, but I'm curious. What happened?" A month had passed since Sam had moved out. They were having dinner together at the Café, downstairs from Eleanor's apartment.

"I was tired of him. I was bored with him," Sam said. He looked tired to Eleanor, as if he hadn't slept well in months. "The second seven-year itch, worse than the first. I'd ask you if that was someone — I mean, something — you ever experienced if I wanted to know. But I don't."

Eleanor thought back to year fourteen of her marriage: 1975. She looked at her middle son, her outlier. She wished Rupert were here to talk to.

"I often ask myself what Dad would say," Sam said. Eleanor smiled. He had often seemed to her to have a direct line to her thoughts, some of her thoughts. "I remember him saying," Sam said, " 'What's most important to you? Do that. And don't give up on it too soon or too easily.' "

"I can understand you wanted to leave,"

Eleanor said. "I don't understand why you're acting as though he never mattered. He was in your life, and our lives too, for years." She paused. "I'm on your side, whatever your reasons for leaving."

Sam asked the waiter for a scotch. He wanted his mother on his side for his reasons, not whatever reasons. The waiter brought him a double.

Looking down at his drink, Sam spoke softly, almost as if he didn't want his mother to hear. "Andrew was the first. Freshman year. He was my TA. We were at a party. I was drunk. So was he. So he said."

"And?" Eleanor said.

"You don't set up housekeeping for four-teen years with your first." He stopped. "I'm being stupid. You married the only man you had sex with — after you were married."

"Did I?"

Sam sat up straighter. "What?"

"You're moving sideways," Eleanor said.

"You never liked Andrew," Sam said.

"Didn't I?" Eleanor said.

"Oh, for chrissakes, Mom, answer a question," Sam said.

Eleanor looked at him, showing no anger, no annoyance, no sympathy. Sam started to speak, then stopped. He took a swallow of scotch.

"Sorry," he said. "You don't like loaded questions."

"No," she said.

"Sometimes I think you and Dad were too respectful of our privacy, not asking questions other parents might ask," he said.

"When was this, upper school? Earlier? Later?"

"Middle school through college," he said.

"Would it have made a difference?" she said.

"Probably not," he said.

"We worried sometimes," she said. "Even after college."

Sam looked sharply at her.

"Dad told me about running into you on Houston Street."

Sam could feel the vein in his neck pulsing. He had been walking with a man, not Andrew, their arms around each other's waist. His father was almost upon him by the time Sam saw him. Sam nodded and walked past. Rupert nodded back. Sam was twenty-nine then, back in New York finally, after Princeton and New Haven, chafing at domesticity.

"Joe Macy," he said. "Two years. After the first seven years with Andrew."

"One of Bill Macy's boys?"

Sam nodded. "He was a class ahead of

me at Trinity. I didn't know he was gay; I should have. He starred in all the musicals. He didn't know I existed."

Susanna was limp in Sam's arms. Briefly, he had a Rhett Butler fantasy of swooping her up in his arms and carrying her away, to safety. Where the hell did that come from? he wondered. He walked her to the sofa, settling her there with pillows and covering her with a blanket. "Rest," he said. "I'll get dinner on." He laid the table, using cloth napkins and place mats. He moved a bowl of flowers from the mantel to the table. He transferred the food to serving dishes. He lit the candles. He put on music, Brahms's Requiem. He brought her a glass of cold Arneis. "Drink this," he said. "Slowly." Susanna took a sip.

"How do you know to do all that?" Susanna asked.

"I watched Andrew," he said.

"Rascal," she said. She smiled at him for the first time, with a look of the old fondness.

"It's the first drink I've had in weeks," she said. Her smile faded; she looked stricken. "Was that it?" she asked. "All the drinking I did in college and after? Or the drugs?"

At Princeton, Susanna had very briefly

tried a very narrow range of drugs: marijuana, Adderall, ecstasy. She didn't care for any of them and had gone cold turkey by the end of freshman year. A friend of a friend had asked if she was a Mormon. Susanna preferred alcohol, sweet drinks that made her drunk in an hour, whiskey sours, margaritas, vodka punches, daiquiris. She would have liked cosmos, but by the time *Sex and the City* hit the airwaves she had left cocktails behind for wine.

"You didn't miscarry because of drink or drugs," Sam said. "There are dozens of reasons women miscarry. Often very good reasons." He wanted to move off the topic of drink and drugs, drugs especially. He didn't want to spook Susanna; he didn't want her worrying about his genetic material. His drug taking, like others who would become doctors, had been catholic and irresponsible. Most of it had been at Princeton but some he kept up through his twenties. He had never injected heroin, he drew the line there, but he had tried almost everything else. He hadn't liked meth; he had used coke only on weekends in social situations; he preferred Percocet to Oxycontin; he loved hallucinogens, especially LSD. He had smoked weed almost every day sophomore year, until his adviser said he was getting a reputation in the department as a druggie. "Does Harry know?" his adviser asked. He had been Harry's sophomore adviser, also Will's. Sam recognized a threat when he heard it. Harry had never used, and took a hard line against all drugs. Sam thought he would tell their parents if he knew. Sam didn't care about his Princeton reputation, only his West Sixty-Seventh Street one. He stopped smoking during the week. He spent the weekends stoned, avoiding Will. The other boys were comparatively abstemious. Will had done a little cocaine. It was hard to close a deal in Hollywood in the '80s and '90s without doing a line. Jack smoked weed, one or two tokes a night. He didn't drink. Tom had had a bad trip with marijuana brownies sophomore year. He became paranoid. He called Sam in a panic. Sam stayed on the phone with him through the night, telling him the next morning he shouldn't do drugs. Sam was in his first year of medical school. Tom took his advice as he would a doctor's. Sam saw it as the dawn of his bedside manner.

"The good news is you got pregnant," Sam said. "You'll get pregnant again. You're not to worry. I have a doctor friend at Mount Sinai, a top-notch fertility specialist and a class human being. He'll make sure you get your baby, whoever the dad is."

"I like women gynecologists," Susanna said.

"For fertility, the best ones are men. The only ones are men. A kind of Frankenstein impulse to create life. Women already create life. They don't have the same test-tube urges. Trust me on this."

"I have a D and C tomorrow," Susanna said.

"I know," Sam said. "I'll take you. Three thirty, right?" Susanna nodded. It had been so long, maybe forever, she thought, since someone had taken care of her. She started to cry again.

Sam took her hand, the way his father had taken his mother's, those times when his emotions got the better of him. "I'll be the second-best father ever, if you give me a chance."

Susanna didn't say anything.

"What's the matter?" he asked.

She shook her head.

"Is it AIDS, HIV?" he asked.

Susanna didn't say anything.

"I was planning to get tested. I'll show you the results."

"OK," she said.

"Was Charles the father?" he asked.

She shook her head.

"Joe?"

She shook her head again. Sam didn't care about Charles. He could push him out. He would have been jealous of Joe.

"Who was it?" he asked.

"Parthenogenesis," she said.

Sam called a Realtor the next morning. "I want two apartments, good-sized, next to each other. A large, rambling, five- or six-bedroom apartment that could be divided in two would also work. Maybe one that belonged to Orthodox Jews. I need two kitchens, or the possibility of two. Each apartment should have at least two bedrooms, preferably three. At least two bathrooms in each and a powder room too. Washer-dryer connections in both. Dining rooms if possible; if not possible, then large living rooms. Southern exposures desirable. Doormen. Live-in super. Elevator. West Village or Gramercy or West End Avenue between Seventy-Second and Ninety-Second. Fourth to eighth floors. Decent condition preferred. Can you do it for three million? How long would it take to find this?"

After speaking with his Realtor, Sam called his lawyer, a junior partner at Maynard, Tandy. Sam asked for a brief tutorial on real estate law and child support. The partner was, as Sam expected, disapproving. Sam got annoyed, the spirit of his father coursing through his body. "I didn't ask for advice," he said, the way his dad might. "I asked for information." As with Rupert, the young partner regressed. "I'm sorry, sir." Sam wondered if he'd have to change lawyers, the humiliation this one now no doubt was feeling being almost complete. Why couldn't he just say, "Right"? Sam thought. Sam apologized for being so short-tempered. "Thanks for your help."

Sam next called Susanna. She was at her office. "I'll take off tomorrow to mourn," she said.

"Would you please meet me for lunch?" Sam said. "I mean, not for lunch. For Perrier. You can't eat. Twelve thirty at Coogan's Bar. I have a proposition. I'd like you to hear it." Susanna agreed.

Sam called his internist, another old pal from medical school, to schedule a checkup. "Also an AIDS test," he said.

"Do you need that?" his doctor asked. "I did one five years ago."

"I need one," Sam said.

"Shit, Sam," his doctor said.

"No, it's not what you think. I broke up with Andrew," Sam said. "I want to be a sperm donor, a father really, for Susanna's baby."

"You both need to go for genetic counseling," his doctor said. "Unmarried couples don't do well with surprises."

Sam was early at Coogan's. Both his parents were punctual, to a fault he had often thought, and both had insisted on the boys being punctual. Even Jack learned to be on time some of the time; his parents would cancel his trumpet lesson if he was late for school more than twice in a week. If any of them was late for dinner — dinner was a command performance most nights, seven o'clock with five minutes' grace, like the theatre — he had a cheese sandwich in the kitchen. Once, there was a palace revolution. They all tripped in at seven thirty. They found the dinner table cleared. Eleanor was in the kitchen putting out the ingredients for cheese sandwiches on the counter. "See you later," she said. She and Rupert went downstairs to the Café. The next night she served cheese sandwiches for dinner. "If you're going to be late," she said, "I don't see the point of serving a proper dinner." The revolution was suppressed. Changing tactics, the boys would tease Eleanor for being so rigid, comparing her to her mother. "Bah. Water off a duck's back,"

Eleanor would say. "Granny is not always wrong. Some standards are worth holding to. Being on time is respectful of other people's time. Being late is disrespectful." Rupert backed her up. "Don't be rude unless you intend it," he said. "Don't waste capital needlessly." In his last year with Andrew, Sam had been late all the time, sometimes as much as an hour. He'd be early for Susanna.

Susanna showed up five minutes later, also early. "Mom got to you too, I see," Sam said.

Susanna laughed. "If it wasn't for your parents, I'd be totally uncouth, still slouching, eating with my mouth open, not standing up when I met someone, doing that silly fork-hand exchange after cutting my meat. I liked that lesson best, eating with two implements."

Over their drinks, Sam outlined his plan for post-baby living. They'd have adjoining apartments, with an interior connection for easy movement in between them. "The little guy," Sam said, assuming, as Harry had, that he'd have a son, "could sleep where he wanted. None of this three-nights-with-me-four-with-you nonsense."

"Who would own 'my' apartment?" Susanna asked.

"I was thinking we'd both own both, a

joint tenancy, the survivor getting it all. If one wanted to sell, we'd sell both and share the proceeds."

"That's some gift," Susanna said.

"You'd be the mother of my child," Sam said, "maybe children. It seems to me a mother should have what a wife would have." He gave her a knowing look. "It's not as if I don't have the money."

"Who pays the mortgage? Maintenance?" Susanna said. "Christ, I sound grasping."

"No mortgage. The plan is to buy them outright. Cash. I assume I'd give you enough child support for the maintenance. You don't have to pay taxes on child support."

"I'd feel remiss if I didn't ask about medical insurance," Susanna said, looking Sam square in the eye.

Sam laughed. "Maybe I should just give you three million outright. Look, we'll make a contract, get it all settled, a kind of prenup. You need to get your own lawyer and you have to pay for him, so I'm not seen as overreaching or suborning or perpetrating some such nefarious act of malfeasance. He or she should be very good. I've made it clear to the Maynard lawyer what I want, but he can't help thinking I'm making a mistake. It's his job, I suppose. My mother has the same problem with them. It's probably the correct instinct for a Wall Street firm, but I don't like their hovering. They want to protect me from myself."

"I may not be an heiress, but it's not as if I don't have money of my own," Susanna said. "Granny Bowles left me a small pile" — she smiled — "and my mother might still come through."

Sam hooted. "What is Prudence planning to do with her money?"

"I'm guessing either a cat sanctuary or an ashram." Susanna said this matter-of-factly, not even allowing herself a sigh. She wasn't making a joke. "She asks me periodically if I need money and then sends me eleven thousand dollars, no gift tax. She said she'd double it if I got married. She might do it for a child."

"One of the best things about college, you find out what's out there in the way of parents. We all found out how lucky we were." Sam paused. "You were not so lucky."

Susanna knew she was very lucky, in the great scheme of things. She was an American; she was a Princeton graduate; she had a good job, with medical insurance; she was probably in the top twenty-five percent in looks. She wished she felt lucky, luckier.

"I need to think about this," Susanna said.

"Yes, of course. I'm just putting in my oar," Sam said. "I don't want you planning another pregnancy without giving me a chance to make an offer, or counteroffer."

" 'Just'? It's plainly unbeatable. You know that," she said.

"That was the plan: to make an offer you couldn't refuse."

"My first reaction? It sounds like concubinage."

"I can see that," Sam said, "but in a good way."

"Oh, Sam, Sam, I missed you so."

They stirred their drinks, occasionally looking at the other and smiling. They were back together, observing the unities of time, space, and action. Sam began mentally kicking himself for his relationship with Andrew.

"Why didn't you leave Andrew for Joe?" Susanna asked, jolting Sam. She's on my wavelength, the way he never was, Sam thought.

"I tried," Sam said. "Andrew kept saying it was a flash-in-the-pan romance. He said it was nostalgia for the high school prom king. He said Joe was like Jack; he called him a black hole of self-absorption. He said he'd dump me within six months. Joe had been in two relationships the year before we met. He'd move in, he'd get a new part, he'd move out." Everyone at Trinity, not only Sam, had had a crush on Joe. He was like James Dean, the universal sex object. Sam thought back to Trinity, wondering if anyone ever recovered from high school. All the people who were fat in high school still thought of themselves as fat. A PhD from Harvard never made up for not getting into Harvard College.

"You never get over your high school sweetheart, even if he didn't know you existed," Sam said. "When Joe made a pass at me when I was twenty-nine, I was jelly. I was sixteen all over again."

"I think that's a Southern experience. Like a Loretta Lynn song. You may be an outlier. In the North, you never get over your first bad boyfriend." Susanna gave him a small smile.

"Well, then, I've nothing to get over. I've never had a bad boyfriend." Sam laughed. "I've been the bad boyfriend."

"I like Joe," Susanna said. "He's a lot of fun, and he's been a good friend, but actors probably don't make the best husbands. Too many other bodies around."

"We keep in touch, a little. You see him more than I do. After we broke up, he started living with a writer. Almost the next day. Since then, there have been at least four others. But who's counting?" Sam detected a peevish note creeping into his voice and tried to shake it off; he remembered the hard feelings he had toward Joe when they broke up. Joe said he was tired of sneaking around. Sam didn't believe him. Joe had liked sneaking around. He had liked spending afternoons at the Carlyle and the St. Moritz. Sam knew how to woo when he wanted to. "He was seeing others when he was seeing me. Of course, I couldn't complain. I kept living with Andrew. Did anyone like Andrew?"

"No," Susanna said. "No one liked him. They all put up with him for you." She looked startled. "I shouldn't have said that. It was cruel."

"It's OK. It's strange. I'm finished with him. Completely. He's like 'yesterday's mashed potatoes.' I have no feelings toward him. I have no interest in him. How does that happen?" Sam stopped.

"How does it happen?" Susanna said.

Sam took a big breath. "I hated who I was with him. He always had me on the defensive. He never bought me a present. He said I had everything already. So I stopped buying him presents." Sam paused. "I was myself with Joe, the way I am with you. It was a huge relief. 'It's really hard to be roommates with people if your suitcases are much better than theirs.' " He gave a small smile. "Holden Caulfield."

"So that's been my problem," Susanna said. "Not liking men with expensive luggage. Except you."

"Like to like. It's easier," Sam said.

"Is there anyone with money you are interested in?" Susanna asked. Sam didn't answer. "Other than Joe?" she asked. Sam shrugged.

"We have to be responsible and discreet about significant and insignificant others in the apartments," she said. "No uncles showing up for breakfast in a bathrobe."

Sam nodded. "My doctor said we should go for genetic counseling."

"What about the Wolinskis?" Susanna said. "Could they find out the results?"

Sam looked surprised. "Do you really think they could be Dad's sons?"

"I don't know," Susanna said. "I don't know."

# CHAPTER 6
## JIM

---

What's gone and what's past help/Should
be past grief.

WILLIAM SHAKESPEARE,
*THE WINTER'S TALE*

When she first saw the five Falkes boys,
standing in front of the Hotel des Artistes,
Anne Cardozo knew Jim was their father.
They looked so much like him. Eyes didn't
lie. She started to hyperventilate.

The little boys were jostling each other
and pulling on their mother's arms; the bigger ones were trying to talk to her. Rooted
to the sidewalk, riveted and winded, Anne
struggled to regain mental footing. She
hadn't been expecting five children, five
boys. She had imagined two, maybe three.
People didn't have five children anymore,
not since the pill. She took in a deep breath
and held it for ten seconds. They couldn't
be Jim's, she told herself. Eleanor might

have had one child with Jim, the first out of
anguish or the last out of nostalgia, but not
five, not in her world. She watched the older
boys walk down the street. Could those two,
the oldest two, be Jim's sons? The resemblance was spooky. She felt light-headed
and panicky. Am I losing my mind? she
wondered. She had a sudden vision of her
brain cells, resolving into sand and sliding
down her spinal column. Education was
useless, she thought. Being a neurobiologist
had given her no special understanding of
her thoughts, feelings, or perceptions; all it
had provided was a topographic map of an
overactive brain. She leaned against a
parked car. It was an old story with her, the
triumph of the amygdala over the cortex.
The first time she studied the cerebrum and
its hemispheres at Vassar, she thought she
heard the professor say that the two halves
"commiserated" with each other. When she
realized, reading her notes, that he must
have said "communicated," she was disappointed — in the professor, in the course,
in science. Barely into her major, she already
suspected that Freud was more interesting
than Broca. There was elegance in science
but no poetry. Ten years later, she thought
she might benefit from therapy if her Ger-
manic upbringing and her scientific train-

ing, a practical redundancy, had permitted it. Her internist prescribed Ativan.

After weeks of spying, on and off the tennis field, Anne was forced to reject theories of Cardozo paternity. In the ways the boys looked like Eleanor, they looked like Jim, at least from a distance, staring into the sun. In the ways the boys didn't look like their mother, they didn't look like him. They were not Jewish children. They were Lapp or Cossack. They had high cheekbones and Tatar eyes, lending them an exoticism beyond the genetic possibilities of the Cardozos. These must be Rupert's contributions, his phenotypes, she decided.

Anne didn't remember meeting him at her wedding; she barely remembered anything of the day. Had she danced with Jim? What music did the band play? Had she eaten? She didn't remember having a good time. She remembered that her feet and head hurt. It was a late-morning wedding with lunch. She and Jim left at five, the band played until six, then packed up and left along with her parents. There had been so many people, at least six hundred, more than a hundred of them relatives. Henry Kissinger came; so did Jacob Javits, Charlie Rangel, John Lindsay, and Bess Myerson. Other people she also didn't know came.

She had left the invitation list to her mother, who'd given Jim's side a hundred guests, more than generous in Mrs. Lehman's view. They weren't Cardozo Cardozos.

One of Anne's cousins, Ben Straus, had sat next to Eleanor at the wedding. At a family dinner, not long afterward, Ben burst out: "There was this gorgeous WASP, thirty-something, with five sons at our table. She sure had Mrs. Robinson beat." Everyone laughed. Eleanor had come in on the Cardozo quota. Anne didn't think then to ask who she was.

With Falkeses on the brain, Anne checked the seating arrangements. Eleanor and Rupert had been seated at a table with the Strauses; also at the table were the Javitses and "some et ceteras," as her mother referred to the B-listers. The tables sat twelve; they were all made up of mixed groups. "That way, there are no good tables, no bad tables," Mrs. Lehman said. "Every table is good and bad." She believed that making everyone unhappy to the same degree was better than making only some very unhappy. The one exception she made was with the Cardozos; she had Jim's mother seat most of them. "I don't know them," she said, "I can't be responsible for them." She put the Cardozo tables in the middle of the floor.

Anne's spying was amateurish and boring, like most spying. Her methods, culled from film noir, were shoe leather and perseverance. Occasionally she did library research; she was reluctant to interview anyone for fear of looking insane. When she couldn't pick out Rupert from the men streaming out of the Hotel des Artistes in the morning, she looked for the Falkses' wedding announcement in the *Times* microfiche. Eleanor was beautiful in the photo despite the airbrushing. Rupert was clerking then for Judge Friendly. She asked her father how she could find out where lawyers worked. He raised an eyebrow and sent her to Martindale Hubbell. Maynard, Tandy was an old WASP firm. Eleanor had reverted to type, Anne saw with satisfaction. For two weeks, she stood outside Maynard's offices on Wall Street in the evening to see if anyone she recognized from West Sixty-Seventh Street came out the door. It was hopeless. The only person she recognized was the delivery boy from the corner coffee shop. She wished she had the spine to hire a private investigator.

She found Rupert, by accident, after a day of reconnaissance on the Upper West Side. She often loitered at the bar at Gray's Papaya, in her brown hat, after tennis practice. Most days, the older boys stopped there before going home. One afternoon, as they were eating their hot dogs on the street, a tall blond man came toward them from the subway. "Dad," Harry said. "What are you doing here? It's too early." He pointed at the sun still overhead. "Are you allowed out in daylight?" Will asked, flapping his arms and screeching like a bat. The three headed down Broadway, the boys on either side of their father, chattering and laughing. Anne didn't follow; she had seen what she needed to see: the cheekbones, the eyes.

"Did we dance at our wedding," she asked Jim a few nights later. He didn't remember. "I remember stepping on the glass," he said. "I remember shaking hands with Kissinger and not saying anything to him, except 'Thank you for coming.' " As Jim talked, Anne remembered the cantor coming through the receiving line. He shook hands with Jim and offered him congratulations. Then he turned to her and, leaning in as if to kiss her cheek, whispered, "When you come to a fork in the road, take it."

Jim thought Eleanor's boys looked like him, and though he knew they weren't his sons, he felt cheated. They should have been his. Grieving his loss and feeding his grudge, he took an unhealthy interest in the Falkes boys. He couldn't help it. At least once a month, he would find himself at Sunday services at St. Thomas. He'd arrive early and take a seat in the back on a side aisle. From there, he'd watch the Falkeses come in and go out. Eleanor would hold the littlest ones' hands as she walked to their seats. Rupert would keep the older ones moving down the aisle, a sheepdog prodding his sheep. The boys wore their school blazers and ties. They didn't go to Sunday school. Rupert didn't believe in it. Religion was music, mystery, and ritual. Bible stories were no different from Greek myths. He left both to the d'Aulaires.

Sometimes after a morning surgery, Jim would go to an afternoon movie at Lincoln Plaza, hoping he would run into Eleanor. Occasionally he did. She was sometimes with Carlo Benedetti — his successor, as he thought of him. They would chat briefly. He would ask about the boys, wanting to keep up. She never kissed him, as friends might on meeting. Eleanor rarely greeted anyone outside the family, other than Susanna, with a hug or kiss. If she was alone, Jim would invite her to coffee; she would beg off. "Boys to fetch," she'd say. "Take care." As the boys came along, every two years, Jim kept track.

When the fifth was almost four and no sixth appeared, he had a vasectomy. It was an impulsive decision, made more definite when his doctor questioned him. "I don't want children," he said. "I don't like children." The truth was, he didn't want children who weren't Eleanor's. A vasectomy would make sex easier, safer, more pleasurable. He wouldn't have to use condoms if he didn't want to. He feared being trapped by a pregnancy.

To his surprise, the vasectomy was a shock to the system, not physically but emotionally. He felt acutely the ridiculousness of his position. For years, he'd clung to the fantasy that Eleanor would leave her marriage for him. He had to face facts; she wouldn't do it while the boys were young. He decided he would have to marry, if only temporarily, for self-respect. He shrunk at the thought Eleanor might think him pitiful.

In his twenties, Jim was a serial dater, going through ten or more women a year. They were all exceptionally good-looking, tall and lean, like Eleanor, but not Eleanor; they always fell short. He would pick them up at bars or weddings or subway platforms, never the hospital. He had a reputation to keep up there. He was never a boyfriend, only a date, slippery and noncommittal.

He'd call at the last minute, he'd break weekend dates. Heart surgeons had good excuses for not coming across. He rarely took a woman to dinner and he never let a woman cook for him. He didn't like to talk but he would listen if the woman wasn't a chatterer. He didn't understand women; he listened for clues. The women might have been intelligent. His preference was for women who were bankers. They were better-looking than lawyers and not as talkative. He usually took a date to a late movie, then went home to her place, never to his. He was looking for sex, an hour or two. He liked women who liked sex, who were good at it. He was attentive to special tastes. He would ask a woman what she liked and tell her his preferences. "Let's make each other happy," he'd say. He never stayed over. "Early surgery, tomorrow, I mean today, in three hours," he'd say. One woman asked to tie him up. She expanded his repertoire. There were women at the hospital whom he liked, whom he talked to, but until he met Anne, he wasn't interested in dating any of them. Anne made him feel calm. She was smart, undemanding, and adoring, with translucent skin and wonderful breasts: high and firm and larger than his hands. He discovered he was a breast man, not a leg

242

man. She looked nothing like Eleanor. She was nothing like Eleanor. She knew a stent from a shunt. She was Jewish and still she disliked his parents. She laughed at his jokes. No one before her had ever recognized his stabs at humor. Eleanor's humor had made him nervous. Everything about Eleanor had made him nervous, nervous and excited. Eleanor had made herself sexually available to him in a way no twenty-year-old ever imagined. It had ruined other women for him, until Anne, who in her own way was as sexually thrilling. Debutantes were the best.

The Cardozos had put aside enough money to pay all of Jim's medical school costs and to subsidize him during his internship and residency. They wanted him to be a surgeon; they didn't want money worries to drive him into a less prestigious, less demanding specialty. When they said, after he was admitted to Columbia P & S, that he should live at home and not in the dorms — to save money they had saved — he said he would take out a loan and become a dermatologist. They folded. He emptied his closet and drawers, went off in a taxi, and never lived at home again. His father taught accounting at Brooklyn College and did taxes on the side; his mother taught home economics at Washington Irving High School. They had worked and saved all their lives to secure Jim's future. He was their only child, bright and uncommonly handsome, a Jewish Gregory Peck. They lived in Manhattan, on the Upper East Side, in a small rent-controlled walk-up on East Eighty-Ninth between First and Second. They moved there from Flatbush when Jim was a year old. They wanted him to meet a better class of people. Russian and Polish Jews had taken over Brooklyn.

Jim's parents thought it useful for his future medical practice for him to know and socialize with gentiles, but their chief goal was to put him in the way of prominent Jews, Lewisohns, Seligmans, Warburgs, people who could make his career. They joined Temple Emanu-El, so Jim could be bar mitzvahed there, even though it was very expensive. "Tax deductible," Mr. Cardozo would say every time he paid the dues. Jim went to Stuyvesant — private school was beyond their imagination as well as their means — and they expected he would go to City College, then New York Medical College. When he was admitted to Yale, they figured out a way to pay for it and began spinning a fantasy of Columbia medical school. They worked out the numbers. In the long run, they'd be fine; they both had pensions. Their friends envied them. Jim was a credit to the race.

When Jim told his parents junior year he wanted to marry Eleanor Phipps, they threatened to cut him off, no money, no contact. "We'll sit shiva," his mother said. Jim who had dated other gentiles and had gentile friends was shocked. His parents had never said anything to him about marrying Jewish. "We assumed you would. We assumed you would want to," his mother said. "We have been Jews forever, going back to England, to Holland, to Spain, to Babylon, to Solomon for heaven's sakes. We've been in this country for over two hundred years. Your Jewish daughter could join the DAR. You're Sephardic, not some Ashkenazi arriviste who thinks Leon Uris is a genius and Israel is the pinnacle of Jewish civilization." His father let his wife do the heavy work, adding only, "I bet she never saw a circumcised penis before." Jim walked out of the apartment, afraid he would punch his father.

Briefly, Jim and Eleanor plotted to defy their parents. Over Easter vacation junior year, they spun schemes. Plan 1: They would run away to California; Eleanor would work as a secretary, Jim would attend

UCLA's medical school. Plan 2: They would stay in New York and live in the Village. Jim would work for a bank or corporation until he had enough money saved for medical school. Plan 3: They would break their hearts and break up. They chose Plan 3. They couldn't imagine their lives without their parents' support.

Jim didn't introduce Anne to his parents until the wedding invitations had been ordered. He invited them to dinner at the Russian Tea Room; he wanted a festive and noisy place, one that didn't allow for serious conversation. He had put off the meeting for months, dreading his parents' response. They tended in uncomfortable social situations to be cagey and condescending, like a salesclerk at Cartier, trying to size up a badly dressed customer. He saw, from their turned-down mouths, that they were disappointed. Anne wasn't as pretty as they would have liked, and she was short. He ordered Champagne.

"We're getting married in three months," he said, smiling at Anne, "on Sunday, August twenty-fourth."

"Won't it be too hot then?" Mrs. Cardozo said. "September is better. You should do it in September."

"I'm afraid it's too late," Jim said.

A week later, Mrs. Lehman called the Cardozos to discuss their guest list.

"Where is the wedding to be held?" Mrs. Cardozo asked. "And the reception, where will that be?"

Mrs. Lehman was startled by her questions — she had assumed they knew — but she showed no surprise. She never did. "Showing surprise puts you at such a disadvantage," she told her daughters.

"Temple Emanu-El, of course," she said, "and the reception at the Harmonie Club."

"Where's the Armory Club?" Mrs. Cardozo said.

"*Harmonie,* as in musical notes. It's a brisk three-minute walk down Fifth," Mrs. Lehman said, her tone taking on its own briskness. Jim's list had fifty people on it. Mrs. Lehman told the Cardozos they could invite another fifty. When Mrs. Cardozo offered to pay for more guests, Mrs. Lehman stopped her. "We wouldn't think of it. I know how hard it is to decide whom to leave off," she said. "Could you send the names and addresses by the end of the week?" Until the Cardozos showed up at Temple Emanu-El and saw the packed sanctuary, they had thought the wedding would have no more than two hundred guests.

Anne knew many passive-aggressive men; both her father and brother, at home, in their easy chairs, were adept practitioners. Their specialty was a mix of chagrin and forgetfulness. Mr. Lehman would slap his forehead when one of his daughters told him that, once again, he'd forgotten his wife's birthday. Her brother would look dazed, a rabbit in headlights, when he found out he had booked a golf game on Mother's Day. Jim dispensed with chagrin. His art was forgetting. He forgot everything that made unwanted demands on him. Anne thought of him as aggressive-passive. She was almost admiring. She hadn't realized she might, without remorse, without apologies, treat another person as though his feelings didn't matter. When she occasionally remonstrated against his high-handedness, he would shrug. "Occupational hazard. Hanging around with surgeons. We're an arrogant lot."

Jim had half played with the idea of keeping the wedding small, just Anne's parents and siblings, and not inviting his parents. Mrs. Lehman wouldn't hear of it. "A small wedding is out of the question; with relatives alone, there are at least a hundred and fifty, and they all expect to be invited and fed." She shook her head as if she were the victim of circumstances and not their master. "But that is beside the point," she said. "Small or large, your parents have to be there. To exclude them would be to make a scene. You'd find yourself the object of criticism, the Ungrateful Son instead of the Happy Groom." She paused, rifling her brain for a trouncing bon mot. Finding no quotation on point, she improvised: "I've always found that elaborate courtesy makes most people behave." Anne laughed. "Well done, Mum," she said. "You can retire Bartlett's." Her mother shook her head. "No. Someone somewhere at some time said something like that. I always credit my authors. 'Honor among thieves.' Anonymous. I'll find it."

The next day, Mrs. Lehman left a message with Jim's answering service: " 'There can be no defense like elaborate courtesy.' Edward Verrall Lucas."

All the years he lived in his monk's studio, Jim saved money for the purpose of paying back his parents every cent they ever spent on his education, with interest. The thought of being indebted to them, of being reminded of their sacrifices for him, shriveled his soul. He estimated four years at Yale at fifteen thousand dollars; four years at Columbia P & S at twenty thousand; and seven years of internship and residency subsidized at thirty-five thousand. In 1975, on the eve of his wedding, he sent his parents a certified check for eighty thousand dollars. Taking his cue from his future mother-in-law, he included a note. "This is to thank you for your support through college, medical school, and advanced training. I recognize the sacrifices you made for me. I wouldn't want you in old age to find yourselves in straitened circumstances because of them." After depositing the money, his parents mildly protested. "Can you really afford this? Is your practice doing that well?" they asked. They used the money to buy a co-op in a doorman building on East Eighty-Seventh and a condo in Delray Beach. As their wedding present, they gave Anne and Jim leather-bound, autographed copies of Stephen Birmingham's popular histories, *The Grandees: America's Sephardic Elite* and *Our Crowd: The Great Jewish Families of New York.* "He's writing about the two of you!" Mrs. Cardozo wrote in the note she sent with the books. Despite her disappointment in Anne's plainness, she was deeply gratified by the match. The Temple Emanu-El membership had paid off; all her friends were envious. Writing to Jim separately, she said: "Now, aren't you glad you didn't marry that pretty gentile?"

Jim called his parents every Sunday morning. On their birthdays, he sent them presents — cashmere sweaters for his mother, golf clubs for his father — and every other month, he and Anne would take them to dinner at an expensive restaurant with hovering waiters, hoping to forestall complaints that he neglected them. "We really must do this more often," his mother would say, like clockwork, as the main course was being served. "The hospital keeps us busy," Jim would respond. "Don't let your lobster get cold."

Jim was surprised that Eleanor accepted his wedding invitation. He had thought of the invitation as a letter in a bottle, unlikely to reach shore. The Falkeses' wedding gift was more surprising; she had chosen the fish server in her parents' pattern. She remembered, he thought. He had admired it the one time he had had dinner at her parents' apartment, days before the breakup. Against all reason, he began to spin fantasies again of stolen moments together at 106th Street; she would tell him she had never stopped loving him; she would know he had never stopped loving her. Catching sight of her at the reception, as she stood in the receiving line, he felt his hands getting sweaty, his breath shortening, his mind kaleidoscoping. He signaled to a waiter for a drink. "Hot in here, isn't it," he said to his mother-in-law, who stood to his right. "No," she said. "It must be the excitement." He waited impatiently for Eleanor to reach him, counting down with every handshake. When she was only four people away, he saw that Rupert was standing behind her. He hadn't figured on Rupert.

"Congratulations, Jim," she said. "I'd like you to meet my husband, Rupert Falkes." Jim knew who Rupert was, from his St. Thomas hauntings. The men shook hands. Jim introduced Eleanor to Anne. "A friend from my college days," he said, "Eleanor Phipps." She would be Eleanor Phipps if she couldn't be Eleanor Cardozo. Why had she come? he asked himself. What did she want? He couldn't think straight. His eyes followed her as she joined the swarms buzzing the food tables. He saw his parents approach her; she said something, then turned away. She still hates them, he thought. His mind began to break up again. They would run off together, today, his wedding day, like Dustin Hoffman and Katharine Ross in *The Graduate*. They'd get divorced; they'd get married. To hell with everyone else. He reached into his trouser pocket to make sure he had his wallet. A scant second later, he felt his mother-in-law's hand on his arm, pulling him down to earth. "Look," she said. "Henry Kissinger's next in line. Now, no antiwar confrontation. He's your guest."

The rest of the wedding passed in a blur for Jim. It reminded him of his bar mitzvah party: too many people he didn't know or like. After Kissinger, his mind quieted, an unexpected response to the surprisingly bonhomous Secretary. He drank too much Champagne. He danced with Anne, then with his mother, then with his mother-in-law. The best man, an orthopedic surgeon, made a toast that some people thought funny, others vulgar. The waiters cut the cake. He and Anne slowly made the rounds of the tables. As they approached the table where Eleanor sat, Jim's pulse began to race again. The Falkeses were surrounded by Strauses and Javitses. They had all pulled their chairs out so they could talk together. The other guests at the table sat silently, watching the A-listers with the grim stares of lifeboat survivors. As Anne leaned over to kiss her uncle's cheek, her aunt Pauline beckoned to Jim.

"Thank you for seating us here." She spoke very softly so no one else might hear.

"The Falkeses, Eleanor and Rupert, are the most charming people. I asked them their connection to the bride and groom. I didn't recognize either of them. Eleanor said laughingly she was an old girlfriend of yours, 'five small boys ago.' I don't know why you let her get away. Lucky for Anne. And the rest of us."

For months after the wedding, Jim found himself thinking too often of Eleanor. He would buy flowers for his studio in the brilliant hues he knew she liked. For her twentieth birthday, he had taken her to a flower shop on Madison Avenue to buy her a dozen roses. He had pointed to some pale yellow ones. "No, no," she said, laughing. "Those are flowers for good girls. I'm a wild anemone girl."

When she called him, more than a year after his wedding, he found himself getting agitated. She wanted the name of a cardiologist. Her mother had had a silent heart attack and wasn't doing anything about it. "She said she'd trust your recommendation," Eleanor said. Jim gave her a name and said he'd call him for her.

"I can't thank you enough," she said.

"How about a movie?" he asked.

Eleanor paused. "I only go to movies in the afternoon," she said.

"I can do that," he said.

They made a date to see *The Story of Adele H.* the following Tuesday. They would meet at the theater.

Jim was early. When he wasn't in surgery that week, he had thought of nothing else. "Do you ever think of the old days," he asked her as they settled into their seats. "Who has time?" she said. "I'm up to my eyebrows in boys. Tell me about your work." Jim shrugged. "Heart repair."

After the movie was over, Jim suggested a quick supper. "Not possible," she said. "Dinner is a command performance, for everyone, including Rupert." She gave a half smile. "The boys sometimes compare me to their grandmother."

"Let's do this again sometime," Jim said.

"Yes," Eleanor said. She turned and walked away.

Six months later, Jim called to find out how Mrs. Phipps was doing. Did she like the cardiologist he had recommended? Eleanor apologized. "She died a month ago. Suddenly. She saw your colleague, Dr. Schwinn. He said she had a congenital defect. She could go anytime. I should have let you know. I'm sorry." Jim didn't invite her to another movie. He stopped buying flowers for his studio. Eleanor made a donation in Jim's name to the Cardiac Center at Presbyterian Hospital.

Nathan Isaac Lehman Cardozo was born on Thanksgiving Day 1977. He had Jim's dark hair and eyes and Anne's sturdy build. Nate excited feelings in Jim he didn't know he had; life took on meaning outside the operating room. He would die for him; he would live for him. Nate laughed whenever he saw his father, his whole body crinkling with happiness. Holding Nate to his chest, Jim would feel his heart miss a beat. Until Nate, he had disliked the overworked "heartfelt" metaphors his patients bandied about in the examining room, playing down their panic. Their "hearts in their mouths," they spoke jokingly of themselves as "brokenhearted," "heavyhearted," "fainthearted," "lighthearted," "halfhearted." Jim would nod and half smile, thinking, The heart is a muscle; if you want love, look to the brain. Nate upended his scientific literalism; he had stolen Jim's heart.

For Nate's first birthday, the Lehmans threw an afternoon party for all his aunts and uncles and cousins. They invited Jim's parents. Mrs. Lehman insisted. "It's practical good manners. If we include them, as we should, you may not have to see them again for two months." Many small children cry at their birthday parties. Nathan, holding on to his mother's hand, wobbled about the room, beaming and chirping, happily accepting coos and kisses from relatives. All the Lehmans agreed: Nate was the most charming baby they'd ever seen. Jim wondered if he too might have been that way had he been raised with different parents. He looked at his wife, beaming as brightly as her baby. He needed to thank her.

"It's too bad Nathan isn't blond and blue-eyed like his mother," Mrs. Cardozo said to Mrs. Lehman as they watched their small grandson on parade. "He should have had Anne's coloring and Jim's body type. He's so plump, don't you think? And a bit plain." Mrs. Lehman stiffened. It was a family rule: all babies were beautiful, all grandmothers doting. " 'Beauty in things exists merely in the mind which contemplates them.' David Hume," she said. Her tone was brisk but not openly hostile. "Also Shakespeare: 'Love looks not with the eyes but with the mind.' " She smiled, showing her teeth. Mrs. Cardozo fumbled with her hanky, coloring with anger at her hostess's correction. She always felt at a disadvantage in the presence of the Lehmans, her Sephardic pedigree no match for their German pile. Blowing her nose, she massaged her grievance against the Lehmans. Arrivistes, thinking money was the same thing as class. She signaled to her husband it was time to leave. They missed the cake and candles.

The Lehman and Lewisohn grandchildren called their grandparents Oma and Opa, in the German fashion. It was an old family custom, going back to 1843, when their forefathers landed in the New World, "on *die Maiblume,*" Anne told Jim, only half joking. The only exception was one of Mr. Lehman's great-aunts, who insisted on being called Grossmutter. "She was a Seligman," he'd say, no other explanation being needed. Like all the old German Jewish banking families, the Lehmans and Lewisohns had married so determinedly among themselves, they'd become unhealthily inbred. By the fourth generation, first cousins who didn't marry first cousins were the outliers, teased for marrying auslanders and diluting the bloodline. Anne's parents had been second cousins; her grandmother's had been first cousins. "My mother is also my second cousin once removed," she explained to Jim. "That is true of my father as well." She laughed. "My sisters and brother are also my third cousins." When her sisters married Hungarian and Czech Jews, Mrs. Lehman was relieved. "Thank goodness," she said to her husband. "I was expecting the next baby to be born with hemophilia or the Hapsburg lip." Anne's marriage to a Sephardic Jew was also regarded as a chromosomal boon, though not so groundbreaking. One of her father's sisters had married a Mendes. Mr. and Mrs. Lehman weren't ready yet for a Russian Jew but they knew one was coming. Marriages to gentiles would inevitably follow.

Money aside, not always possible, Jim's parents took the position that he had married down. Certainly in the looks department, there was no comparison. "He looks like a Spanish prince, doesn't he?" his mother would say when anyone told her how handsome he was. "Breeding will out." In safe company, she'd add, with an air of triumph, "Anne and all the Lehmans are squat." She asked Jim to have Nathan call her and her husband Grandmamà and Grandpapà, the accent landing on the last syllable, as an English child might say it. Jim agreed, Nathan couldn't. Try as he might, the best he could manage, accents in place, was Ga-mà and Ga-pà. Jim was delighted. Nathan's Ga-pà sounded like his marble-mouthed "good-bye." "That's my boy," Jim said to Anne. "He announces he's leaving as soon as he says hello."

Anne wanted Nathan to go to Dalton, the neighborhood school, one block north and one block east, an easy drop-off until he was old enough to dash across Park Avenue without getting run over. A friend whose children went there said it was wildly competitive, "starting second semester first grade," but Anne didn't worry about Nathan getting by. He had fierce concentration when he was building with LEGO, and what he might lack in sheer brainpower, he would make up in personality. The most charming baby had grown up to be the most charming child, his parents' love and devotion having done him only good. He was hugely popular at his nursery school at the 92nd Street Y, everyone's favorite playdate, and while he would shove and push if sufficiently provoked, most of the time he avoided scraps. "I run faster than everyone else," he told his father. "They can't catch me." He wasn't a beautiful boy, but his smile was sunshine and he gleamed with sweet self-confidence. He had the vividness and liveliness of a Disney woodland creature, a Bambi boy, soft-eyed and downy. Anne had arranged her work schedule so that she was home on schooldays at four.

Nathan would sit at the kitchen counter, eating berries and graham crackers and reporting on his day. She had never known such happiness. He was a confiding little fellow, guileless in the way of only children. She didn't worry that he wasn't reading yet or that he still wore Pampers at night. She put no stock in precocity.

"He's your child," Jim would say to Anne at least once a month, marveling at Nate's sunniness, grateful to her and her sturdy Lehman genes. "He escaped the Cardozo curse, the envy, the grudge-bearing, the egotism."

"Oh, I don't know about that last item," Anne would answer, as if they were following a comedy script. "He can be egotistical." Once, in a sly mood, she added, "But he's not narcissistic." Jim tousled her hair, deciding she was speaking generally, not about him.

Jim wanted Nathan to go to Trinity, across Central Park, on the way to Presbyterian Hospital. "One of us can easily drop him off on the way to work," he said. Anne wondered if the Falkes connection was behind Jim's thinking; he gave other reasons. Nate was already showing athletic talent. He had learned to ride a two-wheeler when he was three. He could run fast and jump high. On the soccer field, he always knew where the ball was. Jim thought Trinity's athletics were better than Dalton's. He also thought its music program was better; Nathan was agitating to play the upright bass. When Jim asked him, "Why a bass?" Nate said, "It sounds like God." For his sixth birthday, his parents bought him a quarter-size bass.

Jim didn't worry about Nathan getting into Trinity or any other Manhattan private school. There was always an alumnus in Anne's family ready to write the right sort of letter. Lehmans and Lewisohns, as long as they weren't sociopaths, were almost always admitted. As years went by, Jim got used to the benefits of being a Lehman — it opened doors everywhere — and he was almost indignant the few times his father-in-law's secretary couldn't get them a last-minute reservation at the Quilted Giraffe. "Just make sure you tip everyone and tip big," Mr. Lehman said. "The celebrities who eat at these places are lousy tippers; they mostly expect to be comped. The rich, like us, are their bread and butter. We pay to get in, every time."

Anne didn't want Nate to go to Trinity. The memory of the months she had stalked the Falkes boys was mortifying to her. She wanted it buried, beyond recall. She checked the obituary notices regularly, hoping to read that Mr. Phipps had died. She didn't want any surviving witnesses. She tried to talk Jim out of Trinity, without letting on that she knew the Falkes boys went there. She couldn't, and she caved. Nate went to Trinity, where everyone loved him. By the time Nate started kindergarten, Eleanor's two oldest boys had graduated and the younger ones were in the middle school. By the time Nate was in the middle school, she could watch a game at the soccer field without her heart pounding.

Nate decided in tenth grade he would be a doctor — not a surgeon with a grueling schedule, but a family practitioner. He wanted variety in his patients and their diseases, and he wanted to keep playing his bass. He was almost good enough to be a professional. "I can't be in any kind of quartet," he explained to his parents, "if I can't practice with the others regularly." Jim was pleased and proud his son wanted to go into the family business. He wanted Nate to go to Yale, and if not Yale, then Stanford or Harvard. Nate had other ideas. "I'm not the smartest guy in the room," he said to his father, "but I'm the most determined. I'll go to a small school for college. I'll have a better chance that way getting into a good med school." He went to Amherst, where two older Lewisohn cousins had gone, graduating in 2000. He took off a year to work with Paul Farmer in Haiti, then went to Yale for medical school. He admired the dean, David Kessler, who had been the scourge of the tobacco cartel at the FDA. "Maybe I'll do public health," he told his parents. "Yes," Anne said. Jim nodded. His son was a Lehman; he wouldn't have to make money. Jim had tried not to care that Rupert had been appointed to the Yale Corporation. He had money, I don't; not my own at least, he told himself. He didn't care about the money, only everything else, the prestige, the recognition, the honor, Eleanor. He wished she hadn't married so well. He fantasized about Nathan one day joining the Corporation.

Anne's parents adored Nathan. If they had a favorite grandchild, which they wouldn't, he was it. The Cardozo grandparents were not fond. They had been counting on a beautiful grandchild, and Nathan disappointed, one more reason for Jim to keep the family visits brief and infrequent. The last years of Jim's parents' lives, he saw them only when they were in the hospital. He oversaw their medical care. He found he preferred his parents when they were ill. They were like all his other patients, helpless, needy, and afraid.

Anne's news that she was pregnant had surprised Jim, but not in the way he would have expected. He was elated, ready to accept it as vasectomy failure. He knew there were vasectomies that failed — studies showed a one-in-a-thousand pregnancy rate. Like the Honduran murder rate, the highest in the world, he thought, to give the statistic more heft. And he hadn't been tested after the procedure to find out if it had worked. He was, in this way, like many patients and most doctors. Most doctors were notoriously bad patients: they prescribed narcotics and stimulants for themselves; they never got flu shots; they thought checkups were a waste of time and money; they "watched and waited" while their PSA levels went through the roof. Their balkiness wasn't entirely owing to professional cynicism or a sense of invulnerability. They believed in public health — potable water, vaccinations, pasteurized milk, seat belts, birth control — much less in medicines and surgeries. They knew many ailments would go away by themselves, sooner or later. They also knew they would die one day, at home if they were lucky. Hospitals were disease pits, more dangerous than highways, no place to be sick in. Jim often thought of having "Do Not Resuscitate" tattooed on his chest. He was struck how often doctors died of diseases in their specialty. "Best to be a pediatrician," he'd tell medical students. "You'll begin your practice having outlived the condition." Jim suspected he'd die of heart disease. He never took a stress test.

Jim didn't question Nathan's paternity, beyond his first queries to Anne. He couldn't imagine Anne cheating on him, and Nathan himself was the best proof. "Like father, like son," the Lehmans always said. Father and son were both smart without being intellectual, practical without being plodding, analytical without being exacting. They liked working with their hands. Neither had much of a sense of humor, which they admitted privately to each other and came to regard as the secret to their success. Humor was socially useful, professionally distracting. Focus, doggedness, determination, drive, they were the right stuff. By the time there was routine DNA testing, Jim didn't give it more than a minute's thought.

Jim was liked and admired by the nursing

staff at Presbyterian, a distinction rarely paid a surgeon who hadn't previously been hospitalized with a grave and humbling illness. He treated nurses as colleagues and professionals, listening to their concerns, asking their opinion, taking their advice. Before he checked up on a patient on the ward, he would check in at the nurses' station for an update. He believed he owed his success to the ward nurses and often said so, to them and to the other cardiac surgeons. His colleagues mocked him, calling him Dr. Kumbaya. They thought he was breaking ranks with the surgical knighthood by pandering to the yeomanry. "He has a wife with a PhD," they'd say, as if marriage to an educated woman, always a mistake, made men red-eyed, weak-wristed feminists. To no avail, he would explain that his treatment of the nurses was strategic and practical. "I need them," he'd say. Nurses were his early warning system of infections, bleeding, arrhythmias; they also had warmer, more comforting beside manners. His was cool, correct, and fleet: a hand on the shoulder, a nod, a smile. Seconds later, he was gone. He had the best outcomes in the department. Patients came from Rochester, Minnesota, Boston, and San Francisco to see him.

Two days after hearing that Rupert Falkes was dying on the sixth floor at Presbyterian Hospital, Jim dropped by his room. Eleanor was in the hallway, speaking with one of Rupert's doctors. Catching sight of Jim, she smiled at him. "Do I need to introduce the two of you?" The two men nodded at each other, with the chill civility of silverbacks finding themselves in the same clearing: they'd fight it out when the females were gone. "Ah," she said, "I see you know each other. Stephen is Rupert's oncologist; Jim, a college friend." Jim hated that she always added "college" or some other qualifier to her introductions, consigning him to her past. "I'm sorry," she said to Jim, "I need to follow up with Stephen. It shouldn't take long."

Eleanor and Stephen stepped away. They spoke for several minutes. Jim began to feel conspicuously ridiculous. He looked in at Rupert, who was lying very still in bed, his eyes closed. The radio was playing: Bach, he thought. He resisted the urge to read Rupert's file, tucked in a folder on the door. He guessed that Stephen was deliberately taking more time than necessary, to put him in his place, to keep Eleanor to himself. On the oncology wards at Presbyterian, the surgeons and oncologists achieved at best a shaky truce. They had moved past "slash and burn," the tired war metaphors, to literary invective. The surgeons had started calling the oncologists the Brotherhood of Dracula; the oncologists responded by calling the surgeons the Sisterhood of Frankenstein. One morning, in the heat of their schoolyard tiff, mostly played out with plastic body parts and rubber bats stuck in coat pockets, lockers, and mailboxes, the staff found a large engraved metal plaque attached with dental adhesive to the main door of the oncology ward. It read: THE STOKER-SHELLEY MEMORIAL WING. It was too expensive a prank for the residents, the likeliest perpetrators, to have pulled it off; no one else came forward. The doctors, in a rare display of collective good humor, wanted to keep the plaque up. The hospital president ordered it taken down, to protect donors' sensibilities. The chair of oncology decided to auction off the plaque, to raise money for the new children's cancer wing. Jim got it after fierce bidding, for eleven thousand dollars. He knew Eleanor had put it up.

After waiting ten minutes, Jim signaled he was leaving. Eleanor called out, "Thanks for stopping by. Sorry we couldn't talk." Over the next three months, Jim dropped by Rupert's room three or four times a week, hoping to find Eleanor alone. Every time, she was with someone, usually one of Rupert's doctors, sometimes a son or two, occasionally a friend. She was always welcoming, happy to make introductions but never able to talk to him. He knew his behavior was indecent, even if no one but Eleanor knew it. He wasn't there to help her. He was there to woo her, to make love to her, in the presence of her dying husband. Every time he left the oncology ward, he swore he'd keep away. A day later, he'd lost all resolve. He would find himself, in his open hours, drifting down to the sixth floor. I'm only passing through, he'd tell himself. As a discipline and a restraint, he wrote letters to Nathan at college.

Eleanor and Jim met at Columbia summer school the summer before their junior year. He was taking organic chemistry, she was taking the Russian novel. He saw her having lunch in John Jay, bent over *Anna Karenina*. She's beautiful, he thought self-consciously, the same way I am. When he was younger he'd been embarrassed by his looks and the attention they attracted. He had worried that people thought he was a girl. Strangers stopped his mother on the street to tell her what a beautiful child he was. One woman said he looked "just like Elizabeth Taylor in *National Velvet.*" He growled at her. Adolescent gawkiness took the edge off his prettiness, and by the time he was twenty, no one would take him for a girl. Women often still said he was beautiful, but not like Elizabeth Taylor, like Tyrone Power. When he approached Eleanor, he expected a smile, interest. Girls liked him.

"It's better in Russian," he said.

She looked up at him. "Oh, those Russians," she said, unsmiling, "they think Shakespeare is better in Russian." She went back to her book.

He persevered. She was smart as well as beautiful, plainly worth pursuing.

"Do you like it? Do you like Anna?" he said.

She looked up again, her good manners kicking in. "I like it. I don't know if I like Anna. I can't see dying for love. I liked *War and Peace* more. I like Natasha more."

"Do men ever die for love that way, or only women?" he asked. He slid into a chair across the table from her.

Eleanor thought for a moment. It was a more interesting question than she had expected. "Not in novels, only in life."

"I think I might die for love," he said.

She finally smiled at him. "Heroically? Sacrificially?" she said.

"I'd like to think so, but that's not what I meant. I meant dying from loss," he said.

"How can you know that about yourself?" she asked. "Have you ever been in love?"

He shook his head. "Emotions are treacherous. I like to keep things cool."

"I don't know any other way," she said.

They spent every day together that summer. She took him to movies at the Thalia: Bergman, Rossellini, Fellini, Renoir. He read her Chekhov plays and stories. They didn't fall into bed heedlessly, carelessly, drunkenly, like so many young lovers. They planned their first time, with Lancers rosé wine, candles, and, on the bedside tables, a box of condoms. He undressed her slowly. They looked at each other naked. They started at four thirty p.m., after her class, and went on until midnight when she caught sight of the clock, threw on her dress, and caught a cab home. In the fall, she visited him every weekend at Yale. They didn't introduce each other to their parents until the spring and then it all fell apart. They cried. "I'll never get over you," he said. "You must," she said. "You will."

Jim went to Rupert's funeral at St. Thomas.

He had ended his Episcopal surveillance of Eleanor's boys after Nathan was born but he remained too curious about them. He took his old seat on the far edge of the far aisle. The boys looked less alike than they had as children but they were all still dark and lean, plainly Eleanor's children, plainly brothers. There were four wives or girl-friends, all blondes, like Rupert; a sixth dark young man; and two small, white-haired granddaughters, who sat quietly in a front pew, reading books. There was a young woman sitting with the family who looked like the boys; he didn't recognize her. Was she a sister? Had he missed her in his census? Eleanor looked tired and pale. Like a grieving widow, he thought with a start. It had been a mistake to come. The organist started playing. Half listening to the music, Jim plotted. For the last forty years, the boys and Rupert had stood in the way. With the boys grown and Rupert dead, those road-blocks were gone, Eleanor was free. I'll get divorced, he thought, with a stab of pain. He would have to give up Anne.

The eulogies began. The two boys spoke well. Jim found himself wishing Nathan was with him, to hear them speak about their father. He missed his son, off in college, planning a separate life. He wondered what

Nathan would say at his funeral. He hoped he would tell a life-with-old-Dad story, poignant and affectionate. Nathan was the gift of his life. He had never loved, could never love anyone else as much as he loved Nathan. The thought that he might have missed him by marrying Eleanor gave him a thump.

The penultimate speaker, John Earlham, made little impression on Jim. He spoke with a kind of lisp and talked about cricket in New York in the '50s. Rupert was very good at cricket; his swing was deadly. "He held the bat at an odd angle," Earlham said. "When it connected with the ball, the ball flew. When it connected with anything else, call an ambulance. Kidding, sort of." The last speaker was Dominic Byrne. His eulogy made Jim sit up. He sensed a rival, another man with an engaging accent. Byrne spoke about Rupert but also about Eleanor and the way he saw his friends as husband and wife. "I've never married," he said, "and Rupert and Eleanor's marriage was the closest I came to seeing one close up. Eleanor, well we all know Eleanor, she would say, 'Oh, Rupert,' to him or about him, as if she were speaking about a limb or other part of her body. There was in her voice at those times an unembarrassed and unembarrassing intimacy that seemed akin to breathing. Rupert, to me, perhaps not to her, was more explicit and, not surprisingly, less expressive. He called her 'my great good luck.' He would look past me when he said it, as if eye contact might move him to tears."

Jim thought of his wife, his great good luck. Did he love her? He was grateful to her. Did she still love him? He wasn't sure anymore. Their love for Nathan was their strongest bond, but since he went off to Amherst, they seemed untethered. They had become careful with each other, as if a sharp word might sever the connection. Nathan noticed, as an only child will, and asked his mother what had happened. "We're adjusting to a Nathanless life," she said. "Don't worry about us." She wasn't worrying. She had again come to a fork in the road.

For Jim, the adjustment was to a Rupertless life. He tried to imagine his life if Eleanor agreed to marry him, if he divorced Anne. Nathan would be angry, but he'd come around eventually; children always did. Eleanor's boys would be angry too, but that would be more her problem than his. His married friends and colleagues would at first be shocked and disapproving; then they'd be envious. He'd miss the Lehmans. Most of all, he'd miss Anne. He wished he could give up the dream of Eleanor. He would, he knew, be less happy with her than with Anne, but happiness was no longer the point. He was stuck. From the deep recesses of his brain, the words of "The Charge of the Light Brigade," memorized in eighth grade, clamored into consciousness: *Someone had blundered. Theirs not to make reply, Theirs not to reason why, Theirs but . . .* The congregation rose, stepping on the poem's last line. The choir began singing "Jerusalem."

Jim began to think he should cut back on surgeries. He was sixty-four. He'd been practicing for thirty years, since he finished his cardiology fellowship in 1972. He was tired of standing for five hours; his back, which used to ache the last hour of an operation, now ached almost from the beginning and then for hours after. His hands, swelling with arthritis, were clumsier, more likely to make mistakes; his eyes were seeing less clearly even with his magnifiers. He was sweating buckets, from all two million sweat glands it seemed; he thought the nurses shrank from him, repelled by his odor. He talked with Nathan about these changes. Nate had finished his first year of medical school and was itching to start rotations in July. The year had given him enough knowledge to have formed some set opinions. He had always been a boy who kept his eyes open, and in the last year, he had seen many older surgeons resisting assistance in the operating room, risking a malpractice suit, becoming more arrogant as their skills declined. "Two a week, Dad," he said. Jim swallowed hard; he had expected Nathan to argue with him.

"Look," Nathan said, seeing his father's dismay, "you've got a great future as Presbyterian's second-opinion guru."

"You'll be a great doctor," Jim said. "I asked. You answered. Balls."

Nathan looked at his dad. "Are you sure the symptoms are age-related?" he asked. "Not from drugs or drink?"

"What made you say that?" Jim asked. "Has your mother said something to you?"

Nathan paused, giving Jim a start. They both sensed a tectonic shift. Jim wanted Nathan's good opinion.

"Mom is loyal to a fault," Nathan said. "I have eyes, Dad."

Jim roused a small smile. "Don't worry about me."

When Jim made his announcement that he was cutting back on surgeries to do more consulting, he suggested that he thought his colleagues were too quick to operate.

"Why did you do that?" Anne asked.

"Better that they think I'm insulting them than losing my grip," he said.

"When does it end?" she asked. "This chest beating."

"In the grave," he said, smiling at her. She looked blankly back at him. He felt a pang. From the beginning, Jim had counted on Anne's obliging nature. She had said, half joking, not long after they were married, that she came with a lifetime warranty, only his to violate. He had believed her. He couldn't remember an argument that had left either of them raw or jagged. He had always been able to make her see things his way. Her new, sharper edge gave him a feeling of dispossession. It wasn't open rebellion, more like dogged resistance. She was becoming less agreeable and more polite. A note of judgment, hinging on criticism, tinged her conversations with him. She was cooler to him, not adoring, not even admiring. She went along without agreeing, as if the matter didn't matter. "Oh, let's agree to disagree," she would say. She started sleeping in Nathan's room when he went off to Haiti. It was clear Nate no longer needed his parents. Anne had never needed Jim, but she had wanted him. That was no longer clear.

Anne was changing in other ways as well. She had taken up rigorous exercising again, something she hadn't done since she was pregnant. She had gotten prettier as she grew older, hitting her peak in her late forties and early fifties. She's better-looking than I am these days, he thought. He wondered if she knew what he was planning. He wondered if she was making plans of her own. He had a spasm of panic.

His new surgical schedule left him free two afternoons a week to stake out the Lincoln Plaza Theater. The second week he ran into Eleanor going into *Road to Perdition,* the new Mendes. She showed surprise seeing him.

"I've cut back at the hospital," he said. "I wanted to do other things. Going to movies was one of them."

When the movie ended, Jim asked Eleanor if she'd like a cup of coffee. She agreed, no boys or husband to rush home to, and they walked up Columbus to Starbucks. They sat in the window at a high counter. They had to turn to look at each other, a choice both avoided. Jim started sweating. Eleanor shifted in her seat. He had no small talk. He plunged.

"I bought the 'Stoker-Shelley Memorial Wing' plaque," he said. "I was the one."

"I'm sorry, what?" Eleanor said.

"The plaque outside the oncology wing. You must have seen it," he said.

Eleanor shook her head. "No," she said.

She's not giving anything away, Jim thought. That's Eleanor.

"Will you marry me?" he asked, still looking straight ahead.

Eleanor turned to look at him, incredulity in her face. "No," she said.

"Will you see me regularly, then?" he asked.

"No," she said.

"Why not?" he asked. "We're free finally to be together."

"What are you talking about?" she said.

"It's our time, now."

"That was so long ago. I'm not that girl anymore."

"You are. I see her in you."

"Please stop," she said. "That was eons ago. I got over you."

"How could you get over me? We were so much in love." Jim could hear the note of wounded grievance in his voice. He coughed to clear it.

"What can I say?" she said. "That was then."

"Is there someone else?" he said. "Are you seeing Carlo Benedetti?"

"Please stop this, Jim," she said. "You're plowing ancient history."

"Why did you come to my wedding?" Jim asked.

Eleanor took in a deep breath. "I didn't want to; Rupert did. He wanted to meet the Lehmans."

"Why did you send the fish server in your parents' pattern?" he asked.

"It was on your registry," she said. "It was your pattern, yours and Anne's." She moved her chair back a bit.

"You weren't at all curious to see me?"

"No. I hadn't thought about you for years. I had a long, good marriage. Rupert was the right man for me. I was very lucky."

"Why was he right?" he asked. He could hear his voice becoming accusatory. He didn't care.

Eleanor looked out the window, then back at him. She couldn't tell if she was more astonished or annoyed by his suit. She weighed her answer. The conversation had gone on too long. "Rupert would never have given me up."

Jim flinched, as if he'd been slapped. He felt double-crossed, swindled.

"He was the right man for another woman

too." He spoke without thinking. He had seen the *Post* article.

Eleanor stood up. "Don't do this," she said. "Don't make yourself pitiful." She turned and walked out of the shop.

Jim kept his seat, staring out the window, hating himself. It's over, finally, he thought. His relief was as great as his humiliation. His mouth was dry, sticky, sour. This is what gall tastes like. He got up heavily. He felt he'd aged five years in five minutes. A stranger meeting him for the first time would think he was at least seventy. He had an air of collapse about him. He glimpsed his reflection in the window. I look drowned, he thought. He could smell his sweat. I have the stink of defeat. Out on the street, he walked up Columbus until he found a bar. He bought a pack of cigarettes and ordered gin on the rocks. He sat for two hours smoking and drinking. After his sixth gin, he lurched out of the bar. The M11 bus was lumbering down the avenue. He thought about throwing himself in front of it and ruining the driver's life. He stepped off the curb, then stepped back again. What if I don't die? What if I become a quadriplegic? He caught a cab home. Anne was out, at the Y, building muscle. He drank half a bottle of bourbon and passed out.

The next morning he slept in until noon. Feeling hungover, he called his office to cancel appointments. At dinnertime Anne asked him if he wanted anything. He didn't. She saw an empty bottle of bourbon by his bed. The next day he slept in again. It was ten thirty a.m. when he went into the kitchen. Anne was there. He had hoped she would be gone. He wasn't ready to face her. He was visibly hungover, less from bourbon than from a Halcion-Xanax-Oxycontin cocktail.

"Why aren't you at work?" he asked. "How can Fischbach manage without you?" He reached for a playful note, but his unhappiness choked it. Anne had left research fifteen years ago and had gone to work for the dean of the medical school, first as an assistant dean, then an associate dean, then vice dean. She knew how to make herself useful. She was on her third dean. They all loved her.

"I want to talk to you," she said. She looked at his drawn face and wondered if she should pick another time. There's no good time, she thought.

"That sounds serious," he said, wrenching his mouth into a smile.

"Yes," she said. "Please sit down." Jim took the chair at the corner of the table, so he wouldn't have to look directly at her.

"I want a separation," Anne said.

He looked at her, then away, afraid that he might cry. "I don't," he said, turning back to her, "but I'll do whatever you want."

"I'll move out," she said. "It's a trial. For now. We'll see."

"I should be the one to move out," he said.

"No, I need to clear my head. I need a change. I'll borrow or sublet something." She nodded at him, grateful that he hadn't made a scene. She couldn't have taken another lie. "My brother has a pied-à-terre. I can probably stay there. It isn't too hideous."

"I hope you decide to stick with me," Jim said. "When are you going?"

"This weekend. I'll talk to Nathan first."

Jim nodded. "I think I'll go back to bed," he said. "I'm not feeling well." Passing her chair, he wanted to touch her hair; he resisted, not wanting to anger her. He stopped at the doorway.

"You've been wonderful," he said. "I wasn't."

# CHAPTER 7
## VERA

He once called her his basil plant; and
when she asked for an explanation, said
that basil was a plant which had
flourished wonderfully on a murdered
man's brains.
GEORGE ELIOT, *MIDDLEMARCH*

Rupert was a virgin when he met Vera. He
had survived his English schools with
mostly trifling abuse, including the self-
inflicted variety. The one violent exception
exacted violent revenge.

An orphanage is a first-rate training
ground for fending off assaults. Rupert
preferred to ward off attackers with words,
but he was willing to use fists and knees
and even makeshift weapons if they were
needed. He made his reputation his first
week at Longleat, spewing vicious insults
that boys who grew up in respectable homes
blanched at. He thought nothing of calling

285

a sixth-former a cunt, leaving the older boy reeling in shock, feeling the insult without understanding it. He told Dominic that he had introduced the word into the Leater's lexicon, along with Firsters and Publicans. His advantage was his fearlessness and his inventiveness. When his insults fell short, he resorted to threats of dismemberment and disemboweling. He seemed capable of it. The second month he was there, he threatened to eviscerate a fifth-former who tried to suck him off one night in his bed. "I'll knife you in the stomach, I'll make mince of your intestines," he said. "You'll pass out from the pain." A month later, he resorted to physical force, against a more pressing suitor, a sixth-form rugby player who kept groping him, thinking it a great joke. The third time he did it, Rupert kicked him in the balls, rocketing him to his knees. The rugby player took the battering ill, working himself into a rage. "No pissant new boy gets away with that," he told a pal. "Are you in?" The next day, as afternoon services let out, the player and his pal cornered Rupert in the chapel stairwell; securing the door, they took turns buggering him until they got bored.

Rupert took time planning his revenge. Three weeks to the day, on a cloudy afternoon, he took a friend's cricket bat and walked over to the rugby field. Practice was breaking up. Spotting his assailant, Rupert stepped in front of him, holding the bat down with both hands on the handle, poised to swing. The player stopped and laughed. "What's the matter?" he said. "Didn't you learn your lesson?" Looking him in the eye, Rupert brought the bat back, and, angling it with the edge leading, struck his lower leg so hard his shinbone cracked. The player went down writhing and howling. Rupert stood still over him. "I'll kill you next time, you cunt," he said. The player's teammates, having watched the spectacle, made no move toward Rupert or his victim, recognizing in the ways of honorable schoolboys that justice had been done. After a minute of silence, two of them lifted the wailing boy by his arms and carried him to the infirmary. The rest walked back to their houses. No one told. After that, Rupert was left alone; there were many more scared and docile little boys to prey upon.

Self-abuse was rampant at Longleat. One of the masters called it "a cursed bugaboo, more heinous than cheating, a crime against the temple of the body, made in God's image." The boys called him Old Bugger-Boo, which Rupert realized by his third year was neither mocking nor affectionate. The boys knew the masters knew what went on in the houses at night. Their rooms reeked of semen. They reasonably concluded that mutual masturbation was not self-abuse, a relief for the boys with religious scruples or Victorian parents or homosexual desires.

Growing up in an orphanage had made Rupert dislike the close company of other boys. He took up boxing at Longleat so he wouldn't have to wrestle; touching other boys' bodies was repulsive to him, like touching someone else's snot or vomit. When Harry, at two months, peed on him, he almost dropped him. He never changed a diaper; he couldn't. "I was the tenth person in the bathwater," he told Eleanor. "I can never get clean enough." Eleanor mildly objected. "I didn't know little boys minded being dirty." Rupert shook his head. "I didn't mind being dirty. I minded bathing in other boys' piss and shit."

American bathrooms, with their endless hot water pouring from the ceiling, were a refuge and revelation to Rupert. He showered twice a day. When he and Eleanor moved into the Hotel des Artistes, Eleanor saw that he had his own bathroom. It was the best gift ever, he told her. His bathroom was off limits to everyone in the family, including Eleanor. Only the housekeeper was allowed in. When he was made managing partner at Maynard, Tandy, he moved into an office with a private bathroom. "I'd have given up fifty thousand dollars a year years ago for a private bathroom at the office," he told Eleanor. He regarded American plumbing as the pinnacle of its civilization, more impressive than its dentistry, its skyscrapers, even its air-conditioning. He loved air-conditioning. "It can never be too cold in summer," he would say. He thought American homes were overheated and, in the winter, he was always opening the windows in the apartment, to let in fresh air. What fresh air? Eleanor thought. She followed behind at a discreet distance, closing them. Brought up in the city, she was most comfortable, summer or winter, at eighty degrees.

Rupert arrived by freighter in New York in July 1955, with two hundred pounds sterling, the remnant of his legacy from Father Falkes. The exchange rate was in his favor, providing him with more than five hundred and fifty dollars, enough, he reckoned, to carry him at least six months. He had read the classified ads in the New York newspapers regularly before he left England. He thought he would be able to rent a room with two meals a day, pension-style, for sixty-five dollars a month in Manhattan, less in one of the boroughs. He was confident he would find a job in six months. He could teach history; he had read history at Cambridge. If he had to, he'd wait tables or tend bar, anything except clean. He needed a job to get a green card, a green card to get a job. He'd find a cricket club or a bar where English expats hung out. He'd offer his services to an Episcopal church with a serious choir; he'd sing for his supper and other meals as well. Someone would help him; someone always had.

His first night in New York, Rupert slept in a Times Square hotel, one step up from a flophouse. He checked in as Robert Fairchild, under a wary premonition that he might not want to be remembered by his earliest New York acquaintances. The admitting clerk sat in a cage. The charge for a private single with a toilet was seventy-five cents. The bathtub was down the hall. Rupert had put two crumpled dollars in his pocket so he would have to reach inside it only to pay the bill. He flattened out a one carefully, giving the impression that he was hoarding his last dollars. He had worn an old pair of khaki trousers, a worn tweed jacket, a fedora, and an oversized shabby raincoat, a legacy from Father Falkes. The rest of his clothes and his toiletries were in a straw suitcase. He didn't look like someone worth robbing, though he was clean and unblemished and not drunk. The room smelled of stale cigarettes, the bed was unmade, the sheets stained with food and human emissions. Rupert locked the door and moved the dresser against it. He slept on top of the bedspread with his money belt, underwear, and shoes on. He checked out at seven a.m. and walked to Penn Station, where he brushed his teeth and washed his face. He then walked ten blocks down Seventh Avenue to the McBurney Y. A room there was a dollar fifty. He figured he could stay four nights. He checked in again as Robert Fairchild. He took a twenty-minute shower.

Everyone spoke English, but no one was. He was in a foreign country where no one knew him or understood him. He felt lightheaded. Anything was possible.

Stefan, one of the Y lifeguards, told Rupert about a room in a house in Brooklyn, in Greenpoint. "It's a Polish neighborhood, nice people mostly," he said. "They don't like blacks or Jews, but you'll be fine. They'll like your fancy accent. Where'd you get that?"

Rupert phoned the owner, Ruta Wolinski, and made an appointment to see the room. "I don't let just anyone stay, Mr. Fairchild," she said. "Stefan said you were nice, clean. I run a decent house. I cook simple food. Two meals a day, breakfast at seven thirty a.m., dinner at five thirty. You share a bathroom. I clean the house. I keep it very clean. I make your bed and give you fresh sheets and towels once a week. Two dollars a night. Some months sixty dollars, some months sixty-two. February, a bargain, fifty-six." Her voice had a slight inflection, not a full-blown accent, as if she were a native speaker who had learned English from immigrants. She sounded not warm but not unpleasant, which suited Rupert. He didn't want a relationship with his landlady.

The house was on the five hundred block of Leonard Street, a working-class neighborhood. It had four floors. The front was faced with peeling clapboard and crumbling brick. The entryway was on the ground floor. Mrs. Wolinski eyed Rupert through a keyhole, then let him in. He took off his hat, sealing the deal for her. She was a bad judge of character, showing a childlike reliance on extravagant compliments and florid manners. "Mrs." was an honorific, like the French "Madame," belonging to age not status. She had had two children with three men, none of them the marrying kind, none of them still on the scene. "Their fathers were gentlemen," she told Rupert. "They had refinement. You can see it in my girls. Vera, come here. Meet the new tenant." Vera glided into the room. At seventeen, she was golden and silky, Greenpoint's Lana Turner. Her older sister, Daria, lived down the street. She was a plainer version of Vera, already faded at twenty-four, the mother of three children under three. Her husband, an electrician, didn't beat her when he was drunk, but he was tight-fisted, a skinflint.

Men were always buzzing around Vera, but she knew her value and, for the most part, swatted them away. She wasn't going to have her mother's life or her sister's. She was meant for bigger things. Setting her eyes on Rupert as her mother showed him around the house, she sized him up in a glance. He's it, she thought. He's my ticket. She was wearing a cherry-red cotton sundress, which displayed a riveting cleavage. Even as his pulse raced, Rupert recognized the moment as kitsch film noir: the femme fatale meets the sap. His instinct for self-preservation kicked in. He was curt to her, on the border of rude, the Englishman's standard response to a threat. Any other manner, he knew, would show him to be clueless, feckless, hapless. Mrs. Wolinski approved. He wasn't interested in Vera, she said to herself; he wouldn't ruin her. Vera knew better. "We need to Americanize you," she said. She didn't smile at him; she didn't flirt with him. They had to come to her, preferably on their knees. She walked out of the room, brushing his arm with her breast. He lowered his hat to cover his erection.

Rupert spent his first week in Greenpoint walking the neighborhood. He took the GG train to the Fort Greene post office, and rented a PO box in his own name. He found the local Carnegie library, around the corner from the Wolinskis, and took out a card in the name of Robert Fairchild, using a letter from Ruta Wolinski as his identification. The librarians, he discovered, were helpful, especially when he told them he was looking for a church to join. He explained that his father had been an Anglican minister and he wanted to find a church that might offer the kinds of prayer services he was used to. "Do you know of any Episcopal churches with good music?" he asked. "With evensong? With choristers?" He saw that a willingness to ask for help served him, though less successfully than sincerity. What is it with Americans? he thought. They overvalue sincerity. He saw sincerity as a portal to egoism.

Talking to the librarians gave him practice talking to women, though all of them were old enough to be his mother. Or maybe my grandmother, he thought. One of the librarians, Betty Frost, took him on as a special project. She called the Episcopal Diocesan office. A priest in the office recommended St. Thomas. "Best music in New York. No question." She reported back to Rupert. "St. Thomas is the church for you. There's a choir school and a men's and boys' choir. They must take their worship" — she paused — "if not their religion, seriously." Miss Frost took her religion seriously. "If you don't like it," she said, "cross the street and try St. Patrick's." Rupert was moved. There are people who like being helpful, he thought, people who like doing favors for others. His old world had been so dog-eat-dog. Those who had been helpful to him he saw as extreme altruists, like Father Falkes. In the librarians, he recognized a new category of human being: the matter-of-fact, neither kind nor unkind, useful person. He ascribed it to the American character. He would do his best to be that kind of American.

Rupert called the British consulate. He said he was looking to play cricket in New York; could anyone help him? He was passed along to John Earlham, a young officer who pronounced his *r*'s like *w*'s. Rupert wondered if it was an affectation, an aspirational impediment. Probably not, he decided. The Diplomatic service preferred the real thing. Earlham was cool until Rupert had established his bona fides: Longleat cricket, King's College Cambridge cricket. "What are you doing in New York?" Earlham asked. "Not sure yet," Rupert said. Earlham would have liked a straighter answer, but he invited Rupert to play the following Sunday at Walker Park on Staten Island. Rupert was making his way. He had found a church and a cricket team.

By the end of his second week, Rupert had made three decisions. First, he would go to law school, he would be a lawyer; lawyers, even solicitors, were respected in America and they made good money. Second, he would find a working-class job, as a waiter or bartender, a job that wasn't taxing, a job that gave him free time in the day, that paid off the books. Third, he would get laid, preferably without having to pay for it.

He fell asleep at night thinking of Vera. He asked Miss Frost about law schools. She suggested Fordham and St. John's. "Are you trying to convert me," he said, when he found out they were Catholic schools. "Yes," she said. "You're too good to be a Protestant." He smiled at her, shaking his head. "I need your help. Don't let me down," he said. She gave him a list of top law schools. "What is the Ivy League?" he asked a day later. "What is a standardized test?"

In between his law school research, he read *Nip Ahoy,* a book on mixing cocktails. He learned forty of the most popular. Six years of memorizing Latin cases at Longleat turned out to have its uses. The first drink he was ever paid to make was a Beam and Coke. "Right," he said, suppressing the impulse to offer a Manhattan instead. He never understood the popularity of Coke drinks: the Cuba Libre, Jack and Coke, CCC. The English sweet tooth hadn't yet swerved to sugary cocktails. The English still liked their drinks warm, rough, and alcoholic.

In his fourth American week, he found a job as a bartender at Farrell's in Windsor Terrace. It was out of the neighborhood but on the GG line, an easy commute. He wanted a crash course on America; a bar was the place to find it. He'd talk to strangers. He'd break up fights. He'd be sincere. Bartending was a time-out occupation, a postwar non–Grand Tour adventure. It had more cachet than waiting tables. He could say, "I finished Cambridge. I wanted a break. I'm discovering America from the ground up." Earlham, the real thing it turned out, a baron's son and not a bad sort, seemed envious. "I have to learn to speak French to stay in the Service. Tell me how I'm to do that when I can't pronounce my *r*'s?"

Rupert opened a bank account in Fort Greene, in his own name, the day after he got his first week's pay. He had worked thirty-two hours, earning twenty-four dollars in wages and twenty-four in tips, all of it in cash. The work was tiring. Listening was the most tiring. It will get easier, he thought. He worried about money. He'd spent a hundred and sixty dollars in five weeks, though that included two months' rent. He took twenty dollars and bought himself a pair of khakis, two white shirts, two white T-shirts, underwear, and a pair of tan suede desert boots. He deposited the rest of his inheritance, three hundred and fifty dollars, in a savings account. He was living on the edge. He had worked out a monthly budget: sixty dollars for rent, eight dollars for subway fares, thirty dollars for lunches and snacks, bringing his expenses, not including toothpaste and a movie, to ninety-eight dollars. His monthly income, he calculated, was two hundred dollars. He wanted to save a hundred and twenty-five dollars a month for law school. He wondered whether he could get by some days on two meals. He doubted it. Mrs. Wolinski's meals were missing essential food groups. She piled on the rice, potatoes, and noodles, lubricating them with margarine and tiny dollops of gamey meat whose provenance was doubtful. Rupert suspected horse; he'd eaten it often during the war. Vegetables, when she served them, were turnips, sprouts, and parsnips, boiled for thirty minutes. Dessert was a butter cookie and canned peaches or pineapple slices. Fresh fruit never entered her house. Breakfast was always the same, scrambled eggs and sausage and a fried tomato, out of a can. Dinner, in theory, had a fourteen-day rotation, but it seemed always the same, barely better than the sodden meals served at his English schools. Mrs. Wolinski was also living on the edge.

There was another lodger, an old Polish

man, in his late sixties, who came out of his room only for dinner. He paid an extra five dollars a week to have Vera and not Ruta clean his room. For ten dollars a week, Vera let him grope her breasts above her clothes as she dusted. She didn't tell her mother, but Ruta knew and collected another five dollars a week in hush money. "Vera's jailbait," Ruta would remind the groper. "I'd hate to have to report you to the vice squad."

As the days passed, Rupert found Vera almost blindingly distracting. He had never known such longing. Meals were a trial, the worst part of his days. Vera always sat next to him. "The old Pole is so disgusting," she'd say. "You don't mind, do you, Robbie?" He inhaled her even as he stared down at his plate. Sometimes, reaching across him for the salt or mustard, she grazed his chest with her hand. At other times, she turned toward him, brushing her breast against his arm. He fought the attraction by ignoring her, never looking at her directly, never speaking to her. Miss Frost stepped outside her librarian's role and warned him against the Wolinskis. "Don't stay too long. There'll be a baby and it will be yours no matter who the father is."

After eight weeks, Vera, gauging that his

will was greater than his desire, decided to make a move. He got home from work at two thirty a.m. Everyone else in the house was asleep. She listened as he washed up, then went to his door and waited until he had turned out the light. She stepped silently into his room. She slipped off her nightie and slithered between the sheets. Rupert froze; his heart raced. "Go away," he said. Vera took his hand and placed it on her breast. "I want you to make love to me," she said. He took his hand back. "No," he said. "I can't." "Yes, yes, you can," she said. "I'm not a virgin." Afraid to look at her, Rupert spoke to the ceiling. "Virgin or no, you're only seventeen. Come back when you're eighteen if you want to." Vera got out of the bed. She pulled back the sheet to look at his erection. She leaned over and kissed it, as she might a baby's head. "Until my birthday then," she said.

Rupert had been tested and had survived. He knew he wouldn't survive a second test. He went to a drugstore near Farrell's and bought ten condoms. "One girl? Ten girls?" the pharmacist said. Taking Miss Frost's warning, Rupert sounded out the bar owner about the possibility of sleeping in the bar's back room. It had a bed, a sink, and a light-bulb. He could use the bar's restroom and shower at the Brooklyn Y. He explained he was likely to lose his lease in a few months. The owner said he could have it. "Five bucks a week. Get your own linens. And locks."

Rupert began to grow less afraid of Vera. She was becoming fawning in her attention to him. Staying up one evening until he came home from the bar, she leapt up as the door closed. "What do you do when you go out at night?" she asked him. "I see friends," he said. "Do you see women?" she asked. He didn't answer but walked up the stairs to his room. Despite his inexperience with women, he saw his advantage. He would let her pursue him. She was experienced. He didn't want a virgin; one in the bed was enough. Not to show his ignorance at the hour, he went to pornographic movies on Forty-Second Street. They mystified him as much as they aroused him. He understood the nun fantasies but not the men who kept their clothes on. He would try it. He wondered if he'd like to bugger a woman. The movies made it exciting for the man and he was never physically repelled by girls or women, the way he was with boys and men. He thought of visiting a prostitute, but he was afraid of the clap. Vera was so clean, so young. He would wait for her.

The evening of her eighteenth birthday, Vera went out with friends. She didn't go to Rupert's room. He knew it was her birthday; there was a cake with candles at dinner. The old Pole bought her a gold bracelet. A weight had been lifted; he might paw Vera without the threat of the vice squad. Mrs. Wolinski raised his rent the next week to eighty dollars a month. Vera also raised her rate, to twenty dollars a week, and let him grope her under her blouse. She stopped cleaning his room.

A week passed, then two. Vera stayed away. Rupert ignored her. Finally, in the third week, he found her one evening in his bed when he got back from work. She was naked under the covers. He pulled back the blanket. He had never seen anything so beautiful. "Do you like what you see?" she said. "I do," he said. "Stand in the middle of the room, for me," he said. "I want to look at all of you." She did as he asked. He walked around her. She was flawless. "Don't you want to touch me?" she said. "Everywhere," he said. She lay down on the bed on her back and crooked her finger at him. He unzipped his fly and put on a condom. "Come lie on me," she said. "I'll make you happy." The porn instruction manual in his head, he lay on top of her. It was over in thirty seconds, leaving him exhilarated and exhausted. He rolled off her. "I think you should go," he said. "Your mother might come in."

"Only once," she said. "That was like lightning. Don't you want to do it again? And again?"

Rupert flushed in the dark. He thought only men in porn movies did it more than once a night. He didn't know how long it would take him to recover. He leaned over and felt her breasts. "Let's take your clothes off," she said, unbuttoning his shirt.

Over the next three hours, he and Vera went at it in every way he could think of. The porn movies had been instructive enough, and Vera was also instructive. He used two more condoms and would have gone on all day if she hadn't worried that her mother might find them. Rupert was past worrying when she left at five a.m. She had to wrench herself out of his arms. "Stay, stay," he said. "I must have you again." He lay in bed in a state of perilous ecstasy. He understood for the first time all the Church's fulminations against sex. A man might ruin himself for sex. He knew he would do almost anything asked of him to have sex again with Vera.

Vera stayed away the next two nights.

When she showed up on the third night, he told her to go away. "Why did you stay away?" he said. "I don't want to play games with you. Games are for the Pole." Vera took off her blouse and bra. He didn't move. She took off her skirt and underpants. "Take me," she said.

"No games," he said.

"No games," she said.

"Can I believe you?" he said. He turned his back to her, not wanting her to see his erection. She came up close behind him. "I'm sorry," she said. "I won't do it again." He turned to face her. "What will you do?" he said. "Anything you want," she said, and placed his hands on her breasts. He almost came standing there. He led her to the bed and lay down. He unzipped his fly and put on a condom. "Would you get on top of me?" he said. "I want to look at your beautiful breasts."

Rupert decided to look at Columbia Law School. He would aim high. His brief residence in America had shown him that his accent would open doors that were shut to the huddled masses. He found his way to the admissions office, guessing it was the admittance office.

"I was wondering if I might speak to

someone," he said to the receptionist. "I'm a foreigner and I'm not sure at all of the procedures for applying to the law school." He spoke in a clipped voice, pruned of all ingratiating notes and implying, ever so slightly, that the procedures and not his ignorance were the problem. "Let me check, sir," the receptionist said, in spite of herself.

The director of admissions met with Rupert. Rupert told him he had an honors BA from Cambridge. The director mumbled "very good, very good," not wishing to display his ignorance of English university degrees. When Rupert asked him if he'd have to take the LSAT exam, the director said he didn't think it would be necessary. "I've never taken a standardized exam," Rupert said. "I haven't a clue what they're like. What do they tell you about the candidate?" The director smiled, without answering, as if they both knew the answer. The director said he'd look out for Rupert's application. They shook hands and parted.

Rupert's research had identified Columbia, Harvard, Yale, and Michigan as the top law schools in the country. After his visit to Columbia, he thought he should look at one of the out-of-town schools; he decided on Yale as the cheapest train ticket. On a damp, drizzly November morning, he caught an early train to New Haven. He took along, to keep him occupied on the train, a copy of Karl Llewellyn's *The Bramble Bush,* a grating and canny handbook on the study of law. The train was crowded. He found a seat in the last car, next to a shortish, balding man, with shrewd, crinkly eyes and ears that stuck out. Rupert took out his book.

"Are you a law student?" his neighbor asked, looking over at the book's title.

"Embryonic," Rupert said. "At least, I hope so."

"Brit?"

"Yes," Rupert said.

"Where are you going now?"

"New Haven. I want to look at Yale Law School."

"Are they expecting you?"

"No. I'll look around and see if I might beard someone."

"Where were you at university?"

Rupert looked at his interrogator with interest. Americans never went to university; they went to college.

"I was at Cambridge, King's," he said, testing to see if his shorthand answer would answer.

"Ha," the man said. "I was there in '33, '34, on a fellowship. Never so cold in my life. Chilblains." He held up his left hand.

"See this, permanent damage." All Rupert could see was a prominent writer's bump on his middle finger. The man smiled at Rupert as if they shared a secret. Rupert smiled back; for all the man's friendliness, he knew he was being coolly appraised, as if he were a racehorse of doubtful pedigree. Well, of course, I am, Rupert thought. He waited for the verdict. It came seconds later, expressed in a small "hmmph" of satisfaction, as if once again the man's instincts had proved him right. "Gene Rostow," the man said, holding out his hand to Rupert, "dean of Yale Law."

Rupert's heart started beating wildly. *O God, Thou art the father of the fatherless . . .* The orphan's prayer came to him unbidden. "Rupert Falkes," he said, shaking the dean's hand, "illegal alien."

The dean smiled again, as if the last bit of information had been part of his calculations. "Shall we do some business?" he said.

Rupert told him he had read for the Historical Tripos and had come away with a double first.

"Good, good," Rostow said. "Do you know any American history?"

"Scant and invidious. Puritans, the Tea Party, a written Constitution, cotton, slavery, Lincoln, the slaughter of Indians,

308

Manifest Destiny, Jim Crow, Hiroshima, McCarthy. We English are sore losers."

"I've always thought history should be taught from texts written by a country's enemies," Rostow said. "American exceptionalism does invite taking us down a peg or two."

"I've read Carlyle on the French Revolution and Guizot on English history. Oh, and Tocqueville," Rupert said. "He approved of all your charities. I hope to be a beneficiary." Rupert had never before spoken so unreservedly to anyone. His usual offensive with men was to retreat into watchful silence, letting the other person fill up the space. Rostow, with his charm and warmth and interest, had made him, or let him, drop his guard. He looked down at his book as though he might have dropped it in his lap. He felt uneasy in his ease, worried he was showing himself to be a chatterer and a show-off and an egoist. He looked up at the dean, who was still smiling at him. He would go on; this was his best shot. "I'm not only illegal, I'm an orphan, a foundling."

Dean Rostow agreed that Rupert shouldn't have to take the LSAT. "It's a test that tests standardized test-taking ability," the dean said. "You'd be terrible at it." Money was the big problem. "You need a full ride," the dean said, "and living expenses too." Rupert nodded. "Tuitions and fees are approaching a thousand dollars a year. You'll get that. In addition, for room and board — we'll put you in the dorms, if you don't mind — we can provide a hundred and fifty dollars a month. You'll have to get summer jobs after the first and second years. I'll help you. Will that do it for you?" Rupert nodded again. His heart was racing; he could feel it pounding in his rib cage. His mouth was dry; he couldn't speak. "Oh, yes," the dean said, "green card. We'll help you with that."

The dean looked at him, locking his eyes on Rupert's. "You're capable of having a distinguished career. I'm counting on it."

At Union Station, the dean and Rupert caught a cab to the law school. The dean asked his assistant to show Rupert around the school. "Come back to see me, when you've seen the place," he said.

Rostow's assistant gave Rupert the nickel tour; his nose was out of joint at having to babysit an applicant, even a Cambridge grad. After twenty minutes, he told Rupert he should walk around the campus. "At first, everything looks the same," he said. "The dean will see you at two." Yale was, Rupert thought, Errol Flynn gothic, with gargoyles, carillons, central heating, and most blessed hot showers. He felt almost giddy.

He was back at the law school at two. "We're set then," the dean said. He handed Rupert a copy of the application. "Send it to me, in this envelope. Yale is the best law school in the country and we're only going to get better."

Rupert hated to thank anyone, almost as much as he hated to apologize. The dean made it easy. As Rupert started to speak, Rostow waved him away. "No. You'll give back. I know that. See you next September."

Rupert walked to the train station. He wished he had someone in his life he could tell about his phenomenal luck. He'd have to settle for Vera in his bed. He had pushed her out of his thoughts until then. She was too arousing, too distracting. On the ride home, he thought about what he'd do to her that night, what she'd do for him. He wondered if he owed God a word of thanks, more grateful, more intentional, than the Psalmist's spontaneous intercession on the train. Prayer had never been easy for Rupert. God would have to judge him by his works.

Rupert liked a fight after a strike of exceptional luck, to appease the envious evil spirit who, like Sleeping Beauty's bad fairy, had cursed him in the cradle. The day he heard he'd been admitted to the Prebendal School, he spit at an older, bigger boy, who duly thrashed him. The bloody nose was expiating. The day he was admitted to Longleat, he threw himself into the riling waters off Hayling Island. He didn't know how to swim. A passing fishing boat saved him. The fisherman asked him why he'd done it. "A dare," Rupert said. The fisherman took a liking to him. "I'm going to teach you to swim," he said. "Come see me Sunday, at one p.m., after church." Rupert knew how to swim and sail by the time he started at Longleat. The day he heard he was admitted to King's, Rupert crawled out of his house window after hours and took himself to the local pub, where he drank up all his spending money and got so drunk he pissed himself before passing out on the front steps. When he woke at four a.m., he walked back to school. His classmates snuck him back in. "Jesus," one said to him, "what are you, some kind of kamikaze?" He had a black eye from the fall. When a master asked him about it, Rupert answered simply, "Too embarrassing to talk about, sir." The master let it go.

At the Wolinskis' dinner table that evening,

still high from his New Haven triumph, Rupert eyed Vera, spilling out of her white blouse, a gold cross between her breasts. She had lifted the look from the Hollywood starlet playbook, the teenage temptress, bent on driving him and his ancient Polish tablemate mad with desire. It worked. He could tell the old Pole was rubbing himself under the table. Worried he'd betray himself to her mother, Rupert struggled to tamp down his erection. He pushed the sodden vegetables around his plate. Ruta, sensing his unease, watched him closely. "Don't you like my dinner?" she said. "I think I may have caught a chill today," he said. He took a Brussels sprout into his mouth; bile rose up in his throat. Forcing the sprout down, he thought about the ways he might punish himself for getting into Yale Law School. The stakes were higher than they'd ever been, but he was no longer willing to pay with a punctured lung or a black eye or a bloody nose. The evil spirit must be assuaged, but not by violence. No brawling, no life-threatening stunts, no alcoholic binges: the fight would have to be against himself. He stabbed a second sprout with his fork and looked again at Vera. I won't have her for a week, he vowed. He choked down the second sprout, as if sealing his pledge. Seven days, he told himself. A week has at least the odor of penance, if not the bite. As soon as he made his pledge, he was awash with doubt and regret. Under the table, she put her hand on his thigh. He couldn't stand up.

Sitting in his room after dinner, trying to read *The Bramble Bush,* his thoughts occupied and preoccupied by Vera, he worried that the evil spirit would not understand his suffering. The evil spirit was a creature of the Grimm Brothers, not the Bible; it had little respect for resisting temptation; it preferred payment in the body. I shall have to give my body over entirely to self-abnegation, he thought. He revised his plan. For seven days, he would not only deny himself Vera, he would subdue and mortify his flesh. He would fast during the day; he would take cold baths; he would sleep naked on the floor, without bedclothes; he would not touch himself; he would scourge his body with ropes. Throughout Rupert's childhood, Father Falkes had flagellated himself with a cat-o'-nine-tails, leaving huge bloody welts on his back. At the time, Rupert had thought the practice was homage to his crypto-Catholicism. Years later, he came to believe the beatings were meant to suppress his longings for young men.

Growing up in the British boys' cloistered world of boarding schools, Rupert had thought all men were heterosexual, all boys homosexual. Homosexuality was a phase, like acne or involuntary erections, outgrown if not entirely forgotten, once a man was lucky enough to find a woman who would let him in.

A little after one a.m., Vera slipped into Rupert's room. He hadn't locked the door, a slipup in his plan. He was asleep on his back, lying on the hard floor, naked and exposed, the window open, the room cold and damp. She lay down beside him and started stroking him. He awoke with a start and sat up. "Please go away," he said. "I can't tonight. I'm doing penance." He thought she would understand, being Catholic. She continued stroking him. "I want to stay," she said. "Are you playing games with me?" She looked down. "He doesn't want to do penance." Vera slipped off her nightie and went down on him. Rupert was in agony. "Not that, please," he said. She looked up at him. "You don't really mean that," she said, and went down again.

"Oh, God," he said, his pleasure gaining on his agony. He made one last brave try to save himself. "Please, stop. We need to talk." Vera lifted her head. "You can stay," he said, "only if you let me come in behind." Vera had refused to let him sodomize her, her one act of resistance. She got on her hands and knees in front of him. "Do it, do it now. I'm yours," she said.

Satan had offered Jesus all the kingdoms of the world and their glory; he had not offered him Vera. That night, Rupert did everything with Vera he had ever imagined doing. He did it with her standing, sitting, lying under him, lying on top of him, backward, forward, on the floor, on the bed, in a chair, against the wall. He never used a condom. "You don't need a rubber," she said to him. "It's much better without, for both of us." At five, she left the room, barely able to stand. "What a night," she said to him. "You were a tiger." Lying on the bed, after she'd left, he cursed the evil spirit. "Do your worst," he said out loud. "I'm done with you."

The next afternoon, Rupert took Vera to Forty-Second Street, to a porn movie. "Watch carefully," he said. "I want us to do everything they do." Looking around the darkened theater, Vera was nervous and excited. She was the only female in the place. "Don't worry," he said. "I won't let any of them touch you." She took his hand and placed it under her blouse. "I hope

you'll touch me," she said. "I'll touch you."
Afterward, he bought her an éclair at Toffenetti's. She had brought a camera with
her, a Brownie. She asked a man on the
street to take their picture. Vera smiled into
the lens; Rupert looked down and sideways.

Vera was pregnant. She'd been to a clinic.
"The rabbit died," she told Rupert. "Early
Valentine's present." He had noticed that
Vera's breasts had gotten larger, more sensitive. He had loved them only more. The
news threw him into a tailspin. The evil
spirit had done his worst.

"Who's the father?" he said.

"Don't be an idiot," she said.

"How can this be?" he asked. "We've only
had sex for a couple of months."

She looked at him with disbelief. *Was* he
an idiot? "Don't you know how babies are
made?"

"Why didn't you use something?" he said.

"I always relied on you," she said.

"You must have known you'd get pregnant
if I didn't use a condom."

"We got carried away."

Vera sat on his bed. She started undress-
ing. "We can still have sex, and we won't
need condoms." She took off her blouse and
bra. Her breasts were the most beautiful

things Rupert had ever seen. She slipped off her skirt and panties and lay down on the bed. "Come lie on top of me," she said.

Afterward, as they lay on the bed, Vera started planning their future.

"We should get married soon," she said. "Before I show. We can live here until you find a job. I'll work to put you through college. You're very smart, Robbie. You could be successful. Would your parents be able to come to the wedding? Where do they live in Scotland?"

Rupert sat up. "I can't marry you," he said. He was sweating. He pulled the blanket up. He thought he might throw up. He could feel his heart pulsing in his ears.

"What are you saying?" she said. "You have to marry me."

"No, I can't," he said.

"You just made love to me again," she said.

"I can't."

"What do I do?" she said. She started to cry.

Rupert took her hand. It was cool and dry. "Don't cry," he said. "I'll think of something." They sat without speaking. Rupert's mind raced.

"I'll be a good wife," Vera said.

Rupert took a large breath. "We'll talk

tonight. I'll do what's best for us. Don't say anything to anyone yet. Go to bed now. Get some sleep." Vera smiled at him.

"Don't you want to do it again?" she said.

"I need to think," he said. "You should go."

"I want you," she said. She began stroking him.

"Don't, don't," he said, "I need to think."

"Think later," she said.

She left his room at four a.m. At five, he went off to the bar, slipping out of the house while everyone was still asleep. He took his suitcase with him. The owner was getting ready to open. "You're twelve hours early, Robert," he said.

"I think I'll take the back room tonight," he said.

The owner nodded. "Don't forget linens. And locks. You'll need two, one for inside when you're inside, one for outside when you're outside. Get sturdy ones. Drunks break into rooms for the hell of it. Don't leave the suitcase until you've got the locks. I don't want to be responsible. Too many sinners here." Robert handed the owner a five-dollar bill to cover his first week's rent.

Rupert got breakfast around the corner, at Spanky's Diner. He ordered pancakes with real maple syrup and bacon. It was the best meal he'd eaten in America. At nine, he went to his bank in Fort Greene and bought a four-hundred-dollar certified check, made out to Vera. I've squandered my inheritance, thrown it away on a woman, he thought. Then he remembered her breasts. She had been worth it; the whole experience had been worth it. He'd have paid double. He wondered what Father Falkes would think. He thought he'd understand. Around the corner from the bank, at Sammy's Discount, he bought sheets, a blanket, a towel, and two locks. Back at the bar at ten, he stashed his suitcase and linens in the back room and fastened the lock to the outside hinge. He pulled on it several times. It held.

He was back in Greenpoint by eleven. Ruta and Vera were not home. They were probably at Daria's. They usually spent their weekday mornings with her and her children, smoking, cooking, ironing, and gossiping. Rupert wrote Ruta a note, using his left hand, paranoia creeping in. "I'm sorry I didn't get a chance to say good-bye. A family emergency has made it necessary for me to leave. Thank you for your hospitality. I will always remember the months on Leonard Street. Yours, Robert Fairchild." Rupert was not unaware of the ironies in his letter,

the family emergency, the necessary depar-
ture, Ruta's hospitality, the memories.
Molière would make it a comedy, Chekhov
a tragedy. Rupert had paid his rent to Ruta
through the month. She'd think she got the
better of him, even if Vera got the worse. He
wrote Vera a left-handed note as well. "I
cannot marry you. I cannot say more. I'm
leaving New York. Here is $400, all I have.
I'll never forget you. Robert."

Rupert made the bed and straightened the
room, making sure no trace of him remained. He put the check and note for Vera
under her pillow, the note for Ruta on the
kitchen table. He left the house and slipped
the key through the mail slot. He walked
around the corner to the subway. He didn't
look back.

Four years later, with Eleanor sitting
beside him at the Thalia, he watched, in a
state of arousal and self-disgust, the movie
version of John Osborne's *Look Back in Anger.*

"I'm Jimmy," he said to Eleanor as they
walked out of the movie house. "With a
posh education."

"Yes and no," she said.

"The 'yes' part, you don't mind," he said.

"No. It's all right."

"Where shall we go for dinner?" he said.

"Let's buy sandwiches and go to your rooms," she said. "I'm not wearing underwear."

He had not expected her to say that. "I thought you were a good girl," he said.

"I am," she said. "Very good."

Rupert pulled her to him and kissed her, one hand gripping her lower back, the other, in front, reaching under her skirt and snaking between her legs. He proposed that night and she accepted. Am I marrying him because of a movie? she wondered as they lay tired and almost happy on his bed. I went to Vassar because of *Women in Love.* She remembered then that Lawrence's hero was named Rupert. "Do you like D. H. Lawrence?" she asked Rupert. "He wants to have his cake and eat it too," he said. He leaned down to kiss her. "You are my cake," he said.

Vera haunted Rupert for months after he left Greenpoint. He missed her breasts, her thighs, her mouth on him, her submissiveness. He wondered if she'd had the baby or an abortion. He wondered if his father had left his mother pregnant like that. Was that their story, his story? He didn't want to think about it. They had been well matched, he and Vera, a pair of young brutes, using each other for their own purposes. He had been better at it. He had been longer at it. He couldn't get pregnant. Would she know where to get an abortion? He wouldn't think about it.

At the bar, he took to having sex with married women, older young women in their late twenties and early thirties. He'd take them into his little back room at closing. Afterward, they'd go home to their husbands, who worked the late shift. He never had sex with any of them more than three or four times. He didn't want an angry husband pounding on his door. He didn't want a relationship. "I don't have much conversation," he'd say. They taught him things he couldn't learn from porn movies.

At Yale, he slept mostly with graduate English students, bluestockings in black tights. They were competent, obliging, undemanding. He used condoms, not willing to find himself cornered again. He talked books with them and read what they recommended, American authors he didn't know, Melville, Hawthorne, Cather. They rounded some of his edges. His vanity made him a decent lover; he liked being good at the things he did. He learned by doing.

Eleanor was the only woman he had sex with who made him please her. "I like that," she'd say. "Would you do it again?" In her desire and her pleasure seeking, she brought a level of wantonness that made him, to his surprise, wild with wanting. It was almost as enthralling as Vera's surrender.

Sex was an important part of the Falkeses' marriage, as important as the boys. Even in their last year, they had stirring encounters. Eleanor's voice, husky and intimate, with a sly hint of laughter at its edges, filled him with desire, from the first day to the last. Her phone calls could give him erections, even when she didn't talk dirty, which she often did in the early years. It took him years not to mind going to cocktail parties with her. Other men were always seeking her out; he knew they wanted her, as he did. She was a MILF before there was a word for it. In the late '80s, at a Maynard, Tandy Christmas party, a drunk, thirty-year-old associate took Eleanor's hand as they were talking and pressed it against his crotch. Quietly, she removed her hand and poured her glass of red wine on his pants front. He stood moaning as she walked away, "Come back. I'm sorry. Come back." Rupert fired him the next day. The associate didn't protest. All he said was "How did you get to be such a lucky son of a bitch?"

A month after their wedding, Eleanor

dropped by his office, late in the afternoon. "Do you mind?" she said as she locked the door behind her. She opened her coat. She was wearing her mother's pearls, a wedding gift, red high heels, and nothing else. He could barely stand up. She lay down on the floor by his chair. Afterward, she said, "We've baptized it." "Baptism" became one of their sexual tropes. They had sex in every room in their apartment, except the boys' rooms and Rupert's private bathroom. They had sex in every office he ever had. They had sex in his hospital rooms. In hotels, before they unpacked, they had sex. "Quick and Dirty" was another trope. "I want sex with you every way," Eleanor whispered to him at their engagement party. "Let's try quick and dirty." After the toasts, when most of the guests were drunk, she took him into a powder room. "Don't let's waste this occasion." She opened his fly. He kissed her neck and pulled down her underpants. At parties, when the attention she was receiving from other men became too exciting to him, he'd signal to her. They'd meet in the powder room. Afterward, she'd say to other guests who made inquiries, "I needed his help. No. Nothing's wrong." At home, they often had sex half-dressed. She liked to come up behind him unawares and reach into his pants in front, whispering all the things she wanted to do with him; he would sink to the ground, pulling her with him. She would try anything he wanted at least once, and nothing disgusted her, though he always felt she held herself back, just a little, adding, perversely, to his pleasure. She was a sexual adventurer. He would never tire of her. In all their thousands of couplings, she failed him only in failing to be submissive.

Rupert had known she wasn't a virgin when they first had sex, and he wondered, after her tubal ligation, whether she might be sleeping with other men — gamekeepers or cardiologists or Italian lawyers — when she said she was at the movies; the thought aroused him. He was sure the children were his; she was too honorable to cuckold him. Did he love her? He couldn't imagine life without her. Did she love him? Did anyone?

Their marriage hit a bump in its fifteenth year. They had been together a long time. At the office, Rupert was discontented; at home, Eleanor was at loose ends. Neither acknowledged their unease, waiting for the other to speak, hoping the skies would clear. Rupert couldn't remember why he had wanted to be a lawyer. His work had become boring, his partners irritating. He thought of teaching instead, perhaps at Yale, and started coming into the office late and leaving early. Eleanor had too much time on her hands. She went to the movies almost every day, sometimes twice in one day. The boys were growing up. The youngest was in kindergarten. The older ones had secret lives. The trip to England made things worse. Rupert hadn't wanted to go; Eleanor had insisted. "You need to go the first time," she said. His mood was unhappy the whole time they were there, his premonitions all fulfilled. He hated England and the English. For the first time in their marriage, they didn't baptize the hotel room. Everywhere he went, he felt exposed and derided for the fraud he was. He was sure everyone, the hotel concierge, the maître d' at Simpson's, the taxi drivers, knew he was an orphan and an outcast, their English antennae always alert to the striver, the parvenu. He felt everyone blamed him for not having parents, for not deserving parents, for not being able to keep them. He blamed himself too. And he blamed Eleanor. She had taken all the relatives for herself, generations of Phippses, Deerings, Livingstons, and Porters, going back past the Mayflower Compact to the Domesday Book.

Jim Cardozo's wedding, coming on the heels of the English debacle, was the trip wire. Rupert wasn't sure why he had wanted to go. The food was delicious, unheard-of at an English wedding, and the company lively. He liked the Strauses especially. I'm better with Jews than with Christians, he thought. The problem was the groom. His slavering over Eleanor, while offering minor satisfaction, excited jealousy where he hadn't thought it existed. When he asked Eleanor that evening, whether she'd ever had an affair, she didn't answer but unzipped his fly, slipped off her underpants, and lay down in her silk dress on the floor, in front of him. "Do you want me to touch myself?" she asked. He nodded. "God is in the details," he thought, watching her. Afterward, lying on the floor, he remembered lying clothed on his bed in Greenpoint with Vera sitting on top of him, naked, aroused, yielding. He tried to conjure her physical memory but his skin had shed it, leaving behind only the visual, unspooling in his mind as soft-core porn, slightly out of focus. He felt a shaft of terrible longing and loss.

Over the next few weeks, every time he and Eleanor had sex, he thought of Vera. Before long, he was thinking about her all the time. The subway ride became torture. Every blurry young blonde on the train reminded him of her, making him ache. He fought the urge to rub against them from behind, to clutch their breasts and breathe into their necks. After a month, he decided he would have to find her. There was no other resolution.

He wanted to look for her himself, but the risk, he knew, was too great. He wouldn't be careful enough. He hired a private investigator. He gave him her name and the Greenpoint address. "I want to know everything," he told the PI. "Where is she living? Where is she working? What does she do? Is she married, divorced, engaged? Has she ever been married? Is there a man in her life? If so, who is he, what does he do? Does she have any children? Did she have any children? And get me a picture. I'll give you two weeks. I'll pay for three weeks if you can do it in two. I don't think she's strayed far from Leonard Street."

The PI was back to him in ten days. His report was vague on some points. He had been diligent. Vera was careless:

Vera Wolinski, aka Vera Wolinski Koslowski, still lives at 536 Leonard Street, Greenpoint, with her mother and her widowed sister. She has often claimed that she too is a widow. When she was very young, she told neighbors, she married an old Polish man, Adam Koslowski, a boarder in the family home; he died six months after the nuptials, leaving her $10,000. There is no record of that marriage or any other. There have been many men in her life since then but no certified husbands. She has no known children and no verified pregnancy or birth, though there was gossip that she married the Pole because she was pregnant. Her current boyfriend, Stefan Malinowski, is the director of the Greenpoint YMCA. He seems a decent fellow. Apparently he's been her on-and-off boyfriend ever since the death of the Polish husband. He always comes back. He's given her three diamond engagement rings. The first two went missing, likely pawned. She's a waitress at the Oyster Bar in Grand Central Station. She's worked there for at least a dozen years. She works both the lunch and rush-hour shifts, coming in at 11:30 a.m., Tuesday through Friday, leaving at 8:30 p.m. Her lunch hour is from 3:30 to 4:30. She makes good money as a waitress, mostly in tips. She also makes extra income on the side. She dates some of her customers, only regulars. The Hotel Coolidge, across the street from Grand Central, is a regular rendezvous spot for illicit couplings. She is known to the clerks, not by name but by her photograph. She makes sure they are tipped regularly and well by her dates. She is very beautiful, as you will see from her picture. She has never been arrested. She does not use drugs. Over the course of the investigation, I was given multiple accounts of events in her life as people heard them from her. Other PIs are said to have investigated her. She was named reportedly as correspondent in two New York State divorces brought on the grounds of adultery, most likely as the designated doxie. I have not found records identifying her as such. She is 37 or 38 years old.

A week after he received the report, Rupert went for a late lunch at the Oyster Bar. Catching sight of Vera, he asked to sit in her section. "Less noisy," he said to the hostess. As he read the menu, he sensed Vera coming up behind him. "Would you like a Greenpoint oyster?" she said. Rupert kept his eyes on the menu. He felt the blood rushing in his ears. "Could you get off work at three thirty?" he said, not looking at her. "Yes," she said, "if it's worth my while." He turned to look at her. She looked scarcely older, still Lana Turner. His eyes went to her cleavage, then to her left hand. She was wearing a cross and a small diamond ring. Keeping his seat, he took out a billfold and handed her five fifties. "It's three now. Meet me across the street in the lobby of the Hotel Coolidge in thirty minutes." Vera counted the bills. "Real money," she said. She leaned down and pressed her hand against his crotch. "Just making sure," she said. He held her hand there for several seconds.

Rupert arranged for a room in the Coolidge in the name of Robert Fairchild. "I expect you to be discreet," he said to the clerk, handing him twenty dollars. "No one will know I'm here. Is that understood? Let me know if anyone asks for me or follows me." The clerk nodded. He had been threatened before by johns but never in an English accent. "Yes sir," he said. "Good," Rupert said. "We can do business. I expect to come regularly. I want a different room each time, but I will always see the same woman. You will show her up. I want the room cleaned with fresh bedding. I will call and pay cash, in advance, and I will pay extra for extra services. Is that understood?" The clerk nodded. "Yes sir." Rupert handed him another twenty. "One last thing," Rupert said. "You will treat her with respect."

■ ■ ■ ■

Rupert and Vera met regularly at the Coolidge over the next six months, at least once a week, often twice, occasionally three times. They came to terms quickly that first afternoon. "Would you mind taking off your clothes while we negotiate," he said. "I want to see all of you. I remember your beautiful body." Vera obliged with a slow striptease. Rupert talked. They would meet in the morning at eight thirty. He would arrange to pay her a thousand dollars a month, deposited directly in her bank account, or in cash if she preferred. She would make herself available to him whenever he wanted her, Tuesday through Friday mornings. He would accommodate her job. She could meet other men as she wished, but not at the Coolidge and not in the morning. He would be her first of the day. She would take the birth control pill. If she got pregnant, if she ever tried to find out where he lived or worked, if she ever talked about their past, he would break off the arrangement.

"Do you agree?" he said. "We exist together only in this room."

"Very professional, very businesslike," Vera said.

333

Rupert said nothing.

She walked over to him. "Do you want to start now? It seems a waste of" — she gestured to her nakedness — "not to."

He nodded. "Lie down on the bed for me, will you, on your back."

"Aren't you going to get undressed?" she said.

"No," he said, unzipping his fly. "Like the first time."

Rupert took feral pleasure in Vera's wondrous, compliant flesh. With her, it was always the first time, bringing him to the brink of ruination. He thought if he died during sex with Vera, it would have been worth it.

Their sessions always began the same way. She would strip in front of him as he sat on the bed, dressed in his shirt and trousers, watching her. He would then lie down, still in his clothes, his fly open, and she would get on top of him so he might look at her breasts. He was as quick as a youth with her.

The rest of the morning followed no plan. Vera was very adept at sex, inventive and improvisational, and she quickly figured out how to please him. She never refused him, realizing that submission was what he wanted. "I'll do anything you want," she'd say. "Everything you want." If he had wanted a dominatrix, she'd have obliged there as well.

At the end of their sessions, Rupert had her wash him in the shower. He would then get dressed. He left the room first, leaving her naked, on her back on the bed so he could have a last look. He would never tire of her.

The end came as it had come before. The session had begun as usual, Vera on top of him naked, he below clothed, looking at her beautiful breasts. They seemed fuller to him, more beautiful than ever. He knew in a flash.

"Please get off me," he said.

"What's the matter?"

"You know what's the matter," he said, his voice low, angry, breaking. "You're pregnant." She slid off him. He sat up. "Why did you do it? I'd have paid you forever." He got up and walked toward the bathroom.

Vera shrugged.

While he dressed, he asked her to lie naked on the bed. "A last look, if you will," he said. He put on his jacket, then sat next to her, stroking her breasts. "God, I love them. You ruined it. You ruined it again." He took out his wallet and gave her twenty

335

fifties. "This is it," he said. He got up to go.

Vera sat up and took hold of his jacket sleeve. "Remember," she said, speaking so softly he had to lean in to hear, "you came looking for me. I never went looking for you." She let go of the jacket and lay back down on the bed. "You'll be back."

Straus's company hired Rupert as their lawyer. The Maynard, Tandy partners elected him to the management committee. Rupert had the PI follow Cardozo. He wasn't sleeping with Eleanor. Rupert thought fleetingly of hiring the PI to follow Eleanor but rejected the idea on grounds of self-respect and self-preservation. "Are you over whatever it was?" she asked him the evening of his first management committee meeting. They were getting ready for bed. He gave her a thin smile. "What doesn't kill you makes you unkinder." He pressed her against the wall and pulled down her underpants. "I always want you," he said. "Yes," she said.

The money going to Vera stopped for six months, then resumed.

# CHAPTER 8
# HUGH

Why bastard? wherefore base?
SHAKESPEARE, *KING LEAR*

Sam called Susanna to give her the good news. "An early Christmas present, of sorts," he said. The reports from the genetic counselor showed no "recessive disorders" percolating in their genes, no AIDS or HIV antibodies steeping in his fluids. Sam wondered why his doctor had insisted on the screenings — probably to scare him. Neither family had a history of genetic diseases, not counting alcoholism and adultery on the Goffe side; nor were they overly inbred for pre-revolutionary whites. The predominant strain in both families was British, but there had been enough German, Scandinavian, French, and Dutch intermarriage to water the stock. Susanna's mother insisted that her grandmother, Susanna's great-grandmother, was an Italian opera singer.

337

"Her name was de Campo," Prudence said. "They changed it to Van Camp to purge the Wop." Susanna didn't believe her. She had never known her mother to tell the truth when a lie was more satisfying. Her father, ashamed of his regicide ancestor, claimed his mother was descended from Ivanhoe. She had said so. "Don't you mean Walter Scott?" Susanna had asked. Her father insisted it was Ivanhoe. "My great-grandfather was Wilfred," he said. On the Falkes side, Rupert was the only wild card, the secret ingredient in their genetic gumbo. "Probably to the good," Susanna said. "I hope the baby has your Arctic eyes."

The report presented a problem, not thought through at the time Sam filled out the forms. At the last minute, he had ordered a DNA test for himself. He wouldn't have taken the test on his own, at least he didn't think so, but it had struck him as skulking and mean not to have asked for it when every other body part was being genetically scrutinized. Harry was incredulous. "Why would you do that?" he said. "You chewed me out for even thinking about it. It would be humiliating to our mother and insulting to our father's memory."

"It doesn't tell us anything about Dad,

you told me that, only about us and the Wolinskis," Sam said. "The test can't prove Dad is their dad, or even our dad."

"Right," Harry said. "We'll find out we're all brothers but Dad isn't our common father. Mom and Vera had, between them, seven children with the same man who we don't know." He paused. "Or maybe we're not related to them and none of us are Dad's sons."

Sam stared at his brother. "I was curious," Sam said. "Aren't you?"

"What do we do?"

"We meet with them, or one of them, and talk about it," Sam said.

"Do we tell Mom we're doing this?" Harry said.

"Mom thinks they're Dad's, I'm pretty sure," Sam said.

"That doesn't answer my question."

"I think we have to," Sam said.

"Report back to me after you've talked to her," Harry said. "I'm not getting burned again."

Eleanor didn't show surprise when Sam told her he'd been tested. "I would have guessed Tom, in a paroxysm of extreme altruism, to be the one to get the test and then push for a meeting with the Wolinskis. It doesn't matter. I understand that you would want to know. I prefer not knowing, and doing what I want about them."

"Do you want to know what we find out?" Sam asked.

"I suppose so," Eleanor said. "After you've gone to so much trouble."

"Why aren't you curious?" Sam asked.

"Dad never said anything to me about Vera or the boys. Either it happened and he didn't want me to know or it didn't happen. I trusted him, I continue to trust him. We were on a need-to-know basis."

"But if it did happen, don't you think he might have said something at some point, before he died?" Sam said.

"Dad and I weren't confessional, not with each other, not with anyone. We took cues from each other."

"You didn't want to know his secrets?" Sam said.

"No. And I didn't want him to know mine."

"When do we learn yours?" Sam asked.

Eleanor didn't answer.

"Weren't you upset by Vera's claim?" Sam asked.

Eleanor shook her head. "It came after," she said. "It didn't change the life I had with your father."

"I don't understand you at all," Sam said.

"It's the angle," Eleanor said. "You can't see me from where you're standing."

Edward Phipps lived to be eighty-four. He died three years before Rupert, a blessing. The loss of Rupert would have pierced his armored complacency. He died at Mrs. Cantwell's, in her bed. "He said he had a bad headache and went to lie down," Mrs. Cantwell told Eleanor. "When I went into the bedroom, he was gone." She wanted his death notice to say he died in her apartment. Rupert told her that wouldn't be possible.

Mr. Phipps's widower years were happy ones. He had Eleanor, Rupert, and the boys down the street on the Upper West Side and Marina Cantwell across the park on the Upper East. He was too early for Viagra but he lost weight, worked out with a trainer, and walked with a springy step. Marina was kind to him, admiring and affectionate. She always laughed at his jokes. She had little use for any of the Falkeses, a boon to all of them. She thought Edward might marry her if Eleanor and the boys were out of the way. She kept lobbying him to move "back to the East Side with all your good friends." When she complained that the Falkeses always came first, ahead of her, Edward would pat her hand. "Now, now, kitten," he'd say. "Let's not ruin a lovely evening."

The funeral was at St. Thomas. The boys took over the planning. Rupert and Eleanor were heartsick. Harry, who had become a serious churchgoer in the hopes of making Christians of his daughters, made all the burial arrangements. Sam planned the service and chose the music. Tom read the Old Testament portion. Will read e.e. cummings's untitled poem that begins "Buffalo Bill's defunct." Eleanor had asked for it. Jack played taps, surprising the priests by reducing most of the mourners to tears. "Danny Boy," with bagpipes, was usually the reliable weeper. Rupert sat at the far end of the front row so as not to be observed.

After the service, friends and family stopped by the Falkeses' apartment. Mrs. Cantwell and Louisa arrived in the first wave. Mrs. Cantwell settled herself in the middle of the living room, in a large wing chair, and prepared to receive her comforters. Louisa brought her mother a glass of wine, then flitted restlessly around the room, picking up photographs and putting them down in different places. She was dressed in full mourning: a black stiff satin suit that crinkled when she walked, black

342

hose, black gloves, a large black hat, and a black draping veil. Spotting Eleanor by the kitchen, she sprung at her. Eleanor had not seen Louisa since her wedding fifteen years earlier, when she'd been all in white. "It's strange we never meet," Louisa said. "Mum used to say she didn't like mixing apples and oranges. I never knew which family was apples. She didn't want to share your father with you. You were the other family."

Eleanor stared at her. "Your mother rarely came round to us, perhaps once a year," she said. "They liked to keep to themselves."

"I saw him at least half a dozen times a year. My mother liked to bring him and me together."

"I think they were happy together," Eleanor said.

"Your father had a gift for happiness," Louisa said.

"Did he?" Eleanor said. "I shall think about that."

"This place is huge," Louisa said. "Mother said it was a wedding present from your father. What are you going to do with his place? It's very nice for a West Side apartment."

Eleanor started to back away. "No plans yet," she said. "Thank you for coming. It must be a comfort to your mother." She turned to speak to another guest.

Louisa caught her arm and leaned into her ear. "I think I'm your sister," she said in a loud whisper. "I think your father was my father." Eleanor turned back to her. Louisa was smiling a death's-head grin.

"I'm sorry. This is terrible of me," Louisa said. "It's been stewing for years, this feeling I've had. My mother never denies it." Her eyes glistened.

"I'm sorry for your pain," Eleanor said, falling, without thinking, into thoughtfulness. "It's too hard to talk here. We'll meet for coffee sometime. Soon. Yes. Soon." Louisa nodded. Eleanor turned from her and walked down the hall toward her bedroom.

Rupert, who'd watched the two talking, followed her. "You're white as a sheet," he said.

"I'd like fresh air," she said.

They stepped out the rear door of the apartment and went onto the roof. Eleanor told Rupert what Louisa had said. Rupert put his arm around her shoulders and pulled her against him. "It could be true," he said. "Edward told me he had an affair with her mother when he was in his early forties. The timing would be right."

"Did my father think Louisa was his daughter?" Eleanor asked.

Rupert gave a flicker of a shrug. "I don't think so. Marina wanted him to believe it, without lying to him. She was always pushing them to spend time together, 'to discover their common bond,' she'd say." Rupert kept his hold on Eleanor. "He resisted. 'We each have a daughter,' he'd say to her. 'Aren't we lucky in them?'"

"Are you saying this to keep my spirits up?" Eleanor said.

"No, your father, whatever his faults, was incapable of false feeling. You know he loved you. Louisa knows he didn't love her."

"I don't know that I would mind, in theory, if he had another daughter," Eleanor said, "but I don't want a sister, not that sister."

"What does she want?" Rupert said.

"Do we throw money at her?" Eleanor said.

"If that will do it, yes," Rupert said.

"My father had dreadful taste in women," Eleanor said.

"Do you want to go back in? Do you want to rest? I can send them all home," Rupert said.

Eleanor straightened her shoulders. "No. I shan't be done in by her."

Will came out on the roof. "Are you all

right?" he said to his mother. "I saw you leave."

"I miss Granddad," Eleanor said.

Louisa and Eleanor met for coffee two weeks later at E.A.T. on the Upper East Side. Eleanor had asked to meet on the Upper East Side, outside her catchment area. "You must think I'm a wretch," Louisa said, "accosting you like that at the funeral." She was smiling overbroadly.

Eleanor sat down. "I did think, I do think, you might have chosen a better moment."

"Do I look like your father," Louisa asked, "or anyone else in your family?"

"No," Eleanor said. "You're nothing like anyone in the family."

"My father, my mother's husband, was much older than my mother. He died when I was nine," Louisa said. "I barely remember him."

"What do you want from me?" Eleanor said. She was tired of Louisa and her feelings.

Louisa looked startled. "I don't know," she said.

"Do you want an inheritance?" Eleanor said.

Louisa's face fell, then turned blotchy. Eleanor couldn't tell if she was enraged or embarrassed.

"Do you think I'm doing it for money?" she said.

"I don't know what you're doing it for," Eleanor said. "I don't know you."

"That's not my fault," Louisa said.

"I can't help you," Eleanor said. She reached for her wallet.

Louisa stopped her hand. "I'll take care of this. I don't want your money."

"You need to take this up with your mother," Eleanor said. "She knows, if anyone does. I haven't a clue." She stood up. "Good-bye."

Eleanor hadn't been so rude to anyone since she had snubbed Jim's parents at his wedding. People can be so annoying, she thought. Next time I'm asked to meet with a putative relation, I'm sending my regrets.

That evening, after supper, she told Rupert about her conversation with Louisa. "I've forgiven my rudeness. She ruined my father's funeral. I thought people only ruined weddings."

"People generally make the most of their opportunities," Rupert said.

"I'm going to be sixty on my next birthday," Eleanor said. "I've decided it's time I stopped smoothing over the rough patches. Rudeness is sometimes the only proper response." She smiled at him. "But you, of course, know that."

Rupert laughed. "So long as you don't give me a hard time."

She gave him a long look. "Too late to start tangling with you."

"No tangling," he said. "I've always relied on your willingness to let things slide." He took her hand. "Your dad too. He let things slide. Differently. I miss him."

"At least he didn't marry Marina," Eleanor said. "Do you think any more shoes will drop?"

Rupert reached out and touched her cheek. "No more shoes will drop."

Susanna thought Sam was crazy to pursue the matter with the Wolinskis.

"But what if they are our brothers?" Sam said. "Shouldn't they get some of Dad's money?"

"Is that what this is about? Money?" Susanna said. "If it is, just give it to them. I'm with your mom."

Harry was having third thoughts. "I haven't time now to think this through," he said to Sam. "And I've pretty much come around to Mom's point of view. I don't want to see the Wolinskis again. I don't want to know."

Sam was startled. "Of course you want to

know," he said.

"No, I don't," Harry said. "I've got to go. We'll talk another time."

Sam was disappointed in Harry but not, as he thought about it, surprised. He had always felt that Harry, like most lawyers, had at best an arm's-length relationship with the truth. He was coming round to Will's position. Will said truth was irrelevant to lawyers. "Justice in America," he said, "is politics, and trials are elections. Two lawyers argue different versions of a story and then ask a dozen ill-informed citizens to vote on the one they like best." When the Supreme Court decided *Bush v. Gore,* Will felt vindicated. "How is this different from a stuffed ballot box?" he said to Harry. "Your ox was gored this time," Harry said. "Next time, it will be someone else's." He looked at his oldest younger brother with affection. "Who knew you were an idealist?"

Harry's balkiness troubled Sam. He decided he should talk to him in person, drop by his office, late in the day. He wouldn't call first; Harry would put him off. They could go for a beer. Harry might even invite him home afterward to have dinner with Lea and the girls. He'd like that. Susanna was pregnant. She was having a girl. He didn't know anything about girls who weren't Susanna. "Will your daughter be like you?" he had asked her. "Are you like your father?" she said.

Late, on a snowy February afternoon, Sam took the subway up to 116th Street. Walking across campus, he wondered if Harry would be unhappy to see him. He had been cranky ever since their DNA conversation, distracted and short-tempered. He cut short phone calls. He didn't have time for lunch. He broke their squash dates, and not because he regularly lost. Harry always went into combat thinking he'd win. Afraid to ask Lea, Sam asked his mother what was up.

"I think he's having what is commonly referred to as a midlife crisis," she said. "He's turned forty, the age of disappointment."

"What does that mean?" There was a querulous edge to Sam's question, creeping disappointment already getting the jump on him.

"Men at forty are often disappointed with their lives and with themselves, not because they haven't achieved what they wanted to, but because they have and it tastes like ashes."

"Did Dad have one?" Sam asked.

"Why would Dad have one?" she asked.

"Why don't you ever answer a personal question?" Sam asked.

"You wouldn't want to know the answer once you knew it," Eleanor said. "I've always thought curiosity was jealousy in sheep's clothing. The will to possess or control or annihilate." Sam stared at his mother.

As he stood outside Harry's office, Sam could hear two voices inside, Harry's and a woman's. He knocked before he could hear what they were saying. "What do you want," Harry called out, his voice deep and brusque, a judge's voice. "I don't have office hours today."

"It's me, Sam," Sam said.

There was no response for several seconds. "What are you doing here?" Harry said.

"I want to talk to you."

"Just a minute. We're winding up," Harry said.

After three or four minutes, the door opened and a young, redheaded woman came out. She looked as though she'd been crying. Harry called after her.

"We can review this again tomorrow," he said. He turned to Sam. "She wrote an execrable paper and now she's crying about the grade."

Sam met his brother's gaze. "I don't

351

believe you," he said. "You're messing around."

"What are you saying?" Harry said.

"Don't mess with me, Harry. I saw it all."

"Christ," Harry said. "Come on in."

"Just tell me she isn't pregnant," Sam said. "No more bastards in the family."

"Her husband found out."

"How?"

"She told him," Harry said.

"That'll do it," Sam said.

Harry was silent.

"Didn't you take the course? Can't she get you for sexual harassment?" Sam said.

"Goddammit," Harry said. "You're a real son of a bitch."

"Don't go high-minded on me. You're the asshole here."

"She's faculty, a historian. We team taught the last few years."

"Is she pregnant?" Sam asked.

Harry didn't answer.

"So this is why you're no longer interested in the Wolinskis," Sam said. "Identifying with Dad, are you? He'd have been about forty then?"

"You're preaching to me?" Harry said. "What about Andrew?"

"I didn't get anyone pregnant until we'd broken up."

"What do I do?" Harry said. His face crumpled.

"You tell her it's over. You tell her if she has the baby and the baby is yours and not her husband's, you'll pay child support, but that's it. You'll tell her you won't be in her life or the baby's. Don't suggest abortion; if she brings it up, tell her it's her decision and it may be the right one for her. Tell her you'll pay for it, if she wants it, so she doesn't have to use her insurance. Tell her you made a mistake, tell her you love your wife and children, tell her you're not going to leave them. Tell her you won't see her anymore."

Harry didn't say anything.

"Don't tell me you're in love with her," Sam said.

Harry shook his head. "She's so young, so undemanding."

"She looks like Lea. Except the red hair."

"She looks like Lea? She looks nothing like Lea."

"What were you thinking? Bartenders, waitresses, secretaries, trainers, never your colleagues, never your colleagues' wives."

"Do I tell Lea?" Harry looked like he might cry.

"No blurting to clear your conscience. And if Lea asks, you lie to her too unless your historian says she's going to tell her. If you do wind up telling her" — Sam shot Harry a squint-eyed look — "tell her you were at a party and drunk and stupid and careless. It meant nothing to you, it means nothing to you. She and the girls are your world."

"How do you know all this?" Harry said.

"I've never been faithful, not since I left Princeton. I didn't love Andrew, not 'truly madly deeply,' but even if I did, I don't think I could be faithful. I don't like being tied down. Susanna is the only person outside the family I love and I can't marry her. All very self-serving, I know. I think Will is the only one of us capable of being faithful to the end. Maybe Jack. His trumpet comes first."

"Is Tom messing around?" Harry asked.

"No, but he could. With Dorothy Day or Mother Teresa. He'd say he was furthering the cause. Caroline might believe him. A woman born to suffer."

"You don't think well of any of us, do you?" Harry said.

"I'd die for you, for any one of you. Isn't that enough?"

Jim Cardozo died six months after Anne moved out, in early February 2003. He died at the kitchen table. He'd been reading the *Times.* When he didn't show up for his afternoon appointments, his secretary called Anne. Anne was distraught and at first blamed herself. Mrs. Lehman, canny as always, offered consolation. "Men have died and worms have eaten them, but not for love. Shakespeare."

The autopsy showed three of the arteries to his heart were blocked. "He should have had open-heart surgery," Dr. Schwinn told her. "Didn't he ever have an EKG? A stress test?"

Anne shook her head. "He never went to a doctor, not even for a flu shot," she said.

Nathan was bereft. He too blamed himself. "I shouldn't have told him to stop doing surgery. That's what he lived for," he said to his mother. "That and, of course, us."

"No," she said. "He should have gotten checkups."

"His colleagues should have seen how ill he was," Nathan said.

"I think he knew he had a blockage," Anne said. "He gave up at some point, with himself, with me." She smiled at Nathan, a small, sad smile. "Never with you. You were the bright spot always, the best thing that ever happened to him and me. You must know that."

"Why didn't I notice? His color was so bad," Nathan said.

"There was nothing you could have done," Anne said. She wondered if Nathan knew about his father's drinking and drug taking. They'd never spoken about it. "He had set his course. You couldn't have saved him."

Nathan looked as if he might cry. He was supposed to save people. It was his job. "I didn't try," he said.

"Oh, Nathan," Anne said. "He was beyond saving."

Nathan stared at his mother, rattled by the ambivalence of her remark. "Don't you care that he's dead?" he said. "Don't you miss him?"

"I'm sad for him," Anne said, "and sad for us."

"I wish I knew him better," Nathan said.

Going through Jim's papers, Anne found a sealed envelope addressed to Eleanor. Her first impulse was to read it; her second, to toss it. She resisted both. She felt surprised, then disappointed, then slighted that she hadn't received a sympathy note from Eleanor. The omission seemed out of character for someone overbred. Perhaps Jim's letter explained its absence. His death had been, once her feelings of guilt dissipated, a relief to Anne. The letter to Eleanor was unsettling, igniting old feelings of envy and jealousy, feelings that shouldn't have outlived Jim. The Wolinski lawsuit had given no satisfaction. Anne decided to deliver the letter in person.

When Jim died, Eleanor was in Los Angeles, visiting Will and Francie and their infant daughter, Mary Phipps Gore Falkes, who, everyone agreed, was the spitting image of Rupert, with her white fuzz and pale eyes. "Dad would chide me for gene packing," Eleanor said to Will, laughing. "He's getting his own in the next generation. And all girls." Francie liked her mother-in-law and allowed her to hold the baby. She even agreed to go out to dinner one night and let Eleanor babysit. "I shall deliver her as I found her, I promise," Eleanor said. "Oh, it's not you," Francie said. "It's me. She'll be fine without me. I might die."

Eleanor had begun reading the obituaries and death notices in the *Times* when Rupert was dying. Her father's death, three years earlier, had been painful but expected. He was old. Rupert's death at sixty-six was unexpected, unnatural, unfair. She had counted on them living into their eighties, downsizing to three bedrooms, perhaps moving to the East Side, a West Sider's idea of assisted living, where everything could be ordered by phone and delivered to the door. With Rupert gone, she felt trapped in their huge apartment. Anyone might die at any time. So long as I don't outlive the boys, she thought.

On Sundays, after browsing the wedding notices to find out whose children had married, she browsed the death notices to find out whose husbands and wives had died. When did I become the last generation before death? she wondered. She envied the lucky dead, those who lived to eighty-eight, the perfect age to die after a brief, chemo-free illness, leaving just enough time to say good-bye and good luck. Those who lived longer she pitied; they were too likely to have outlived their friends, their money, their arteries, and their wits.

Eleanor didn't see Jim's notice when she was in L.A. She found out only when Anne called her to ask if they might meet. "Jim left you a letter."

Eleanor agreed as agreeably as she could manage. She couldn't see her way to denying a grieving widow bearing a letter meant for another woman. "Does morning coffee work for you this Saturday, ten a.m.? We could meet at E.A.T."

After their last dreadful time together,

Eleanor had never wanted to see Jim again. She got her wish, though she'd never wished him dead. As a girl, she had wished her mother dead, dreaming violent ends for her as she fell asleep at night. Eaten by tigers was her favorite. Tigers would succeed. She found herself relieved by Jim's death. He'd become an albatross. She had not minded his mooning over her, at St. Thomas, at his wedding, at the movies, not until Rupert was dying. He kept dropping by the hospital room as if she wanted to see him. Rupert's oncologist noticed it. Eleanor shrugged it off. "Does he?" She had given up, temporarily, her budding rudeness. There were so many people whose goodwill she needed for Rupert's care; she couldn't let rudeness take over. Rudeness, she had discovered, was an earthquake emotion, growing exponentially with each eruption. She held her temper even as she wished she could get a TRO against Jim. What had she seen in him, she wondered. We were twenty. He was beautiful. Our mothers were harridans. He'd read *Anna Karenina* in Russian.

As she walked across the park to meet Anne, Eleanor wondered what about her encouraged postmortem confessions. She had never heard from Louisa again after their last encounter. She imagined Louisa hadn't the stomach to confront her mother. She had heard from the mother only once after her father's funeral, a month later. Mrs. Cantwell had phoned to ask for three items from Mr. Phipps's apartment, a pair of Nefertiti-head bookends, a silver candlestick, and a Persian prayer rug. Mrs. Cantwell giggled when she asked for the last item. "Your father said he worshipped me," she said. Rupert wanted to say no "on principle," the lawyer's aversion to making distributions outside the will to people he didn't approve of. Eleanor said to let her have them. "My principle is expediency. I want to be done with her." Nothing in her father's new apartment meant anything to her, and Mrs. Cantwell's claims on the items had made them repellent to Eleanor. She hoped she might part with Anne as easily, if more cordially. She would walk out of E.A.T. again if she needed to.

"I'm sorry for your loss," Eleanor said as she sat down. Anne had gotten to the restaurant first and taken a table in the back. Eleanor silently gauged the number of footsteps to the exit. "I hadn't heard until you called," she said. "I was in Los Angeles, visiting my son Will, and his wife and their new infant daughter." Anne sat up straighter at this personal opening, fearing for a moment that Eleanor knew from her father about her stalking days. Officially this was only their second encounter.

"It was sudden," Anne said. "Blocked arteries. No one knew. He never got check-ups. He didn't believe in stress tests. He didn't believe in doctors."

"My mother died of a heart defect," Eleanor said, "though she knew about it. She was younger than Jim. Dr. Schwinn — do you know him? — was her doctor. Jim found him for me."

"Schwinn reviewed the autopsy report," Anne said. "If you die at home alone, too young, they do an autopsy." She reached into her purse and pulled out an envelope. It said "Eleanor Falkes."

"Do you mind if I read it here?" Eleanor said. She didn't want to take the letter with her.

The note was written by hand:

Dear Eleanor,
I'm sorry for being so out of sorts the last time we met. I didn't much care for Road to Perdition and it made me irritable and no doubt irritating. I know I talked too much about Nathan. I was still recovering from his year in Haiti. Anne and I worried all the time, even

though he's the most sensible and practical young man I know. It's a huge relief to have him safe in medical school. He'll be an excellent doctor. We feel very lucky in him and each other. I don't know how you managed with five.

I've cut back on my surgeries. My hands are getting arthritic, my eyes are growing cataracts. Getting old surprised me. You never seem to change. Anne only gets better. Wishing you all the best.

Jim

Eleanor handed the note to Anne. Anne shook her head. "No, no," Eleanor said. "Please read it."

Anne read the note. "I promised myself I wouldn't cry," she said, her eyes watering.

"We went for coffee after the movie. Jim talked about Nathan the whole time," Eleanor said. "He was so proud of him, so happy he was going to be a doctor." Anne handed her back the letter. "No, keep it," Eleanor said.

"I always thought I was in the looking-glass version of *Pride and Prejudice*," Anne said, "the one where Charlotte Lucas and not Lizzy Bennet marries Mr. Darcy."

"Funny," Eleanor said. "I thought of myself as Isabel Archer in a bowdlerized

*Portrait of a Lady.* She accepts Lord Warburton's proposal on the spot."

"A Vassar education does that," Anne said.

"Yes," Eleanor said. "It allowed us somehow to think of ourselves as both heroines and wives."

Anne shifted in her seat. "Jim was Heathcliff," she said, "in Philip Roth's *Wuthering Heights.*" She didn't mean to be witty or malicious, though she knew she might be accused of being both.

Without thinking, Eleanor reached across the table and touched Anne's hand. "Don't rewrite," she said. "Don't let the present get in the way of the past."

Anne's eyes watered again. She folded the letter and put it away in her purse. Would she now have to mourn him, miss him? she wondered. She didn't believe the letter but it moved her, the effort he'd made, writing it for her.

"I'm afraid I have to run," Eleanor said. "I promised to look after my son Harry's two girls. I had five sons and now I have four granddaughters, with a fifth on the way." She stood up. "He saw you, you know, as his great good luck." Anne looked away to keep from crying. "He did," Eleanor said.

Lea called Sam. "Harry told me he had a

fling with a colleague, Mary Ann Evans, like George Eliot. He says it's over."

Sam groaned. "He's a schmuck, Lea. He's always been a schmuck, he'll always be a schmuck. You married the schmuck. He's yours."

Lea laughed. "I like that, the Schmuck Theory of Matrimony. Like the sign in the antique store: 'You Break It, You Own It.' "

"He told me about it. He was heartsore. He was ashamed and sorry and so afraid you'd leave him," Sam said.

"She was pregnant," Lea said. "She miscarried. She has a husband. It might have been his."

"I told him not to tell you," Sam said. "I told him to man up and live with his guilt."

"Yes, well, the schmuck is also the blurter, as we all know."

"What did you do?" Sam asked.

"I told him he had to move out, at least for a while. I needed to get my head clear. He asked your mother if he could stay with her. She said no. She said, 'If you're old enough to mess around in your marriage, you're too old to live with your mother. Or, your mother is too old to live with you.' "

"Good old Mom," Sam said.

Lea liked talking to Sam. Unlike her women friends, he didn't commiserate. He didn't make her feel sorry for herself.

"Did you meet her?" Lea asked. "Did you see her? Was she pretty?"

"I saw her once, at the law school. She was crying. I think she was pretty. Hard to say when they're crying. She looked like you."

"Have you heard from him?" Lea said.

"No, I saw him maybe two weeks ago. We talked about talking to the Wolinskis."

"Harry told me. You got tested. Harry's not so angry now with your father. He's not sure he wants to do anything about it."

"I'm not angry at Dad. I never was. I'm curious."

"She was younger than me," Lea said.

"They always are. That's their great appeal. Also, they're not the wife or the husband. In an affair, you don't have to talk to them. Better, you don't have to listen to them."

"Oh, Sam," Lea said, "you've lived a very sophisticated life."

"Take him back, Lea. You're good for each other. He's a dog."

"I don't like him right now. I need to like him again before I can let him come home."

"That sounds like something my mother would say," Sam said.

"Harry pays attention better when I sound

like your mother," Lea said.

Harry needed to confess to his mother, his confession to Lea providing little relief. Eleanor wasn't interested. "No details," she told him. "I don't like confessions." They were having dinner downstairs from her apartment, at the Café des Artistes, the farthest Eleanor felt like going to be with Harry.

Harry was hurt. He didn't understand. "I feel awful. I wish I hadn't done it."

"I wish you hadn't done it, but more, I wish you hadn't told me," Eleanor said.

"I was miserable the whole time."

"What did you expect?" Eleanor said. "Happiness? It's not in the cards. One person might be happy, but never both. The whole point of adultery is to be unhappy — excited, guilty, and unhappy. Sex, new sex, is the point."

Harry winced. He hated when his mother said anything about sex.

"Do you think I was in it only for the sex?" he said.

"Are you saying you wanted to marry the woman?" Eleanor said.

"No, no," he said. "But we talked too."

"How did she get pregnant?" Eleanor asked.

Harry was quiet. Eleanor waited.

"I don't think it was mine," he said.

"Did you use condoms?" she asked.

He shook his head.

"Do you want to stay in your marriage?" Eleanor said.

Harry nodded.

"Will Lea take you back?"

Harry lowered his head and started crying silently into his napkin.

Harry agreed to go with Sam to meet Hugh Wolinski. He was, he admitted, curious. Iain couldn't make it; he was at sea. Hugh was reluctant. "What's the point?" he said. "Please," Sam said. "We'd like to have a better ending than the one last year in the Surrogate's Court." They made a date for the Saturday before Easter at the Parlour Bar on West Eighty-Sixth. Rupert had been dead for three years, almost to the day.

Sam and Harry got there early, taking a table in back. Watching Hugh walk toward them, Sam thought, He could be Dad's son. Sam and Harry stood up. They shook hands with Hugh. They ordered beers.

Hugh waited. This wasn't his show.

"I've taken a DNA test," Sam said. "If you take one, we can find out if we are brothers" — Sam paused — "and we could make some kind of amends."

"And if I'm not your brother?" Hugh said.

"We think our father knew your mother," Harry said. "We think there was some kind of relationship."

"I don't see what's in it for Iain and me," Hugh said.

"There's family money," Sam said.

"Look," he said, "I don't care. It's too late. A father might have been useful when we were younger. But whoever took care of us financially — we called him Daddy Warbucks — took care of us well enough. Vera sent us to Catholic schools. Good places, Catholic schools. They make you read one Shakespeare play a year. They teach you to write sentences. Then we both went to the Coast Guard Academy. We love being on the water. We like our work. We like our lives." Hugh stopped, then added shyly, "I'm getting married in June." He laughed. "I think I'm the first person in the family in three generations to marry."

"Congratulations," Sam said.

"Money is useful," Harry said.

"It was our mother's idea to sue your father's estate. We didn't want to. She insisted. It was humiliating, I'll say that outright. I find this conversation humiliating."

"I'm sorry," Sam said. "We want to do right by you."

"If your father fathered us, he did right enough by us. I have no interest in becoming officially the bastard son of a rich man. I'd rather be the bastard son of no one. Our mother might have had children with half a dozen pricks who wouldn't have supported her or us. After Iain was born, she had her tubes tied."

"I want to make sure you know what you're giving up," Sam said.

"If we got any money from your father's estate, we'd give it to Vera. You want to do us good, start sending her money, like before."

"We can do that," Sam said.

"No, no, I'm just talking. Iain and I, we don't want your money. Listen. You seem like decent guys. I liked your mother. She made me think your father, if he was our father, wasn't a complete shit. You'll pardon me. Our mother is something. Vera. The name means 'truth.' She wasn't a bad mother; she may even love us in her way, but she couldn't tell the truth if her life depended on it. Or mine. Or Iain's. You five get all the money. I'm OK with that. Iain too. Men cycled through our house. 'Uncles,' we called them. One, Stefan, looked out for us when we were young. Vera almost married him. Three times. She couldn't do it. She said she liked her freedom. There was talk that Vera was pregnant long before us, back in the mid-'50s, when she was seventeen. The story had many endings. Everyone told different versions, none agreeing. She got pregnant by a fireman who bought her a ring. He was a Baptist; she couldn't marry him. She got pregnant by a young GI who was going off to Korea the next day; he died on a secret mission there. She married an old Pole, Koslowski, who beat her, forcing her to give birth prematurely. She was sent away to a home for wayward girls and gave the baby up for adoption. She miscarried. She had an abortion. The baby was stillborn. The baby died at three months, stopped breathing, crib death. She sold the baby to a rich Westchester family. The baby was a boy, the baby was a girl, the baby was two babies. Who knew what was true and what wasn't? She liked being the heroine-slash-victim of everyone's stories. It made her feel like a celebrity. She never cried over that baby, if there was a baby, not to us, and, I'll give her this, she never cried for herself. She said our father was Scottish, a gentleman. But we're not even sure we're full brothers. You might test the wrong brother." He stopped to make sure he'd made his point. "We never heard of Rupert Falkes growing up. The first time we heard his name, our grandmother showed us a picture from the *New York Times,* his obituary. I don't know how she got it. It was months after he died. 'Isn't that Robert Fairchild?' she said to Vera. Vera got a lawyer the next day."

Hugh stood up and reached for his wallet. "We don't need any more family, Iain and me. We're fine the way we are." He put down a twenty. "I'd like to treat you guys."

# Chapter 9
# The Heirs

Who is it that can tell me who I am.

SHAKESPEARE, *KING LEAR*

Sam reported the conversation with Hugh to his mother. "Dad-like," Eleanor said. "Dad never wanted to find his parents. He dreaded them finding him."

"Did he know anything about them?" Sam said.

"When he was twenty, Father Falkes told him he had come from a 'good' family. He stood out from the other St. Pancras found-lings. He was plump, healthy, clean; his clothes were nicely made and unpatched." Eleanor paused. "I've no doubt his looks and appearance attracted Father Falkes's interest and attachment, and Father Falkes only meant to be kind, but the story hard-ened Dad against his parents. He could have understood better a poor family abandon-ing a child."

"What are you going to do?" Sam asked. Eleanor said nothing.

"Are you still going to give them money?"

"Stop it, Sam," she said. "He was my husband."

Eleanor decided to fire Maynard, Tandy. They kept throwing up roadblocks to her plan to give money to the Wolinskis and then blaming the roadblocks when they did nothing. Jack used to do that as a small boy. He would never do anything he didn't want to do if there was any way of not doing it. In the early years, until he became fully himself, self-interest looked a lot like self-sabotage. When he was nine, he tore up a homework assignment and then told his mother he couldn't do the work because the assignment was torn up. Eleanor surveyed the crime scene.

"You'll have to tape it together if you want to go to your trumpet lesson on Tuesday," she said.

"I didn't do it on purpose," he said. "It was a mistake."

"Of course," she said, "but you still need to tape it together."

"It will take too long, it's in too many pieces," he said.

"Better get to work then," she said.

Jack looked down at the floor, covered with bits of torn paper. He started to cry. Eleanor handed him a tissue. "The tape's on my desk," she said.

By the time he was thirteen, Jack had stopped tearing up his homework assignments. He did what he wanted to do, to hell with everyone and everything else. Eleanor held out stoutly against his iron will, buckling no more than half the time. He'd steal from her, if he needed to, to pay his trumpet teacher. It was addict's behavior but admirable, she knew, in its way. "It's my life," he told her.

In mid-August 2002, Jack's wife, Kate, gave birth to a baby girl, Ingrid, another blonde. A month later, Jack won a MacArthur grant. "Good God," Sam said, "now he's a certified genius." Shortly before Christmas, Eleanor flew to Austin to meet her new granddaughter. She rented a car, a convertible; she never depended on Jack for rides. Something more important always came up. "Do you mind taking a cab?" he'd say. "I've got a gig." She arrived at his house late morning and found him outside on the lawn, jiggling the baby and crooning Irving Berlin. "We've been waiting for you," he said. "I could have picked you up."

They went inside. Eleanor smiled at Ingrid

but made no attempt to nuzzle her or hold her. "Do you want her?" Jack asked. Eleanor shook her head. "Let's give her time to get used to me."

"I didn't want a child," Jack said, settling on the sofa, "but Kate did. I did something, sort of, for someone else." Eleanor sat in a chair across from Jack. Ingrid stared at her grandmother. "At first, I was afraid I'd be displaced," Jack said. "The baby would get all the attention. What about me? What about me? Then, I was afraid I'd have one like me." He gave a half smile. "I don't know why you and Dad didn't beat me, or lock me in one of the Hotel's attic rooms, or ship me off to a military school."

"Your brothers dented your consciousness, but Dad and I couldn't," Eleanor said. "It was good you were the fourth and not the first. I didn't take it personally."

"Why is it we're always afraid of the wrong things?" he said. He looked at his mother, then looked away. "I left Ingrid at home alone when she was only three weeks old. I forgot I was babysitting and went out to a last-minute gig." He paused. "When I got home, six hours later, Kate and Ingrid were gone. Kate left a note. It was very short: 'I was half-tempted to call Children's Services on you.' " Eleanor said nothing. "We're still separated, but Kate lets me see Ingrid so long as someone else is in the house." He paused again. "I hired a full-time nanny. Kate can't forgive me. She said I was a monstrous egoist. I don't know what to do." He started crying. Ingrid looked up at him, then started crying. Eleanor reached over and took the baby from him, murmuring softly, as if to both of them, "It's OK, it's OK, it's OK."

"Kate's thinking of moving to DC, near her folks," Jack said. "My playing's gone to hell." He looked at his mother, tears streaming down his face. "I'm so ashamed."

"Did you tell that to Kate?" Eleanor asked.

"I've apologized," he said.

"Did you tell Kate you were ashamed?" she asked. He shook his head. "I'd start there," she said. He opened his mouth to speak. "No," she said. "I won't."

"I'm an exuberant trumpet player. I need to be happy to play," Jack said.

He got up and went to the phone.

Eleanor stood up; the baby tucked her head into her grandmother's neck. "Ingrid and I are going to take the morning air."

Kate returned with Ingrid a month after Eleanor's visit. "I'm not optimistic," she said to Jack. "You're on parole."

Jack called his mother. "They're back. For

now." Eleanor couldn't remember a call from Jack that hadn't to do with his trumpet. "I think it was more the full-time nanny than me." He paused. "My playing's getting better. I can't blow this."

Old Gosford, when confronted with the firm's dilatoriness, was patronizing. "It's not so easy a thing to do," he said. "If you give them any money, Mrs. Wolinski will go straight back to the Surrogate and say you're recognizing her boys' claim against Rupert's estate."

He's a useless idiot, Eleanor thought, correcting Rupert's assessment. "Look, Gos," she said, her tone more kindly than she felt, as if she were explaining bathroom hygiene to a four-year-old for the fifth time. "I'm not giving them any of Rupert's money. I'm giving them my money, money I got from my father, my McDonald's money."

"Oh, yes, well, but," Gosford stammered, "setting up a Cayman account is dicey. Possibly illegal."

"I never said anything about a Cayman account. I want to be open about it. Mrs. Wolinski will have to pay taxes. And there will be trustees, people with telephone numbers and addresses in the United States."

Gosford was silent, out of chagrin or cunning Eleanor couldn't say.

"I understand," she said. "The firm doesn't want to do it. I'm fine with that." Eleanor's tone shifted slightly, a cold edge stealing in. "I'm moving law firms, Gos. I've retained Carlo Benedetti. That's why I called." She paused. Her tone shifted again, into a lower register. "I can't imagine I owe you money. In ten months, you haven't done anything."

Gosford sprang to life. "It's a misunderstanding, Eleanor," he said.

"No, Gos, it's not that. You've let me down."

"We'll try again," he said. "We'll do it right."

"No," she said. "If I do owe money, send an itemized bill. We'll speak again, as friends. Regards to all." As she hung up, she wondered whether young Gosford had cried when he found he'd backed himself into a corner.

Carlo Benedetti set up the trust. He, Eleanor, and Will were the trustees. Eleanor funded the trust with seven hundred thousand dollars of her father's McDonald's money. Interest, estimated at seven percent a year, would go to Vera, giving her forty-nine thousand dollars a year before taxes, thirty-eight thousand after. Taxes would be taken out before distribution. She would be paid monthly. There could be no invasion without permission of the trustees. At her death, the trust would settle in equal shares on Hugh and Iain. Carlo notified the Wolinskis, making it clear that Eleanor, and not Rupert's estate, was the funder. Hugh and Iain both wrote brief notes of thanks, their surprise almost overtaking their appreciation. "I don't know what to think or say," Hugh wrote. "Thank you for looking after our mother." Vera sent Eleanor a three-lined note: "Your husband should have provided for me and my sons in his will. What kind of man has his wife pay support to his mistress?"

Carlo proposed to Eleanor the day he filed the trust. "I can't marry my lawyer," Eleanor said. "Conflict of interest."

"I resign," he said.

"You've already been married three times," she said. "Why would you do it again?"

"I want to marry you. I've wanted to marry you for years," he said. "I've loved you for years. Longer than Rupert. I married the others because you wouldn't have me. I divorced them because they weren't

379

you." He paused. "Tell me again why you married Rupert?"

"I liked the way he danced," she said.

Dominic's letter to Eleanor came as a surprise. "I'm getting married," he wrote. "Her name is Bridget Farrell. She's only forty, but kind and good and plainly not marrying me for my money. She teaches history at a local grammar school. We might even have children. My friends here all call me out for marrying someone so young. I tell them I was in love with a woman older than I, but she wouldn't have me."

Eleanor sent Dominic and Bridget a Persian rug, the one from Rupert's library. "Rupert would want you to have this," she wrote in her note. "Wishing you happiness and contentment in each other."

Lea let Harry come home after two months. "Every dog gets one bite," she said to him, "but only one. If you do it again, we're through. That's a promise." Harry had been wretched away from Lea and his daughters. "I won't do it again. I love you," he said. "The girls don't have to go to church."

"I don't know why I did it," he said to Sam. "She came on to me."

"That makes it less your fault, I take it,"

Sam said. He stared at his brother. "You're a good man, Harry, but you're a schmuck. You need to take responsibility for what you do. And, for chrissakes, stop blurting. None of us, Lea, Mom, me, want to hear your confessions. Maybe you should become a Catholic. They have priests who'll listen. Or try analysis."

"I can't help it. I say it before I know I've said it. I do it everywhere. It gets me in trouble at the law school too."

"You could stop justifying what you've blurted. That is in your control."

"I'm a lawyer, Sam," Harry said. "I argue. It's second nature."

"You're doing it again, schmuck," Sam said.

Eleanor called Jack and laid out her plan for the trust. He thought it a great idea. "I liked those boys. If they were our brothers, we could be heroes, seven of us, like *Seven Samurai.*"

"How's Kate?" Eleanor asked.

"Holding," he said. "I think Ingrid has perfect pitch."

"At seven months."

Jack laughed. "An infant prodigy."

Tom also approved of the trust. "Good day's work, Mom," he said. "Didn't Freud say money was shit? We should spread it around, like manure, to make things grow."

The phone went quiet. "Are you there?" Eleanor said.

"I'm changing the subject. I have news," Tom said.

"Yes," Eleanor said.

"We're adopting a little girl. Lila. She's three. She's been in three foster homes. They all wanted to adopt her. Her mother wouldn't allow it. She's finally relinquished her rights. She told the social worker, 'I wanted someone who'd educate her right.' "

"Wonderful news. I'm so happy for you both. I wondered . . ." She stopped.

"Caroline wanted a baby but I couldn't see it; too many humans already on the planet. This will be good. She's very sweet." Tom laughed. "She's blond."

As she hung up, Eleanor wondered at the self-centeredness of her sons. Only Will, most like his father, was exempt. When do they finally grow up? she asked herself. She had thought she had taken the long view with them. She had thought forty was the horizon. "Perhaps it's fifty now." She decided to go to the movies. *Mystic River* was playing around the corner.

Sam and Harry were both annoyed that Will

had been named a Wolinski trustee. "Why Will?"

"He didn't interfere with my plans," Eleanor said.

"Aren't you glad we met with Hugh?" Sam said. "You found out you'll never find out."

"He didn't want the money," Harry said. "You didn't need to do it."

"The money goes to them only if Vera doesn't spend it all," Eleanor said.

"I thought the trust can't be invaded," Harry said.

"Not without permission of the trustees," Eleanor said. "We'll give permission. Another reason not to have either of you as trustee."

"Why are you doing this?" Harry said.

Eleanor stared at him. "I'm settling your father's just debts."

Gemma Bowles Phipps Falkes was born on October 18, 2003. Susanna and Sam were giddy with happiness. She was named for Granny Bowles. Sam handed out Cubans. He had a friend who had a friend who had an acquaintance who had a supplier. "It's easier to get cocaine than Cubans," he said to his mother. "Cheaper too."

"I don't want to know this," Eleanor said.

Gemma was born with a thatch of black hair, "breaking the Rupert spell," Eleanor thought. Four weeks later, her dark hair fell out; the hair coming in was white-blond.

A week after the birth, Andrew called Sam. "How could you do it," he said. "How could you do it?" He was crying. "I wanted a child. We've been over and over this," Sam said. He waited until Andrew caught his breath. "I hope you get what you want too." He hung up.

"Who was that?" Susanna said.

"Rumpelstiltskin," Sam said.

Sam and Susanna had moved into their Siamese apartments two weeks before Gemma was born. They kept the door between them open so Sam could come and go. He hired a full-time housekeeper. He bought groceries and wine and stacked both dishwashers. Eleanor gave them each a set of the Christofle silver.

"I sometimes feel bad about Andrew, but mostly not. He was awful to me," Susanna said. She looked down at her baby lying on her lap, snuffling like a piglet. "Isn't she beautiful," Susanna said.

Sam reached down to stroke Gemma's small head. "Who does she look like?" he asked. "Does she look like me?"

"Around the eyes," Susanna said. "Isn't

she beautiful."

"She's funny-looking," he said, "like all newborns." Susanna glared at him. He backtracked. "Perhaps a little less."

Susanna swatted his hand away. "I require adoration from her father," she said.

"I didn't have that kind of father. We had to do something to get his attention, let alone approval," Sam said.

"I miss him," Susanna said. Sam nodded.

"I still haven't heard from my father," she said. "Or my mother."

"You are a miracle," Sam said. "Gemma is a miracle."

He went out of the room briefly, returning with a small box. "For you," he said. "He'd have wanted it." Susanna opened the box. Inside was Rupert's Patek Philippe watch. "I can't. It's yours," she said.

"You must," he said. "It's right. I claimed it for you." He took the watch out of the box and fastened it on her wrist. It hung loosely, like a bracelet. Holding Gemma against her body, Susanna wept.

Hannah Bigelow's letter, coming on the fourth anniversary of Rupert's death, was a jolt. Everyone had finally settled down. Eleanor held on to it for two weeks before telling the boys. Carlo was indignant. "A

Gypsy fraud if ever I heard of one." He looked at Eleanor. "What is it?" he asked. She had closed her eyes.

"It's the photograph," Eleanor said. "Another wretched photograph."

The photograph had come with the letter. It showed a young family, standing in front of a Gothic church, in coats, probably in the 1930s, a father, a mother holding an infant, and three small children, the oldest no more than three.

The letter read:

10 April 2004

Dear Mrs. Falkes,
I write on behalf of my late mother, Helen Sonnegaard, who died four months ago at age 97. In her will she left five thousand pounds to her son Anders Sonnegaard or, in the event of his death, his heirs. Along with my older brothers, Charles and Antony Sonnegaard, I began a search for Anders. We have good reason to believe he was your late husband, Rupert Falkes.
On March 1, 1934, my parents Bastian and Helen Sonnegaard, gave up a one-month-old baby boy, called Anders, to St. Pancras Orphanage in Chichester,

England, run by the Reverend Henry Falkes. My father, a schoolteacher, had lost his job six months earlier. My mother, also a schoolteacher, had not worked since my oldest brother, Charles, was born. I was 10 months old, Anders was 20 months, Charles was 31 months. My mother's parents, old and ill, had taken in our family in the New Year. It fell to my mother to keep house for everyone. She could not manage with a brand-new baby and three other small children. The times were desperate.

My parents kept track of Anders for the next twenty years. They knew he had been renamed Rupert Falkes. They knew he had gone to the Prebendal School, Longleat and Cambridge. The Reverend Falkes died in 1954. At that point, they lost the connection. Anders/Rupert disappeared. My mother on her deathbed asked that we find him. We didn't remember him. Our parents had never spoken of him. The Internet made a search possible. We found Rupert Falkes's obituary in the New York Times. The details of his life, as described in the obituary, correspond to what we know of our brother. There is no making amends for what was done to Anders, but the family wishes to honour our mother's will and provide his family with knowledge of his parentage. Anders was born January 30, 1934. My parents did not register his birth, knowing they would have to give him up. The enclosed photograph of our family was taken on the day Anders was left at St. Pancras. The church is behind us.

If you sign the enclosed affidavit, we will notify our solicitors and provide you with a copy of the will.

Yours,
Hannah Sonnegaard Bigelow
c/o PO Box 45655, Havant PO9 7AE
England

"I didn't so much mind the Wolinskis. They were Rupert's doing, or not," Eleanor said. "But these people, making themselves known now, after he's dead . . ." She looked to Carlo. "They're seventy years too late. May I throw out the letter?"

"No. You need to stop them. You need to disavow the connection and disclaim the bequest. Anything else opens the door. Signing the affidavit would be acknowledging the relationship. Before you know it, they're on a plane over here, ready to move into the Hotel, threatening to sue for a share of

388

Rupert's estate." Carlo stopped. "It's a lawyer's letter," he said. "I wonder why the solicitor didn't send it."

Eleanor called a family conclave. They thought Hannah Bigelow might be a fraud; still, they'd have liked to meet her and her brothers.

"The children are towheads," Tom said, pointing at the photo, willing to give money to almost anyone.

"All English children are," Sam said.

"They could have reconstructed his history from the obituary and then got hold of his birth certificate. Basic sleuthing," Harry said.

"How did they know about Reverend Falkes?" Jack asked.

"I think his name was on Dad's birth certificate, as guardian or some such," Sam said. "But he was the local priest in Chichester, the head of the orphanage, with, lo, Dad's name."

"Enough money to make the bequest plausible, though not up to the Nigerians," Will said.

"Good letter, dignified with a hint of stoical grief underneath, good photo," Harry said. "If it's really them."

"Do they exist, these Sonnegaard Bigelows?" Sam said.

"There is a Hannah Bigelow in Havant, at 16 Fairfield Road. Carlo found the address," Eleanor said. "I don't know why she only gave a PO."

"Let's call her," Jack said.

All five looked at their mother, their faces full of innocent expectation, as if they were boys again, imploring her to let them stay up past midnight, "Can we, can we? Please, please, please?" Years spent reading Sherlock Holmes, the Hardy Boys, and Encyclopedia Brown had prepared them for this moment.

"Carlo will handle this for now, for me," Eleanor said. "I can't answer for you. Dad never wanted anything to do with them." Disappointment hung in the air.

"We're not Dad's heirs anyway. We're yours. We only have the trusts," Harry said.

"Only?" Tom said. "I can't get rid of the money, it's like sin, 'a huge heap increasing under the very act of diminishing.'"

Carlo had a paralegal find Hannah Bigelow's number in Havant. The paralegal called three times a day for a week. No one answered.

"I ran the letter by an ADA in the Financial Fraud Bureau in the Manhattan DA's Office," Carlo said to Eleanor. "He recommended we CC the Hampshire Constabulary in Havant. Not that they'll do anything, but it should stop the Sonnegaards."

"Why did they do this?" Eleanor asked.

"If they did their research, they might know about the Wolinskis and think, Ha, a helpless widow, a patsy. They might think the Wolinskis were frauds too. There's a reason why people tread beaten tracks."

"I want a designated mail opener, someone like the king's food taster," Eleanor said. She tucked the photo into her wallet.

Eleanor wrote a letter to Hannah Sonnegaard. She didn't want to write the lawyer's letter Carlo recommended, but a widow's letter. She showed a draft, stiff and correct, to Will and Sam. "Do you want to say that?" Will said. "Awfully brisk," Sam said, raising his eyebrows. Eleanor revised the letter, unstiffening it a bit, politening it some. "Better," Will said. "Third time will be the charm," Sam said. Eleanor started from the beginning. She never shared the final version, the letter she sent, with any of her sons. "I wrote only on my own behalf," she said to them. "You must do as you like."

May 21, 2004

Dear Ms. Bigelow,
I write as Rupert Falkes's widow and
heir. If Rupert was Anders, he is no
longer able to claim the family connection or the gift. On a matter of this
seriousness and importance, I cannot
speak for him but only for myself.

Your parents didn't register Anders's
birth. They never spoke of him. They
acted as if he'd never been born. I think
it monstrously self-serving and cowardly
of your mother on her deathbed to ask
you and your brothers to find him. I
understand that you would wish to fulfill
her final wishes but I cannot forgive her
or your father for abandoning him so
completely. I disclaim the bequest, if it
is mine to disclaim.

Yours,
Eleanor Phipps Falkes


I don't believe Rupert could have been
ruder, she thought. I will stop now. She
would miss him every day. She would be all
right.

# EPILOGUE:
## ANDERS

**Play out the play.**
WILLIAM SHAKESPEARE, *KING HENRY IV*

Sam read his mother's letter to Hannah Sonnegaard. He saw a copy on her desk, lying there in the open, an invitation to be read. If she didn't want Harry or me to read it, he said to himself, she'd have put it in a file or destroyed it. He'd come by for Sunday lunch, Gemma in tow. Susanna had begged off. "I need desperately to sleep. Your mother will understand." He walked into the kitchen carrying the baby and the letter.

"I found this," he said. "I wondered what you finally wrote." Eleanor looked at him coolly, not sure if she was annoyed or not. Privacy had always been a trial in an apartment with five boys underfoot, not so much because the boys were curious about their mother but because they were always losing

393

things and looking in the wrong places. "I was thinking of *The Purloined Letter,* hiding in plain sight," she said.

Sam read the letter to Will on the phone. "Doesn't it sound, at the very least, ambivalent about the Sonnegaards: 'I cannot forgive her'?"

"It sounds angry," Will said, "as angry as I've ever known Mom to be."

"Funny, isn't it?" Sam said. "She doesn't mind the Wolinskis, only the Sonnegaards."

"I don't think children are meant to understand their parents," Will said.

Will, Francie, and Mary went to England in early August, to visit Mary's grandparents. When they married, Francie had exacted a promise from Will that they would visit her family at least twice a year, each visit no less than a week. Will often did business on these trips, a relief to all. Rupert-like, he wasn't one to coo over a baby, and he saw that his in-laws longed for time alone with their daughter and granddaughter.

After three days of family, saying he had an author's meeting, Will took an early-morning train down to Havant. Fairfield Road was around the corner from the station. He readily found number 16. The house was detached, a solid, handsome, two-story redbrick structure, with a split flint garden wall and a greenhouse. Gypsies didn't live there. He walked up to the front door and rang the bell. After a minute, a woman in her early seventies opened the door. She was tall, straight, and lean, with graying blond hair and ice-blue wolf's eyes.

# ACKNOWLEDGMENTS

A writer needs an editor, an agent, and a family cheering section. I've been wildly lucky in my set. Thanks to: my editor Lindsay Sagnette who asked after reading a short story I'd written whether I would think about turning it into a novel; my agent Kathy Robbins who read all the many drafts of *The Heirs,* helping me make it better before submitting it to Lindsay who helped me make it even better; and my husband David Denby and my daughter Maggie Pouncey, writers both, who told me I could write a different kind of novel from my first. I also want to acknowledge with thanks the Crown crew: Molly Stern, Annsley Rosner, Rose Fox, Rachelle Mandik, Sarah Breivogel, Danielle Crabtree, Kevin Callahan, and everyone else who worked on turning the manuscript into a book; Kathy Robbins's gang at the Robbins Office, especially Janet Oshiro, Rachelle Bergstein, and Eliza Darnton, for reading the manuscript in its various iterations; my son-in-law Matt who checked regularly on my progress; and my two grandsons, Felix, seven, and Dominic, three, the sunshine of my life.

# ABOUT THE AUTHOR

**Susan Rieger** is the author of the 2014 novel *The Divorce Papers*. She is a graduate of Columbia Law School and has worked as a residential college dean at Yale and as an associate provost at Columbia. She lives in New York City with her husband, the writer David Denby.

1/8